For Lola. Here's your happily ever after. Mahal kita.

Sweetness
AND
MADNESS

Author's Note

Although the characters in these pages are fictional, they do deal with real world issues, such as coping with a miscarriage from the male perspective; ovarian cancer, along with the treatments and its side effects; infertility from the female perspective; and coping with the death of a parent.

Thank you for choosing this book. I hope it takes you on a memorable journey.

Loosely based on a true story.

Sweetness

AND

MADNESS

It was a miracle I got to the theater early. Kaleb and I had been dating for half of my career and had been partners for the last two years. Our moods were usually so in sync with each other, but lately, unease had been radiating off him. I wanted to address it—to clear the air—but our performance was just moments away.

I rushed in through the backstage door, to the hustle and bustle of ballerinas stretching, hairspray clouds, and stagehands moving props around. I'd waited as long as I could for my dad to get home, but leaving Mom, even in the care of a nurse, gnawed at me. Despite the weight of my guilt, my shoulders relaxed just being here.

This theater is my last sanctuary.

I could leave my troubles at the door, freeing my heart and mind.

After rushing into the dressing room, I touched up my hair and makeup and changed into my costume. Amid the familiar routine, thoughts of my mother lying in her bed, frail and fading, consumed me. My father's words replayed in my mind. *I'll be off work soon. Go ahead, I'll take care of Mom.*

She'd been sick for so long. It prevented us from affording hospice care and just added to the list of things I couldn't do for my mother.

Tonight, I dance for you, Mom.

Applause echoed in my ears as I stepped onto the grand stage. The first half went smoothly, but my palms sweated with the pressure of the finale, and my hands shook more than normal. Lost in the whirlwind of thoughts, I faltered. My mistake, a rare occurrence, caused a ripple of surprise. Kaleb's glare was like a sharp rebuke. Thankfully, we managed to recover. The audience remained oblivious to our lapse, but the damage was done. Our mistake hung heavy in the air between us and the other dancers.

After the performance, Kaleb approached me, frustration apparent on his face. "What the hell was that?" His words stung, each one a barb stabbing at my vulnerability.

I pulled a towel out of my duffel and dabbed the perspiration off my forehead. "I'm sorry." I panted, still catching my breath. *He couldn't wait any longer?*

"I stuck my neck out for you to get prima ballerina, and what do you do? You dance like an understudy," he spat.

I swallowed. "What are you saying, Kaleb?"

"Did you think you got here on your talents alone?" His blue-green eyes bored into me.

A quiet gasp escaped me, and my brow furrowed. "That's not true."

"If it weren't for me, you would've never gotten prima," he growled.

"You're a fucking liar," I choked out.

"People die every day. That doesn't mean the rest of us have to stop living too." He ran a hand through his dark hair. "You act like you have *all* the time in the world. You're in your prime right now, and you're wasting it."

How can he fucking say that? I didn't have the heart or energy to respond. His lack of empathy, his insinuations—both personal and professional—cut deep.

He turned his back to me. "Listen, Mia. It's been fun and everything, but I don't think this is working anymore."

"Are you serious? My mother is dying!" I wiped the wetness from my cheeks with the towel and chucked it into my bag.

He still didn't face me. "Yeah, and how long will it take you to recover from that? I just . . . don't have time for that in my career right now. You understand, right?"

I remained in silent disbelief.

"It's over, Mia." He walked away without as much as a backward glance.

My feet moved beneath me through the dimly lit corridor that stretched ahead, shrouded in shadows. The cold, hard floor echoed with each step I took, the sound of my pointes reverberating through the long empty hallway.

Running into a stairwell, I clung to the railing, squeezing

the unyielding metal surface. The weight on my chest made it hard to breathe. *How can he do this?*

My cell buzzed in my sweatshirt pocket. The vibration was jarring amid the silence. I reached for it, hands shaking. The tears blurred my vision. I answered the call. The scent of dust and aged wood lingered with each ragged breath.

"Mia," Dad choked out.

My voice trembled. "Pop, what's wrong?"

"It's Mama." His sobs echoed through the phone and into the stairwell, and I knew.

I knew she was gone. And I hadn't been there for her.

I stepped back until the wall stopped me. Sliding down to the floor, I brought my knees to my chest.

My best friend, Julia, burst through the door. She stared at me. We didn't have to speak to communicate. She crouched, wrapping her arms around me. I shook as my tears soaked the black sweatshirt she wore. She rubbed circles on my back.

"She's gone." My strangled cries resonated off the walls.

Time stood still, and my tears seemed like they would never stop.

Julia's silent embrace was an unspoken empathy of my pain. It was the only semblance of comfort I could feel amid my crumbling world.

Life's unyielding march forward taught me its hardest lesson: it waits for no one. After my mother's death, I stepped away from the ballet company and assisted my best friend, Julia, in launching her dance studio. I was grateful for the opportunity but couldn't shake the feeling of being adrift, unsure of my true calling. So, I resigned.

Lucas Verduce, Julia's husband, had offered me a job at his flourishing record label. My role was mostly behind-the-scenes, but the thrill of being part of something new, something pulsating with potential, was exciting. And it brought me into the orbit of Ethan Miller—a man whose charisma was as unsettling as it was captivating. Over the last year, a strange sort of friendship had formed between us.

My commitment to LV Productions had been unwavering. My boss could make an exception, after all. It wasn't as though I'd ever missed a day. *What am I supposed to do with these?* I stared at the papers for a moment, then remembered I was supposed to distribute them among the parties involved, including Lucas. He still liked keeping physical copies of contracts.

Despite the calming scent of eucalyptus wafting from the diffuser, the office air was heavy with a sense of routine and unspoken expectations. The ticking clock was a constant reminder of the doctor's appointment looming over me. I had an hour left but so much to finish.

I smoothed out my oversize beige waffle sweater and tucked a strand of wavy dark hair behind my ear before picking up the copies from the printer tray.

"Mia."

My gaze trailed up the length of Ethan's sexy frame. From his perfectly tailored black trousers to his royal-blue button-down, this man teetered on the precipice of being a professional and a tease.

Goddammit.

His sleeves were rolled up to his elbows, revealing toned sun-kissed forearms.

I blinked out of my trance. "Hey."

He stopped a few feet from me, close enough that his citrusy bergamot scent filled my nose. "Are you busy?"

This is torture. Absolute fucking torture. Sometimes I questioned my sanity in accepting this job. "Nope, just making copies for that new solo artist you found."

"Sounds exciting. I actually wanted to talk to you about something," he said.

"Oh?" I waited for him to go on.

"It's more of a personal favor."

With an eye roll, I prodded, "Well, spit it out already."

A corner of his mouth tilted up. "My parents hold Thanksgiving dinner at their house every year. And every year, without fail, they try to set me up with someone. I was thinking I could stay ahead of the game and actually bring someone for a change."

I'd met Ethan's family at Lucas and Julia's wedding at the beginning of the year. His mom, dad, sister, and niece seemed to like me well enough. But they knew Ethan and I were just friends.

I cocked a brow and grinned. "What does that have to do with me?"

His lips formed a straight line. "Do I have to spell it out?"

I crossed my arms. "Well, if you're gonna give me attitude, yeah."

He let out a dramatic sigh; luckily, I was immune to his theatrics. "Will you be my date? I really don't want them hassling me about getting married . . . again."

Ethan, like everyone else in this industry, seemed to have an aversion to commitment. In the short time I'd known him, I'd learned he didn't talk about settling down. Not that I was any better. I let out a short breath, reminded of my own reluctance to fall in love ever since Kyle's betrayal. We hadn't been official, but it still hurt like we were.

Julia and I had caught Kyle butt-ass naked, fucking some groupie in the back of one of the tour buses. It had been a painful lesson. My trust in relationships had crumbled, and I'd vowed never to let my heart be crushed like that again.

The wounds had left me wary of diving into anything resembling commitment.

Ethan jutted out his bottom lip, making a pouty face. Taking my hand, he squeezed. "Please? I'll pick up 50 percent of your workload for the next week."

"Make it a month and we have a deal."

He smirked. "You drive a hard bargain, Mia Cruz. But you have a deal."

I pulled my hand away to check my watch. "Shit, I have to go." I gave him the copies of the contract I'd been holding.

He took them. "Where? Do you need a ride?"

I smiled, my boot heels clicking against the tile floor as I made my way toward the exit. "Nope. Why don't you get started on some of my tasks? I'll text you the list."

I ARRIVED AT THE SPECIALIST'S OFFICE IN TIME TO FILL out all the paperwork with the receptionist. This was my second visit in a month. *It's probably nothing.* Just stress from starting a new job. After the No Blood, No Alibi tour last year, thinking it was period cramps, I let it go. Recently, the pain had started to become unbearable. After a visit with my ob-gyn and a few tests, she referred me to a gynecologic oncologist. *Just to be safe due to your family history,* she'd said. Dr. Colton wanted to meet with me in person. In my experience, they usually called with the results.

I sat in front of his modern black desk, unable to speak.

My breaths came out shallow, and lightheadedness swept over me. The word caught in my throat as I sat there in the sterile white office. He'd said the words no one ever wants to hear: *you have cancer.*

The oncologist, Dr. Colton, jotted something down on his tablet, a strand of blond hair falling out of place onto his forehead. "Your treatment plan will begin with surgical intervention, specifically a unilateral oophorectomy. This procedure will involve the removal of one fallopian tube and ovary. After, we'll initiate adjuvant chemotherapy, utilizing a combination of cytotoxic agents tailored to your specific diagnosis."

My head dipped, eyes wide as they flickered between the doctor and the floor.

He stood and began picking brochures off the far wall. "The surgery will be followed by a series of chemotherapy cycles. We'll closely monitor your progress through regular blood tests, imaging studies, and tumor-marker assessments."

Taking the pamphlets from him, I tried to focus on the details, but they blurred in front of my eyes. I blinked back tears, refusing to let them fall in front of him. "Will I be able to have kids?"

Dr. Colton smiled softly. "You should still be able to conceive, but unfortunately, it will be more difficult. The chances we'll have to perform a hysterectomy later in life are high," he said. "We're aiming for maximum efficacy with minimal invasiveness. You're in the early stages, which significantly improves your prognosis."

I cleared my throat, my gaze meeting his once more. "Thank you, Dr. Colton."

"We'll try to get you scheduled after Thanksgiving," he said gently squeezing my arm. "You can get through this, Mia. The best thing to do right now is to live your life as normally as possible."

Normal? All I could do was nod.

We discussed what would come next, but my mind was swirling, unable to focus on what he was saying. Before I knew it, I was stepping outside into the chilly New York air. I looked up at the baby-blue sky, overwhelmed by the enormity of it all. Three words. That was all it took. My life as I knew it had shattered.

THE SILENCE OF MY APARTMENT ECHOED THE VOID gnawing at my heart. *This really sucks.* I sat on my couch staring at the information packet the doctor had given me.

Surgery. Chemotherapy. Radiation.

I read about the type of cancer I had. Tears welled up in my eyes, brimming at the edges before cascading down my cheeks. They fell onto the paper, each droplet landing with a soft tap.

How can I possibly live life normally?

I didn't have family in the States. My father moved back to the Philippines before Thanksgiving last year, but I supposed I'd have to tell him the shitty news. With Mom having passed from cancer, this would hit him hard.

I should tell him, but maybe I could wait a bit. If the doctor could get rid of it as easily as he spoke about it, maybe there was no point in telling anyone. He had the right to know. *He's my father.* But right now, I could only take care of myself.

My cell vibrated on the cushion next to me. Glancing at the screen, I answered the call and did my best to sound normal. "Hey, babe."

"Are we still on for lunch?" Julia's sweet-yet-sometimes-brash voice echoed through the speaker, a quality that made her the perfect ballet teacher.

"I'm gonna need a rain check, Jules," I said, sinking deeper into the sofa. God, I was tired. I'd popped a painkiller before sitting down, and it was starting to kick in. Fast.

"Are you sleeping already?" she asked.

"No. I just got in."

She didn't say anything for a second. "How's work?"

I tried my best not to sound annoyed. "Can we talk about all of this later?" I grabbed the remote from the coffee table in front of me and turned on Netflix.

"Fine." Julia sighed. "When was the last time you were properly fucked?"

Damn, how long has it been? I'd been too wrapped up in the job transition and my stomach cramps to notice. It had probably been a few months at the most.

"Fuck . . . That long?"

I repeated something she'd said to me before she'd

started dating Lucas. "I don't count anyone who can't make me come."

She giggled. "I guess we'll have to find you someone who can, then maybe you'll stop being bitchy."

I hadn't been myself these past weeks, but that was due to the pain I was in. However, I couldn't help but laugh at her stupid remark. It was one of the many things I could count on from her.

A few seconds later, lightheadedness swept through me. "Look, I gotta go, but I'll text you later."

With a groan, she said, "Just tell me you don't wanna talk to me."

"You're being unnecessarily difficult today," I mused.

"Fine, but you better text me."

"Don't you have a husband to annoy now?" I teased.

"Text me," was her final warning before we exchanged goodbyes and hung up.

I tossed my cell onto the cushion next to me. How had everything changed so quickly? Just yesterday, my biggest worry was work, but now it was death. That word alone sent chills down my spine. It felt like I was in a bubble, watching the world move on while I was stuck here, frozen in fear. Julia would try to be there for me in her own way, but she couldn't truly understand. The thought of attending Ethan's family's Thanksgiving dinner lingered in my mind. It was only about four weeks away.

God, I'm exhausted

My eyelids peeled open to the sun streaming through the panoramic window, bathing the room in a warm amber glow of fall. The air carried a mix of last night's activities and just a hint of jasmine, a heady scent that didn't ease my pounding headache. It was further aggravated by the snoring of the dark-haired woman lying naked beneath my sheets, her hair a striking contrast against the white linen.

When did that happen? I couldn't remember calling her, but it wasn't unlike her to just show up on my doorstep. I tossed my legs over the side of the king-size bed, and the cold wooden floor was a shock to my bare feet. Massaging my temples, I tried to alleviate the pain. *God, this time of the year sucks ass.*

"Hey, handsome." Alice's nasally voice rattled my head.

God, I drank too much last night. I buried my face in my hands and didn't respond.

"You have time for breakfast?" she asked, and her weight

left the bed. I listened to the smooth slide of silk and the fumbling of her stilettos as she gathered them from the floor.

I glanced at the clock on my bedside table. "No. I gotta get to the office."

"You're still at LV Productions? Are you *really* gonna take the pay cut?" she asked, but I remained silent with my head in my hands. "You should come back to Sound Sphere."

My gaze snapped to hers, and I bit out, "That's none of your fucking business."

"No, I guess not." She managed to zip her dress up by herself. "But it could be. I'll see you next time." She bent at the waist, planted a brief kiss on my lips, and then walked out, stilettos in hand.

What the hell am I doing? I let out a long breath and wiped my mouth with the back of my hand. It wasn't that long ago I was scolding Lucas about this same fucking behavior. *I am such a fucking hypocrite.*

THE HUM OF THE COFFEE MACHINE FILLED MY BARE kitchen. It gurgled and hissed, releasing the rich aroma of a fresh brew. I leaned against the counter, my gaze wandering across the penthouse.

The kitchen's sleek modern appliances and pristine marble countertops lacked any personality. My living room was an expanse of dull tones. The gray couch was a contemporary piece. *Have I ever sat on it?* The black metal floating shelves held a small library of unread novels. There hadn't been time for reading since I'd started at Lucas's company.

Despite the sunlight filtering through the sheer curtains, the space was cold and lacked the joy that transformed a house into a home. It was just a space—functional, clean, impersonal.

The coffee machine signaled the end of its cycle. I reached into the cupboard above and retrieved the #1 Dad mug Lucas had gifted me before he'd retired from No Blood, No Alibi, the band I'd managed when I worked for Sound Sphere Records. Lucas had told me half-jokingly that I'd taken better care of him than his own father. Grinning at the memory, I poured myself a cup of dark roast, the steam rising in lazy swirls. I sipped the hot bitter liquid and stood in the emptiness of my surroundings.

Just as I set my cup down, the buzz of my cell broke the morning's stillness. Picking it up from the marble counter, I glanced at the screen. There was a string of missed messages, all from Lucas.

Shit. I was supposed to meet him at his personal studio to look at a band he was interested in signing.

After calling for a company car, I ran into my room and threw on my usual attire: blue jeans, a comfortable T-shirt, and a light jacket to ward off the fall chill. As I strode out of the penthouse elevator, the remnants of the warm coffee still coursed through me.

I made my way through the front doors of the lobby.

Fred was waiting in the car just outside my building. I hopped in, settling into the back seat.

"Cutting it a bit close, Mr. Miller," he said, maneuvering the car away from the curb and down the busy street.

Letting out a breath, I said, "It's just one of those days."

The home studio was a high-tech haven with a view. The space was dimly lit with the glow of the sleek mixing console. I usually wasn't late to anything. But these days, life was just kicking my ass, and the weight of Lucas's narrow-eyed gaze only added to my tension.

I closed the door behind me. "Hey, I know I'm late, but I'd very much appreciate it if you didn't give me shit right now."

Lucas, in front of the soundboard, his laptop open on the table next to him, paused a video. He smirked and shifted his gaze to the screen. "We'll talk about it later, fucker. Watch this."

I rolled a plush leather desk chair over and sat next to him as he pressed play.

The camera zoomed in on the faces of the band members, each a beauty. They were a group of diverse women, each with their own individual style. My foot tapped to the rhythm of their music. "They remind me of early 2000s alternative rock, but with an edge. What do they call themselves?"

When the short two-minute song ended, Lucas closed the laptop. "Venom. Their stage names are different snake breeds."

I grinned. "That's awesome. It's refreshing to hear that type of music again. I could see them sparking a new trend."

Lucas nodded in agreement. "The only downside is they're based out of Los Angeles."

"California?"

"No, Michigan." He placed one earbud in and fiddled with the settings on his soundboard. He'd always been pretty damn good at producing.

I deadpanned, "Don't be a smart-ass."

Lucas chuckled, then took on a more serious tone. "You don't have to go alone. Mia's been working her ass off; you should take her with you, show her what it means to be an A&R scout." He ran a hand over the stubble on his chin. "Who knows, she may be a natural. You could potentially go back to Sound Sphere if you train her up enough."

My job with Lucas's record label was meant to be short-term, but I genuinely preferred this work atmosphere. Better morale. The sole issue lay in Lucas's inability to match the salary Sound Sphere offered me. I just nodded, and we said nothing more about it.

Lucas and I decided on a late breakfast at the Morning Brew, one of our favorite little cafés nestled in the heart of downtown. We slid into the back seat of the company car and sat through forty minutes of New York traffic.

The charming spot, known for its cozy ambiance and exceptional breakfast, welcomed us with the comforting aroma of freshly brewed espresso and the hum of quiet conversations. The local pieces of artwork that adorned the walls were mostly abstract, my favorite.

Our waitress, Greta, greeted us with a smile and escorted us to a booth near the window. The late-morning sun filtered through, casting soft patterns across our table.

I was impressed that Greta had our usual orders at our table within twenty minutes of our arrival. My plate was a hearty serving of blueberry pancakes topped with a dollop of butter slowly melting into the stack. The sweet aroma mingled with the savory scents of the café.

A steaming plate of eggs Benedict sat untouched in front of Lucas, the hollandaise sauce glistening under the warm light. He looked disinterested in his food. Instead, he was staring intently at me, his eyes searching as I forked a bite of my delicious fluffy pancakes.

"Why're you looking at me like that? Tired of Julia already?" I teased, still chewing.

He rolled his eyes. "You know what? I'm just gonna come out and say it. You've been totally off after my last tour with No Blood, No Alibi." He finally ate some of his food.

I swallowed and asked, "The fuck you talking about?"

"Weren't you the one telling me I needed to figure my shit out?" He took a sip of water from his glass.

I dropped my fork, and it clattered against the plate. "Yeah. It's just . . ." I wanted to be honest, but how could he ever understand the loss of a love that never had the chance to begin? "You know I don't take my own advice," I said.

Lucas stared at his food, a conflicted expression on his face. He forked another bite into his mouth. "Regardless. I'm here if you need to talk."

I had a feeling he knew what this was about. The corner of my mouth rose. "I know, man. Thanks."

He leaned back in his seat. "So . . . you never said anything about my idea."

"Which one?"

"Mia."

I picked the white cotton napkin off my lap and wiped my mouth before placing it on my empty plate. "I'm sure she'd love to go."

Lucas sighed, taking his wallet out from his coat pocket. "And?"

I raked my hand down my face. "It's fine, I guess."

He cocked a brow. "It's not like you'll be babysitting her. I thought you liked her?"

That's the fucking problem. I liked her a little too much. Her laughter was infectious. She was the kindest person I'd ever met. She had the ability to see good in everything, even me. I was the issue, along with all of my fucked-upness. "I do like her, man."

"Then what's the problem?" Lucas asked.

I waited for the waitress to take his card and the check and then responded, "Just looking out for her."

Lucas groaned, annoyed. "Ethan."

"What?"

"What the fuck are you doing? You better not be stringing her along. Did you forget? I'm married to her best friend. And she *will* kick your ass," he said, pointing his index finger at me.

The volume of my voice rose. "I know—that's why we're

just friends. It wasn't that long ago that Kyle fucked her over."

"It's been over a year, and *you're* not gonna fuck her over." He flicked his lip ring and narrowed his eyes. "Or I will be forced to chop your dick off."

I winced. "That's a bit extreme."

"Have you met Julia?"

Good point. I raised my shoulder. "Touché."

In the year I'd gotten to know Mia, she'd grown to be one of my closest friends. Our daily interactions at work and hanging out during off days had easily become a necessary part of my routine. I'd learned that she took two shots of espresso in her daily coffee. Her favorite color was royal purple. We'd discovered our fondness for reality shows. Spending time with her felt like an escape from the harshness of reality.

A delicate paper airplane glided gracefully through the air before landing on the table in front of me. Curious, I scanned the room, seeking its owner. The café was bustling with activity, the clatter of dishes, and the murmur of conversations.

"Excuse me, mister." A young boy, around ten or eleven years old, approached our table. He fidgeted nervously, his small fingers twiddling. There was an earnestness in his eyes I found endearing.

I couldn't help but smile. "Hey, this is a well-constructed aircraft." I picked up the plane while Lucas watched with an amused grin.

"Thank you," the boy responded, voice full of pride.

Leaning forward, I said, "You know, if you cut slits in the wings and make flaps, it'll twirl when it flies." I demonstrated where to make the adjustments on the plane, then handed it back to him.

His entire face lit up, and he skipped back to his table, where a woman—likely his mother—waved at me in gratitude, a warm smile on her lips.

Lucas's gaze turned thoughtful, his expression reflecting a sorrow that mirrored my own. It was an unspoken understanding of the pain that lingered beneath the surface.

"Jacob would've been about that age." I'd meant to keep that as a thought.

His eyes dropped to his empty plate. "You're gonna be an awesome dad someday."

The urge to leave behind the reminder of what had never been was overwhelming. "Let's get out of here."

After we ate, we traveled back to the studio and spent the next few hours combing through YouTube for potential clients. None of them stood out like Venom. We needed to get them to sign with us.

At around six o'clock, Lucas asked me to do a few tasks since the office was on my way home. He called the car for me, and it arrived within twenty minutes, Fred's personal best. Climbing into the sedan, I said, "That's record time."

He didn't look at me, but I could hear the smirk in his voice when he said, "Where to, Mr. Miller?"

"LV Productions."

He nodded, pulling away from the curb and onto the bustling street.

I stared out the window and watched the city lights flicker. Mia was probably still in the office. *Has she eaten dinner yet?* Recently, I'd found unopened to-go containers on her desk after she had gone home. I had half a mind to stop and pick up food, but I didn't want to miss her.

Lucas had been slow in hiring people to fill some important positions, so Mia was picking up a lot of the slack. She helped with social media, marketing, and sales. She really had been working her ass off, and I felt like a dick for not noticing sooner.

Is she gonna be excited about going to Los Angeles with me?

The car came to a stop in front of the modern brick building. I thanked Fred and stepped out, closing the door behind me. He drove away shortly after. When I strode through the black-metal-framed glass door, I walked into an unusual silence. Mia usually had her music blasting from the portable speaker on her desk. Unease roiled inside me as I made my way down the quiet hallway to her office. Walking in, my heart dropped. Mia lay on the cold tile floor, unmoving.

I rushed to her side and cradled her in my arms "Mia?" I held her close, her shallow breaths drifting across my cheek. "Wake up, Sweetness."

She groaned, and her eyelids fluttered open. Her beautiful dark gaze focused on me. "Ethan?" She stared up at me, a questioning look on her face.

"What happened? Did you fall? Are you hurt?" My eyes roamed the length of her body.

Mia shook her head. "I'm fine, just got a little dizzy. I must've fainted."

I helped her sit up, keeping my hand on her back. "You haven't eaten today, have you?"

"No. I lost track of time," she rasped.

I let out a short breath. "You really need to stop doing that." I placed a hand on her hip, guiding her to stand. "Well, let's order takeout, then." She sat in the nearest swivel chair, and I slipped my cell out of my pocket. "What're you in the mood for?"

Mia rolled herself behind the desk to her open laptop. "How about Chinese?"

"That place on Fifth?"

She nodded. "Pecan chicken, white rice—"

"And stir-fried green beans," I finished with a grin.

Her eyes widened. "Am I that predictable?"

"No." I pulled up the takeout app on my phone. "What can I say? It knows what you like."

A corner of her mouth rose, and her focus went back to the computer screen. "Okay, Mr. Smarty-Pants, what drink do I want?"

Taking into account all the times we'd ordered out at this restaurant, I chose between two of her favorite beverages. "A large taro milk tea with boba."

She sat back in her seat and studied me, crossing one leg over the other. "Wow . . . I had no idea you knew me so well." Turning back to her laptop, she continued to type. I watched in admiration as she tapped each key with quick precision.

What else are those fingers capable of?

After finalizing our order through the mobile app, I walked over and leaned against the desk beside her, our bodies mere inches from each other. Crossing my arms, I leaned closer with a smirk. "Are you impressed?"

She glanced at me with a shrug. "I guess." She stopped, clasping her hands in her lap. "Let's see . . . You ordered crab rangoons, chicken fried rice, and egg drop soup. And to drink . . . Thai tea. No boba."

A grin began to form at the edges of my lips, and warmth spread across my cheeks. "Now that's impressive." I peered over at her screen. "What're you working on?"

She sighed. "Vetting emails from potential clients. I can't believe how many submissions we've received in such a short time."

"Lucas Verduce is a big name. Artists would kill to work with him." I wheeled a chair over and sat close to her. "I need to talk to you about something."

She faced me. "Okay. Shoot."

"Lucas wants us to check out a band in LA this weekend," I said, picking a piece of lint off her oversize beige sweater.

"A band?" She tilted her head. "Am I getting promoted?"

"Um . . . If all goes well, it could lead to that," I replied, waggling my eyebrows.

She let out a loud squeal and lunged toward me, wrapping her arms around my neck and straddling my lap. Her warmth and lilac scent were fucking mesmerizing. All I wanted to do was pull her closer. But I needed to maintain some semblance of control. The fact of the matter was Mia Cruz stirred more than just my cock.

I held her in place, my hands braced on her upper thighs. I hoped to God she couldn't feel the half chub growing in my jeans. *Think of something other than the beautiful woman on my lap. That's not working.* I was still hard.

She seemed oblivious to the impact she had on me. "Thank you so much." She pulled away and stared into my eyes.

With my heart hammering in my chest, I became lost in everything that was Mia. "I can't take all the credit, Sweetness." My cell buzzed in my pocket.

A corner of her mouth rose. Maybe she wasn't so clueless. "You're vibrating." She slid off my lap and plopped back onto her chair.

With a grin, I stood, adjusting my dick as discreetly as possible all while answering the phone. The delivery driver had arrived. I stepped outside, where the crisp evening breeze swept across my cheeks. Collecting our variety of food and drinks, I noted the comforting warmth radiating from the containers. Back inside, I entered Mia's office, where the gentle rhythm of her typing filled the space.

After our meal, I shifted my focus to organizing our upcoming trip to Los Angeles. I browsed through various websites, selecting and booking our plane tickets and hotel room. Mia continued to clear the LV Productions email inbox.

I sat a few feet from her with an ankle crossed over my knee. "Are you excited about LA?"

She glanced at me. "Yeah. I do have to warn you though —I'll probably be a little jet-lagged."

"Me too. We can take a nap when we get to the hotel. Our arrival time is around three p.m.," I said, double-checking the reservations on my phone.

"Sounds like a plan."

"And I hope you don't mind, but we'll be sharing a suite. I checked the surrounding area for two rooms, but they didn't have anything available," I said.

Her long lashes fluttered with each blink of her dark eyes. "It's not like we haven't slept in the same room before."

I recalled falling asleep on her couch a few times when she was going through that whole ordeal with Kyle. "It's settled, then."

"Yup." She turned back to her laptop.

My gaze shamelessly lingered on Mia. The room's ambient lighting emphasized the concentration on her face. Her bewitching charm was weaving its way through my resolve. Keeping my feelings in check was becoming a hell of a lot harder than I'd expected.

I GOT TO THE AIRPORT EARLY FRIDAY MORNING, WHEN the sky was just beginning to lighten with soft hues. The weight of everything was heavy on my shoulders as I waited amid the sea of people in front of the terminal. I leaned on the handle of my purple roller carry-on, exhausted after the long week. *God, I hate flying.*

I didn't notice Ethan until he was just a few feet away. "Good morning," he said, adjusting the strap of his backpack over his shoulder.

I turned to him, offering a forced smile. "Hey."

"You ready to do this thing?" he asked, nodding toward the terminal doors.

We boarded the aircraft and settled into our first-class seats. As the plane ascended, leaving the city behind, Ethan ordered whiskey, and I chose a bottle of water over any alcohol.

Ethan stared at me, sipping his drink. "You sure everything's okay?"

Without looking at him, I replied, "I'm fine, just trying to be healthier."

He raised an eyebrow. "Since when?"

I shot him a sidelong look. "Since now." I took a small swig and then capped the bottle. "So, have you heard Venom's songs?" I asked, deflecting, using his own tactic against him.

He nodded with a smirk. "Yeah, Lucas showed me one of their original songs. I love their sound."

I began to show him the social media profiles of the four girls in the band. They all fit the branding they were aiming for and had been striving for a record deal for a few years now.

Midway through my detailed explanation, a sharp pain exploded in my abdomen. I placed a hand on my stomach, trying my best to mask the pain.

Ethan put his hand on my thigh. "You okay?"

"Yeah, that time of the month." I shifted in my seat before leaning back against the headrest.

"Are you excited about your first scouting assignment?" he asked, breaking the brief silence.

I peeled one eye open, then closed it again. "I guess. I've never been to LA before."

"You'll love it."

Our flight droned on, and the pain settled. I watched patches of white clouds float past the window. My thoughts kept drifting back to Ethan. Had he really noticed how off I'd been lately? *How miserably tired I must look.*

We landed at the busy Los Angeles airport. Despite the doctor's assurance that I was fit to fly, exhaustion wound through me with each step I took through baggage claim. The California sun cast a bright warm glow across the plain white floor.

After Ethan picked up the keys for the rental car, we headed to our hotel. It was a quiet thirty-minute drive through traffic. As I leaned against the passenger window, jet lag and lack of rest finally hit me.

Everything leading up to the moment we entered our shared suite was a blur. Ethan held the door open wide. I walked through, my suitcase rolling along with me. My eyes roamed the lavish sitting room.

"Well, this is our home for the next few days," Ethan said, dropping his bag next to the gray love seat. He scoped out the minibar next to the sliding door that led out to the huge balcony.

He shrugged off his jacket and unbuttoned the top four buttons of his shirt. Biting my bottom lip, I remained quiet, tearing my gaze away before he noticed. "I'm gonna shower."

I carried my suitcase into the bedroom and made my way into the bathroom, the cool tiles a relief to my tired bare feet. Sinking onto the lid of the toilet, I mustered the strength to turn the stainless knobs of the tub.

When the bathroom steamed up, I stripped off my clothes and stepped in. The hot water cascaded down my body, washing away the fatigue for a moment. After the much-needed shower, I took a painkiller, their small, innocuous shape contradicting the heavy significance they held for me.

I still hadn't told my dad about my diagnosis. Wrapped in a soft white towel, I stared at my cell for a moment before picking it up and dialing his number. It would take at least another thirty minutes for the meds to kick in.

It rang once, twice, three times.

"Mia?" Dad's voice rasped through the phone.

The Philippines was fifteen hours ahead. It was about four in the afternoon over there. "Hey, Dad. You busy?"

"No, just getting ready to cook dinner. What's up?"

Inhaling a deep breath, I told him about the pain I'd been experiencing, then about the appointment I'd had with Dr. Colton. There was no easy way to say it. "I've been diagnosed with stage I ovarian cancer."

The line went silent. I'd anticipated that. Dad and I had been here before with Mom.

"It's still early, Dad." I was trying to convince him as much as myself. "My surgery is scheduled for December 1 , and I really want you to be there." My voice shook, tears welling in my eyes.

I could hear a mix of sorrow and disbelief in his tone as he said, "Of course, Mia-bear. I'll be there."

I released a breath, and my shoulders slumped. "Thank you, Pop."

"*Mahal kita, anak.* Stay strong. We can beat this," he said.

I blinked back tears and nodded, though he couldn't see me. "*Mahal kita din.*"

"I need to make sure your *lola* takes her meds, but we'll talk again soon. Call me anytime, okay, *anak?*"

"I will, Pop."

We said our goodbyes and hung up. I dressed in sweats and dried my hair, then made my way out to the adjacent bedroom. The sound of the TV echoed from the sitting room. I assumed Ethan was on the couch, watching it.

Is he watching old episodes of The Bachelor? I grinned.

Too tired to even think about reality TV, I sank into the king-size bed, its sheets cool and soft against my skin. The fluffy pillow cradled my head as the tension in my body began to ease. My breaths deepened, and the chaos of my thoughts drifted away. Gradually, the welcoming embrace of the bed lulled me to sleep, a blissful escape into peaceful nothingness.

I awoke later to a dark room; the only light was the faint glow of the city seeping through the curtains. Disoriented, I wondered how long I'd slept. I glanced at the clock on the bedside table, and it read six o'clock. My stomach grumbled as though on cue.

The bed shifted beneath me as I turned, and the city lights revealed Ethan asleep next to me. His white dress shirt, untucked and partially unbuttoned, gave him a disheveled look that was attractively endearing.

I smiled, observing the rhythmic rise and fall of his chest, the way a strand of his dark hair fell over his forehead, his long lashes and strong jawline.

My heart ached with affection tinged with sorrow. I had it bad for this man, but with my current situation, a relationship was the last thing I needed. Julia could be right.

Maybe I just need a thorough fucking.

I got out of bed and walked to the bathroom, the soft carpet muting my steps. Gazing into the mirror, I couldn't help but see my mother staring back at me. Her hazel eyes, the familiar curve of her nose—her memory lived in my reflection.

It had taken her too soon. Cancer, the relentless thief. Different from mine, yet it steals, takes away from you, sometimes gradually, sometimes brutally fast.

I stood in the bathroom as fear clutched at my heart, its icy fingers paralyzing me. I could almost hear Mama's soft voice saying, *Magiging ayos ang lahat, mahal ko* (everything will be okay, my love). But she was gone. She couldn't guide me through this, couldn't offer her wisdom or her unwavering support. I missed her more than ever, yearning for the comfort she always was, the way she seemed to make even the worst situations feel manageable.

What would she say, knowing her daughter was walking the same difficult path that took her from this world? Standing there, I was lost in the reflection of a life altered forever, wishing for her presence because everything felt too large, too frightening to face alone. Even if I did live through this, I didn't know if I'd ever have a full life. I wiped the wetness away from my cheeks with my palm.

Ethan's knock startled me back to reality. "Mia? You good?" His voice was tinged with concern.

I took a deep breath, blinking back tears. "Yeah, sorry. I'm almost done." My voice was steadier than I felt.

"Did you want me to order takeout? Or we could explore LA a little and go out to dinner?" he suggested, his voice slightly muffled through the wooden barrier.

With a steadying breath, I put on a smile and then opened the door, meeting his handsome gaze.

His blue eyes were filled with a mix of concern and affection. "Have you been crying?"

I shook my head and walked past him. "No, it's allergies. We can go out if you're up to it."

"You know I'm always up for whatever you want, Sweetness." He winked.

I rolled my eyes, a flutter of butterflies stirring in my stomach despite the pain. "Yeah, yeah." I styled my hair into a messy bun using the mirror across from the bed. "Am I underdressed?" I glanced down at my joggers and oversize sweatshirt.

He shook his head. "No, you look fine. I was about to change into something more comfortable myself."

Soon we were out walking the sidewalks of LA, the city alive with lights and sounds. We meandered past several restaurants, eventually settling on a local Mexican place. The flavors of the carne asada tacos were a small delight, and

Ethan's enjoyment of his steak burrito brought a genuine giggle to my lips.

The walk back to the hotel was chilly, a stark difference from the usual New York autumns I was used to. High-rises stood illuminated in the distance, and the streets were relatively quiet, the occasional off-duty cab passing by.

Ethan stopped in the middle of the sidewalk. "You know you can talk to me, right?"

My brow rose, and I nodded, facing him. "I know."

He stuck his hands into his jacket pockets and stared at the ground. "Is everything okay?"

I pursed my lips. "Why?"

"You seem kind of distant lately."

I hated hiding the truth from him, but I was determined to keep my struggles to myself. With a huff, I walked past him. "It's just holiday stress—Christmas is coming up pretty quickly."

He stepped in front of me and stared into my eyes. "Are you sure that's all?"

Hugging myself tighter, I avoided his gaze. "Yeah, I'm sure."

"You'd tell me if something was wrong, right? Or at least Julia?"

My secret lay heavy on my shoulders. I didn't want to be a burden to him—to anyone. Staring at him, I whispered, "Of course."

His eyes softened as they met mine, an indiscernible sorrow in them. "I'm not a fan of the holidays either."

I knew better than to prod, but I was curious. "Why?"

He inhaled deeply, almost as if he was about to open up, to trust me with whatever lay hidden beneath the composed exterior. But just as quickly, he retreated into himself, exhaling slowly, the moment of potential honesty dissipating into the cold LA air. "We should get back to the hotel," he said, his voice reverting to its usual steadiness.

I nodded in response, trying not to show my disappointment.

It was typical Ethan, the king of deflection. Whenever we neared something too personal, something real, he'd skillfully steer the conversation away. Part of me wondered what he was hiding, the untold stories that might explain those fleeting shadows in his eyes. But I respected his boundaries, even as my own heart ached to share our burdens. It seemed we had more in common than I'd thought. We were both extremely cautious with our trust.

We walked back to the hotel in silence. Ethan chose to sleep in the sitting room, leaving me alone with my thoughts in the bedroom. The pain in my stomach returned, more intense than before. I took another painkiller, hoping for relief, but sleep eluded me.

My mind was a wonderland of worries: this scouting assignment, the holidays, surgery, and my treatments. I was determined to face it all—to be strong. Inhaling deeply, I whispered to myself, "You can do this."

Tomorrow will be better. I lay sprawled across the couch in the sitting room of our suite, my hands resting beneath my head in deep contemplation. *Why is Mia so withdrawn lately?* A faint glow from the large flat screen cast shadows across the high ceiling. The light flickered, illuminating the tasteful decor and the lavish furnishings around me. My thoughts swirled around the disheartening start to our trip. It was only the first night, and things already felt . . . tense.

I'd taken some pride in being a trustworthy friend. *Have I misstepped somehow?* She was the one person who could lighten my mood. Her presence was a constant source of cheer and comfort. But being her coworker, there were boundaries that shouldn't be crossed. Yet each day I spent with her tested those limits.

Something to brighten Mia's mood. I stared at the ceiling, a flicker of an idea beginning to take shape in my mind. Mia dancing took the forefront—the way her face lit up, her smile. I could feel it. I needed to take her out, let her lose herself in the rhythm of the music. *It could be the perfect distraction for us.* It was a plan that held promise, a brief escape from reality. With this hopeful thought, I surrendered to slumber, the possibilities of tomorrow lingering like a sweet melody in my dreams.

I WAS JOLTED AWAKE BY THE SOUND OF GAGGING. I squinted at the bright screen of my cell—two in the morning. Groggy, I sat up, rubbed the sleep from my eyes, and stumbled toward the bathroom. She'd left the door open slightly. The sight of Mia hunched over the toilet bowl hit me hard. A wave of panic shot through me. *Is she sick? Oh god, is she pregnant?* I shoved the thought aside, heading to the minibar. After grabbing a bottled water, I placed it on her bedside table.

Before I could retreat, Mia emerged. Her hair was a mess, and the circles under her beautiful dark eyes seemed more prominent in the dim light.

"You okay?" I asked.

It dawned on me she must have been struggling with sleep for a while. We'd been around each other for over a year now. Had I been too wrapped up in my own issues to notice her silent struggles?

Her gaze lingered on my bare chest for a few seconds,

and then she looked into my eyes. "I'm sorry I woke you," she said.

I took a step closer and leaned in. "Are you okay?"

She swayed, still standing in front of the bathroom door. "I'm okay now. Thanks."

"Do you need anything?"

She averted her eyes, hugging her midsection. "Do you think . . ."

We were so close that I could feel the heat emanating from her body. "Yes?"

She exhaled a small huff. "Lie with me until I fall asleep?"

She had to know by now I could never say no to her. The corners of my mouth curled up. "Of course," I murmured, softening my voice.

We lay on the bed, and Mia faced me. The dim light revealed the spattering of freckles across her nose. I stared at her, promising to be more attentive and supportive. When she finally chose to open up to me, I'd be there for her.

"Tell me one thing I don't know about you," she said, resting her head on her hand.

Unfortunately, there were many things she still didn't know about me. Pursing my lips, I replied, "I used to play the guitar. All the time, actually."

Her eyes widened. "Really? Why'd you stop?"

I shrugged. "Just got too busy with work."

She turned onto her back and rested her folded hands on her belly. "Do you miss it?"

All I wanted to do was pull her close and cuddle. She was inches from me, but it felt like a mile, and I didn't want to risk ruining the moment. "Yeah, sometimes. I used to play at open mic nights every so often."

She glanced at me, a grin on her face. "Did you perform your own songs or covers?"

"A little bit of both."

"That's cool. I don't think I could ever write a song," she said.

My eyelids were starting to get heavy. "Why not?" I asked midyawn.

"I'm not talented like that."

The next question I blamed on exhaustion. "Do you miss ballet?"

She stared at the ceiling and breathed in deeply. "Sometimes."

Julia had told me that Mia had quit after her mom died, so I knew it was a touchy subject. *God, I'm such an idiot.* Resting my forearm over my eyes, I said, "I'm sorry I brought it up."

"No. Don't apologize. It's just . . . still hard to talk about," she murmured.

"You don't owe me anything, Sweetness."

I felt her warm hand glide onto the center of my chest. Tingles spread where she was touching me. "Thanks for being such a good friend, Ethan." She removed her hand, and I resisted the urge to grab it and hold it in place.

As cliché as it was, I said, "What are friends for?"

Mia's eyes finally closed, and her breaths fell into a calm, steady rhythm. With a light touch, I swept away the strand of dark hair that lay across her face. Each breath I inhaled was laced with the subtle, sweet scent of lilac. A smile formed on my lips as I listened to the gentle sound of her snoring.

In the quiet room, a thought crept into my mind. *What if I open up to her even more, share my own vulnerabilities? Would she feel comfortable enough to do the same?* The idea lingered, tempting yet disconcerting. It could change everything between us.

I STIRRED AWAKE THE NEXT MORNING, STRETCHING MY arm out to find the sheets beside me cool and untouched, a contrast to the warmth that should've been there. Sunlight filtered through the sheer curtains. I reached for my phone and saw Mia's message. She had gone to a nearby bookstore and would meet me later at the venue where Venom was playing. I'd had plans for us, but then again, there was no *us*, and I wasn't even sure where we stood as friends.

ME

Sounds good. Call me if you need anything.

MIA

I will.

I doubted she would actually call, but what else could I do? *Track her down?* Her independence was one of the many qualities I loved about her. *Love?*

I spent the rest of the day in the suite, lounging in its luxurious comfort. For lunch, I had tacos delivered from the restaurant Mia and I had eaten at the night before. I double-checked the time for Venom's performance, my mind racing with strategies to win them over, though I was confident this contract was a sure thing.

I gazed out from the balcony door at the high-rises reaching skyward, their silhouettes bold against the backdrop of a cloudless sky. My cell's vibrations pulled me from my quiet observation of LA's vast bustling view.

Lucas's familiar tenor voice rang through the speaker. "How're things going?"

I let out a sigh. "They're going."

"I don't like the way you said that. Did something happen?"

I didn't want him to worry. "No. Everything's going as planned."

"Have you met with the band yet?"

"We're gonna watch them perform tonight," I replied, brushing my fingers through my hair.

"Keep me posted. I just received word that Sound Sphere offered them a contract a few days ago. Do everything you can to convince them to sign with us," he said.

Great, I had to compete with my old label. Letting out a breath, I assured him, "It's in the bag."

We said our goodbyes, and I headed to the bathroom to get ready.

How the fuck am I supposed to pull this off? Maybe I'll invite them to have some drinks in our suite. I hoped Mia would be okay with that.

Showered and clad in my usual laid-back attire, I gave my hair a final tousle in the mirror, trying to look presentable. Stepping out of the room, I took the elevator to the lobby.

I drove through the busy streets of LA, the city's nightlife unfolding like a vivid painting. Neon signs flickered in a symphony of colors. Towering buildings with windows aglow and the lively energy of the city pulsated around me.

I parked and could feel the bass in my chest as I walked into the lounge. Colorful lights painted vibrant streaks across the walls and ceiling. The crowd was an eclectic mix, each person seemingly more interesting and animated than the last.

I couldn't believe how much I missed Mia even though we'd only been apart for a few hours. Anticipation buzzed through me, heightening my senses as I scanned the crowd, searching for her face. My heart leaped at the gentle tap on my shoulder.

I turned to find Mia standing there, casual yet stunning in her fitted jeans, burgundy sweater, and brown UGG boots. Her wavy dark hair was pulled over one shoulder. She hadn't put on makeup, but her natural beauty shone through. I was breathless. Though even in the dim lighting, I couldn't miss the dark circles still under her eyes.

Mia greeted me with a soft smile.

"How was the bookstore? Did you buy anything?" I asked as we made our way to a high-top table where she had already ordered our drinks—a whiskey sour for her, a craft beer for me.

She blinked, seemingly lost in thought before she said, "Oh. It was fine. Nothing caught my attention."

My chest tightened at the thought of her wandering LA by herself, but she was a grown woman and had proved time and time again that she could take care of herself.

The moment was interrupted by the MC taking to the small wooden stage, his voice booming over the speakers, thanking everyone and introducing Venom.

The band members, each with their unique snake-themed nicknames, took their places. Gia, known as Viper, commanded attention as the lead singer and guitarist, her fingers dancing over the strings with a fierce intensity. Beside her, Liv, nicknamed Python, harmonized as the backup vocalist and rhythm guitarist, adding a layer of richness to their sound. Behind them, Krissy, or Mamba, rocked the drums, her beats resonating through the crowd. Completing the ensemble, Sam—Cobra—produced deep reverberating rhythms on the bass.

Their performance was a blend of original songs and covers that rocked the room. I stole a glance at Mia, noticing her finger tapping in time with the music, a sign she was enjoying the show.

Without much thought, driven by their melody and the moment, I took Mia's hand and led her to the dance floor.

She stumbled into me. I placed my hands on her hips, steadying her. She wrapped her arms around my neck. We moved in sync with the music, and the world around us faded into a blur. Our eyes locked, breaths mingling.

Her warm body pressed against me, and my dick twitched against the zipper of my jeans. *Fuck, not a great time to get a boner.* I leaned close, my lips grazing her ear. "Are you okay? Do you wanna keep dancing?"

She eased back, her mouth curving up. Her hazel eyes connected with mine, a spark of something real and unguarded in her gaze. "I'm fine. Thank you, Ethan."

As we continued to dance, her laughter mixed with the beat, each note weaving through the air and wrapping around my heart. A surge of hope filled me as my chest tightened. My fondness for this woman was growing with every second I spent with her.

The moment Venom's last note echoed through the lounge, the room crackled with applause. The scent of sweat and excitement was heavy in the air. Mia and I weaved our way through the crowd toward the stage, where the band was already talking with a few enthusiastic fans and an intern from Sound Sphere.

"Hey, great show, ladies," I said. "I'm Ethan Miller, this is Mia Cruz. We're from LV Productions. I believe I spoke with Gia on the phone."

The lead singer of the band, still glowing with the energy from her performance, greeted me with a confident handshake. "It's nice to finally meet you. I'm Gia," she said, then quickly introduced her bandmates. Each of them exuded a unique charm. Their collective energy was inviting, making Mia and me feel welcome in their circle.

Mia said, "You all sounded awesome."

Liv, still holding her guitar, leaned in. "Glad you enjoyed it. That's what we aim for."

Mia canted her head at me, something unreadable in her eyes. I didn't dwell on it though. Sure, Liv was attractive, but I had a firm rule against getting involved with clients. That and no eating or drinking in my Camaro. Those were the two most important rules in my book.

Sam, with her bass guitar still strapped over her shoulder, added, "Yeah, nothing beats the feeling of a live audience."

Krissy massaged her arms. "Especially when they're as enthusiastic as tonight's crowd." She shot me a flirtatious wink.

Seizing the opportunity, I suggested, "How about we all head to our hotel suite for some drinks and wind down after that amazing performance?" *I'm laying it on thick.*

Gia exchanged quick glances with her bandmates and then smiled. "We're down for that."

The intern from Sound Sphere said, "Maybe you should call Alice and invite her along."

My face went icy. "I don't think that's necessary." The intern hit call on her cell phone, and I stepped in and tapped end call. Leaning closer, so only she could hear me, I said, "Why don't you head back to Sound Sphere and let Alice know I'll be handling Venom from now on." I flipped her my card and sent her on her way.

After helping them pack up their instruments and equipment, we all made our way out of the lounge. The cool night air brushed against my face, a refreshing contrast to the stuffy warmth we'd left behind. I wasn't going to let Lucas down. I was prepared to win over these ladies and ink a deal with LV Productions.

How in the hell were we supposed to convince this group of girls to choose the smaller label? Sound Sphere, with their impressive client list, had more of everything. On the other hand, Lucas had a massively successful music career behind him. Ethan appeared undeterred, assuring me on our way back to the hotel that he had a plan. I just wished he'd shared it with me, to ease the knot in my stomach.

Walking into the grand lobby of our hotel was a contrast to the intimate setting of the lounge we had just left. Opulent chandeliers bathed the marble floors in a soft inviting light. Venom sat waiting, their youthful energy palpable even from a distance. We led them to our suite. The compact elevator was an interesting challenge, but we all managed to squeeze in, a tangle of limbs and laughter.

My ass was pressed against Ethan's groin, his proximity sending a rush of warmth into my cheeks. He slid his hand up to my waist and squeezed. I imagined him holding on to me like this, pushing his hard length into my wet pussy.

I didn't dare look over my shoulder. I couldn't let him see my blush. Though I could've used the excuse of too much body heat in the cramped metal box.

Liv was standing in front of me. She stepped back, pushing me flush against Ethan, my back colliding with his hard chest. I could've sworn a low rumble escaped him.

Liv apologized but didn't move.

His hand lowered and slipped beneath my sweater. His finger traced small circles along my hip. I cleared my throat, disguising the moan that slipped past my lips.

Sex would probably help me sleep better. Especially sex with Ethan.

The band members were still buzzing with post-performance adrenaline, their chatter filling the small space. I remembered that same rush from my days in ballet, a thrill I missed.

The elevator door opened on our floor, and Ethan's hand dropped from my waist. I walked out and led the way to our suite. With a quick tap of my card key on the reader, the lock beeped, and I opened the door. It beeped, and I opened the door. The girls immediately scoped out the huge place.

"This is bigger than two of my apartments," Gia said, her hands stuffed into her black jacket. The rest of the girls started taking off their layers and making themselves at home.

"Help yourselves to the minibar," Ethan said, kicking his shoes off by the door.

I grinned, knowing he'd picked up that habit from me. Growing up in my Asian home, shoes weren't allowed.

"Oh my god, look at that balcony." Gia opened the sliding glass door, letting a cold breeze sweep through.

"Shit. Close the door, Gia," Liv said, hugging herself.

I made my way across the spacious living room. Reaching Gia, I stepped out onto the balcony and promptly shut the sliding door behind us, cutting off the flow of the night air into the suite. The chill of Los Angeles was a far cry from New York's biting cold, yet the cool breeze was enough to make me shiver.

Through the window, I caught a glimpse of Ethan. He was in his element, skillfully concocting drinks for Liv, Krissy, and Sam. The way he moved, with such ease and confidence, caught my attention before I turned back to the view.

Gia stood beside me, her gaze fixed on the cityscape. "I could get used to this," she remarked, a note of awe in her voice.

I moved closer to the railing, standing next to her. The wind played with her short black hair. She drew in a deep breath of the crisp air, visibly shivering despite the protection her heavy coat offered.

The skyline, marked by illuminated buildings and billboards, created a dazzling urban picture. Below us, the streets were filled with neon signs and shifting car lights weaving through the city, resembling glowing arteries. Above, the stars twinkled faintly, competing with the vibrant luminance encapsulating the dynamic energy of LA.

"This is beautiful, and it kind of reminds me of New York, though it's a tad bit colder there," I mused.

She glanced at me. "I've always wanted to go to New York." She turned to face me. "Do you like working at LV Productions?"

I hugged myself and gave a noncommittal shrug. "Totally. I'm lucky to have a job with people I love. My best friend is married to Lucas, and he's been a great boss," I said. "Everyone there is passionate about the music, and I think that's a huge benefit to our artists. Lucas is an awesome producer."

Her brows rose. "I like hearing that. I've always been a fan of No Blood, No Alibi."

"Their music rocks. I was lucky enough to go on tour with them over a year ago," I mentioned. "It was a great adventure, but I'm still trying to find my place."

She studied me, a grin on her lovely face as she turned back to the view. "I get it, trust me."

"You do?"

"Yeah. It took me a while to finally realize making music is my calling. Even though my parents don't exactly approve of it," she said. "They wanted me to be a doctor or nurse or lawyer. All great occupations, but not for me."

I thought about my short career as a ballerina, the dream that faded when my mother passed. A melancholic smile pulled at the corners of my mouth. The reminder of my absence during her last moments made returning to dance too painful. The irony of my changed life weighed heavily on my chest—from a dancer in the spotlight to someone battling their shadows.

Gia stepped toward me. "Are you okay?"

My gaze snapped to hers. "Yeah, I'm fine."

Laughter spilled out onto the balcony from inside the suite. Turning, I caught sight of Krissy. She stood so close to Ethan that all he had to do was look down for an eyeful of boob action. With each giggle and expressive gesture, she subtly invaded his personal space, her flirtation unmistakable.

An ugly, unsettling sensation started to twist my stomach, like the early stirrings of stage fright. The more I watched, the harder it became to think clearly. *Why is this bothering me?* Ethan's and Krissy's laughter seemed to grow louder, taunting me. I had to look away and force myself to focus on the city lights, but the image of the two flirting lingered in my mind.

"God, she gets so loud when she drinks." Gia's gaze turned back to the cityscape. "So, what's the deal with you two?"

"Me and who?" I asked, even though I knew what she was implying.

"You and Ethan. Are you two a couple?" She said it low, like it was some kind of secret.

I chortled. "No. We're just friends."

She cocked a brow. "Really?"

"Is that so hard to believe?" I leaned my forearms on the railing.

Gia grinned. "I just thought you two were together from the way you were staring at each other on the dance floor."

My mind flashed back to when I'd stumbled into him. I had no idea she'd seen us among all those people. "I don't know what you're talking about."

Her gaze met mine, and she tilted her head. "I'm sure. Well then, that saves me the trouble of telling Krissy to lay off. She's a sucker for a man in a suit."

Another chill crawled up my spine. I said nothing and stared off into the distance.

I felt Gia's eyes on me. "I could still tell her to lay off," she said.

I inhaled, then exhaled. "No." I hadn't intended for the word to come out so angry. "I mean . . . I don't care either way."

She shrugged. "Okay. If you say so."

This was it. I needed to talk to her about signing with LV Productions. Clearing my throat, I started, "So, have you considered our deal over Sound Sphere?"

She faced me, a hand on her hip. "The girls and I have talked about it, but we haven't made any official decisions."

I straightened. "I know Sound Sphere Records is the big time every artist is eyeing, but LV Productions can give you something they can't."

"And what's that?"

What would Ethan say? I did my best to put myself in his shoes. "Priority. LV won't just sign you and forget you. You'll be our priority, not just another band in the lineup."

Her brows rose. "That sounds great and all, but do you

have the reach? Could you guys give us what Sound Sphere can in terms of exposure?"

Biting my lip, I thought about that question for a moment before replying, "We have heart, and we'll work twice as hard. We're all about personal touch and really getting behind our artists. Lucas wants our artists to be more involved in the production process. With Sound Sphere, you risk getting lost in the shuffle. LV Productions, though small, has some serious industry respect. We could be the springboard you need."

Gia crossed her arms, her jacket rustling with the movement. "I don't know. It's a gamble. A big one."

Shit. What else could I possibly say? Maybe I needed to take a different approach. I remembered reading about her heritage on her social media. "Look, I know the struggle—what it's like being judged because of the way you look. I used to be a ballerina, and not one of the premier companies wanted to give me a chance."

That caught her attention. She stepped closer. "What happened?"

I stuffed my hands into my coat pockets. "Aurora Ballet, an inner-city company, gave me a chance, and eventually, I made it to prima ballerina. My point is, they took that chance on me, and I took the chance on them, even though they weren't the New York City Ballet. That choice allowed me to grow in ways I couldn't have imagined."

"I won't lie, the idea of being a priority and not just another headliner is extremely tempting. But what if we sign with LV and it doesn't work out?"

Placing a hand on her arm, I replied, "We won't let you girls down. You're all amazing, and we can see that. We want this to work *for you* just as much. And we're not interested in changing who you are—which Sound Sphere has been notorious for."

Gia smiled as her hands fell to her sides. "You're pretty cool, Mia Cruz. If LV Productions is ready to take a chance on a bunch of wild California girls, then I'm game."

I blinked in surprise. "Wait, does that mean you're agreeing to sign with us?" A smile spread across my face, a mix of relief and disbelief. I couldn't pinpoint exactly what had convinced her, but I was thankful I hadn't held back. Talking with Gia Razon had been easy, maybe because we shared some common ground. Navigating life as a Filipino American woman had its challenges, and maybe that shared experience had forged a subtle bond between us.

"I'll have to talk with the rest of the band, but I'm pretty sure you can consider us a sure deal," she replied with a grin.

The evening seemed to speed past, each moment slipping away faster than the last. I stuck to ice water from the minibar, the cold liquid in the tumbler serving as a prop more than anything else.

I couldn't help but notice Ethan. He and Krissy were engrossed in a lively chat, their laughter ringing out and mingling with the ambient sounds of the suite. Their easy rapport was evident. Their conversation flowed as naturally as the music that had played earlier.

I tried to rationalize these hideous feelings away, telling myself it was just fatigue or maybe the side effects of my meds. But deep down, I knew it was neither. Ethan with someone else, the way he smiled at her . . .

I continued to sip my water, the coolness doing nothing to quell the pirouettes of emotions I didn't want to face.

The members of Venom ended up leaving at three in the morning. They all confirmed that they'd decided to sign with LV Productions. Ethan told them to come back at noon that day to sign the contract.

I cleaned up the sitting room, placing all the used glasses next to the minibar for room service to pick up the next day. Krissy had given Ethan her number before she left, and I wondered if he was interested in her.

"What did you say to Gia?"

I turned to see Ethan leaning against the doorpost of the bedroom. My lips curved up. "That's between us."

He moved to the couch and plopped down. "Fine. Keep your secrets."

The next words came out without much thought. "You and Krissy seemed to be getting cozy."

He raised an eyebrow, sinking into the cushions of the couch. "She's a sweet girl."

Placing the last of the glass tumblers on the bar, I asked, "Do you think you'll hook up with her?"

He stared at me, a glimmer of curiosity in his eyes. "She lives across the country."

I crossed my arms. "You don't remember that girl from Colorado? You literally flew over for the weekend."

"If I'd known she was married, I wouldn't have gone." He leaned forward, resting his forearms on his thighs.

I sat next to him, exhaling sharply. "Wait a second, let me get this straight. You actually saw a future with her?"

He shrugged. "I saw potential. It was probably just me being desperate."

I stifled a laugh and then pressed my lips together. "Why didn't you tell me?"

"We were just getting to know each other, and you were going through that whole thing with Kyle," he replied.

Now that I thought about it, Kyle fucking that groupie was the best thing he did for me. I wasn't in love with him. It was lust. "I still wish you would've told me. It probably would've gotten my mind off the jackass."

Ethan turned, his beautiful eyes meeting mine. "What Kyle did to you was fucked-up. I'm sorry."

"Julia tried to warn me, I should've listened," I muttered, crossing one leg over the other.

"That's one thing I've always liked about you," he said.

"What's that?" I asked, pushing my hair over one shoulder.

He scooted closer. "You're not easily influenced. You follow your heart. Something I seem to have trouble with."

Did I really follow my heart, or was I just stubborn? I knew he wouldn't elaborate, but I had to ask. "Why is that?"

He sat back, not breaking eye contact with me. "It's a long story."

That meant he didn't want to talk about it. Uncrossing my legs, I stood and said, "Maybe a story for another time, then."

He nodded and rasped, "Yeah."

"Good night, Ethan." I started toward the bedroom.

"Good night, Sweetness."

As I lay in bed, Ethan's words echoed in my mind. *You follow your heart.* Did I really? I'd followed my passion for ballet, even when it led me away from a secure life. Maybe he was right about me. But what about him? Why did he find it so difficult? That question gnawed at me, making it hard to sleep. Maybe one day he'd trust me enough to talk to me.

THE NEXT MORNING BRIMMED WITH A NEW BEGINNING. Ethan and I were about to turn dreams into reality for Venom. Stepping into the hotel's chic conference room, awash with the morning rays, I felt a rush of excitement. The band sat waiting, vibrating with anticipation, a mirror of our own eagerness. It was more than just a contract; it was the start of something big—something that felt like destiny. I had a good feeling about this girl band. They were going to take New York by storm.

Ethan unfolded the contract with practiced ease, his demeanor a perfect blend of businesslike efficiency and approachable warmth. He connected his tablet to the projector on the wall and pulled up a digital copy of the contract. Glancing at each member of Venom, he started by thanking them for choosing us and then moved on to read each item. "This clause ensures you retain creative control over your music."

Gia's brow furrowed. "So, we keep all our rights to the songs we write?"

"Yes," Ethan said, a reassuring smile spreading across his face. "Full ownership. We're here to support you, not control you."

I watched the band members exchange looks of anticipation. Krissy leaned forward, her fingers tapping lightly on the table. "And how much input do we have in regard to touring?"

"You'll have a say in your touring schedule. We'll provide the resources, but the final decisions will always be yours," he said.

As Ethan continued to explain, his tone conveyed a genuine interest in making the process as transparent and comfortable as possible for all parties involved. He wasn't just reciting legal jargon; he was making sure they felt confident and secure in their decision.

The band members listened attentively, occasionally exchanging looks of nervous excitement. When it came time to sign, each member took their turn, making their moment of commitment significant. A partnership.

A collective exhale filled the room as the pen was set down after the last signature. Hands were extended, each handshake firm and meaningful.

"Welcome to LV Productions," Ethan said with a warm smile.

"Congratulations," I added, my lips turning up. The tension that had hung in the air moments before dissolved into a chorus of relieved laughter and excited chatter.

Despite the complex emotions lingering from the previous night, I couldn't help but share in the optimism of the moment—the sense of hope for what the future held for both LV Productions and Venom.

Gia and I were the last to walk out of the conference room. She looped her arm through mine, slowing her pace and letting the rest of the group get farther away from us.

Once they were out of earshot, she said, "I work at a restaurant part-time. You and Ethan should have dinner there tonight. It's on me."

I glanced at the time on my phone and clicked my tongue. "I wish we could, but our flight is in a few hours. We need to get back to New York. Rain check?"

"Yeah, for sure," she said with a grin.

"Give me your phone." I held my palm out to her.

She handed her cell to me.

Typing my number into her contacts, I said, "If you want to talk, or end up in New York and need a place to stay, call me." I gave her cell back.

"Thanks, Mia. I will."

We caught up with the rest of the group. Ethan and I bid the girls goodbye and watched them drive away in their old-school minivan. I wished we could've stayed longer, but with LV Productions being short-staffed, we needed to get back home.

Carrying the uplifting energy from the successful meeting, my mind gradually shifted to the more personal challenges awaiting me. Our flight back to New York loomed ahead, and I was *not* looking forward to the ride home.

Back in the suite, I started packing up all my toiletries, which were scattered along the bathroom counter. *How many emails are in LVP's inbox? I should probably check it before we board.* I went through a task list in my mind of things that needed to be done, including my laundry.

"So, what do you think?"

I jolted, sending my toothpaste into the air. It landed in the shower. "Fuck, Ethan." I placed a hand to my chest.

A corner of his mouth rose. "I mean, we can if you want."

My cheeks warmed as I turned away. "What do I think about what?"

He stood in the doorway. "About your first scouting assignment."

Zipping up my small makeup pouch, I moved on to pack my face wash and moisturizer. "I had fun."

"Not every assignment is going to be successful, of course, but you gotta take the wins with the losses," he said.

I nodded, a faint grin tugging at my lips. Honestly, I wasn't in the mood to talk about anything. The pain in my stomach had returned, but I needed to wait until we got onto the plane to take my meds.

He continued to study me. "Is something wrong?" He leaned against the doorframe with his arms crossed, staring at my reflection in the full-wall mirror.

I stopped what I was doing and looked at him. "Why do you keep asking me that?"

A muscle in his jaw ticked. "Why do you keep deflecting?"

Maybe I should just come out and tell him. But the

stubborn part of me said this wasn't his burden to carry. I didn't need to worry anyone else with this. I was worried enough for all of us. Inhaling and then exhaling, I finished packing up the rest of my toiletries before facing him. "I already told you I'm fine."

"What you're saying and how you're acting doesn't make sense," he replied, taking a step closer.

I held my ground, eyes narrowed. "And how am I acting?"

"I don't know how to explain it. Not like yourself, that's for damn sure."

"Maybe you don't know me as well as you think," I said, staring straight into his feisty blue eyes.

He leaned in, bringing his face just inches from mine. "Keep telling yourself that, Sweetness. Whether you want to admit it or not, we've become inseparable this past year. I'm an important person in your life now."

I scoffed and averted my gaze. "You're such a cocky motherfucker."

He grabbed my chin and forced me to look at him again. "Tell me I'm wrong."

I wasn't going to give him the satisfaction, so I said nothing. My eyes widened as he brought his nose to the curve of my neck. It sent gooseflesh down my arms. My lips parted, releasing a faint breath.

"Why do you always smell so fucking good?" His hand drifted to my waist, and he gripped it tightly.

I felt his lips against my neck. He worked his mouth against my skin, sucking and nibbling his way to the sensitive spot behind my ear. A moan escaped me, and that seemed to make him snap.

He lifted me onto the counter by the backs of my thighs, setting me on its edge. I let out a small squeal. He continued to caress me and ground his hard dick against my pussy.

This couldn't go farther no matter how much I wanted him. I pulled away. "We can't . . ."

He stared at me with a conflicted gaze, then stepped back. "Shit . . . I'm sorry."

Recognizing the regret in his eyes, I hopped off the counter and grabbed my toiletries bag. Before walking out, I said, "Let's just forget this ever happened, okay?"

I settled into my seat on the plane as reality snuck up on me. *It was nice while it lasted.* The day of my "minor" surgery was approaching, and I just wanted it to be over, to be free from the pain and uncertainty that clouded my days. Despite my wishes, some things were out of my control. It was a harsh truth to accept, but acceptance was all I had.

As the plane readied to take off for New York, Ethan sat next to me in the window seat and leaned back against the plush first-class cushions. He offered me a faint smile before closing his eyes.

My gaze lingered on the contours of his jaw and the

tempting shape of his lips. His brown hair fell in a relaxed manner across his forehead.

So fucking handsome.

Now that I knew the feel of his lips, my body wanted more. Shaking my head, I refused to let myself go there. *Why torture myself?*

I quickly took my painkillers. Drinking water, I stared at the white label of the medicine bottle. Once he learned about this illness, that I might not be able to have kids . . . *Why would he want me?* Not that he wanted me in the first place.

"Are we not gonna talk the whole ride home?" I asked once our plane leveled.

He didn't open his eyes. "What would you like to talk about?"

"Are things gonna be awkward between us?" I crossed my arms, goose bumps spreading over them. *Damn, that air is cold.* I closed the vent above me.

Ethan's eyes opened. He looked at my forearm and the hair standing on end. Without a word, he unzipped his cotton hoodie and placed it over me.

I became lost in his citrusy bergamot scent. "Thanks," I muttered.

He kept his gaze on me as though thinking about his next words. "I promise we're okay, Sweetness. No awkwardness here."

My chest constricted. *This is for the best.* Not to mention he had a no-dating-coworkers rule. From everything I knew about him, he stuck to it. No exception.

Hours later, the plane touched down, wheels hitting the tarmac with a jolt. I unbuckled my seat belt and glanced at Ethan beside me. His face was a mask of calm, but I could sense the underlying tension between us.

As I stepped into the terminal, the noise and chaos of the airport enveloped me—hurried footsteps, distant announcements, and the hum of countless conversations.

Ethan and I parted ways. I needed space, a break from the complexity of our interactions. Each conversation with him brought an urge to reveal my struggles, yet I feared he would pity me or shift how he saw me.

It took my taxi driver forty-five minutes to finally reach my building. I paid the fare, grabbed my bag, and headed inside. Unlocking the door, I stepped into my apartment. It was a sanctuary of solitude, where the only sounds were the soft creaks of the floorboards beneath my feet and the distant hum of NYC faintly echoing through the windows.

I rolled my suitcase into my room, promising myself to unpack it later. My stomach grumbled, the pang of hunger hitting me. *Shit . . . I should've stopped for takeout.*

The fridge greeted me with its barren shelves. With a sigh, I grabbed peanut butter and crackers from the cupboard and settled onto my well-worn thrifted couch. The room was engulfed in silence so profound that the sudden vibration of my phone made me jump. I picked it up, the screen casting a faint glow in the dim room, breaking the stillness for a moment.

JULIA

Hey, babe, checking in. How was your trip?

ME

It was fine. We signed Venom.

JULIA

Awesome! We need a girls' night soon. Lucas is getting on my nerves.

ME

As usual. Lol. And a girls' night sounds great. Gossip Girl and junk food?

JULIA

Sounds good. Talk soon!

I placed my phone on the coffee table and sank into the cushions with a sigh. I did not want to go to work the next day. The pain in my stomach had returned. It was only bearable with medication that left me feeling drowsy and disconnected. I hated how those pills made me feel.

That night, exhaustion took over. I fell asleep on the couch, still in my travel clothes, too weary to move. The faint serenade of the city outside my window lulled me into a restless slumber, filled with dreams and fears too tangled to untwine.

WE HAD OUR FUTURE LAID OUT PERFECTLY BEFORE US, and I couldn't wait. My girlfriend, Hailey, the most amazing girl in school, was always by my side. As captain of the hockey team, I was the big man on campus. I scored winning goals, and our victories were legendary. My heart pounded with a mix of nerves and excitement; all those hockey victories paled in comparison to this. In a matter of months, I'd gone from high school hero to soon-to-be dad.

Christmas music played low on the radio as I gripped the steering wheel of my Camaro. Hailey was about to give me the greatest win of all: we were having a baby boy. Heart racing, I darted through the sliding doors of the hospital, making a beeline for the maternity ward. When I reached the waiting room, the sight of Hailey's parents, faces etched with worry, stopped me cold.

My blood turned icy. "What happened?"

"There've been complications," her dad said, his voice heavy.

The hallway stretched into infinity as I paced its length, each step echoing my mounting fears. Time warped into an agonizingly slow crawl, each tick of the clock a sharp reminder that Hailey was alone in the delivery room, battling complications I couldn't fight with her—for her.

Doctors and nurses whizzed by in a blur, their faces a mix of focus and concern, but I stayed rooted in place, utterly fucking powerless. Waiting, the not knowing . . . It gnawed at me, tearing at my insides.

I'd faced nerve-racking playoff games, stared into the eyes of fierce opponents on the ice, but this? This was a whole new level of dread. The kind that grips deep in your gut, twisting tighter with every passing minute. Never in my life had I felt so sidelined, so desperate for a win that I had no hand in securing. Every second she was behind those closed doors, my heart raced faster.

The moment the ob-gyn emerged, my world stood still. He approached us, a solemn look on his face. "Hailey is doing well, but . . . I'm sorry, the baby . . . was stillborn." His words hit me like a ton of bricks.

The muffled sobs of Hailey's parents pierced the thick, suffocating air, their grief a tangible presence wrapping around me. Sorrow echoed in my hollow chest in response to my unshed tears. Through the fog of disbelief, the doctor's words about Hailey holding on to our son seemed distant, yet it jolted me into motion.

My legs, heavy as if weighed down by concrete blocks,

carried me in a slow surreal march to the delivery room. I pushed the door open, revealing Hailey, a silhouette in the dimly lit room. She was clutching our dark-haired little boy to her chest, her body shaking with sobs that cut through the silence. Her tears traced wet trails down her face, glistening in the faint light.

"Hailey," I whispered, my voice unsteady—foreign to my own ears.

She didn't respond.

Walking over to her bedside, I placed my hand on her shoulder. "Hailey, love . . ." It was all I could muster. Words caught in my throat, strangling the air out of me. My heart pounded against my rib cage, a frantic drumming in the quiet of the room. My other hand trembled at my side. I stood there, torn between an instinctive urge to take our son into my arms and the crushing reality of his stillness.

She looked up, her eyes a well of sorrow. "Ethan, he was perfect," she sobbed.

My heart broke for her, for us. "He *is* perfect, babe," I whispered, reaching for his tiny body. His feet weren't even the length of my pinky.

She pulled away from me. "No."

"Please," I choked out, using my index finger to brush a strand of blond hair behind her ear. It took everything in my soul not to lose it, to be strong in this moment for her.

Hailey's features softened, and she conceded.

I reached for my son, cradling him in my arms. He was so small, too still. Tears brimmed in my eyes and threatened to shatter my barrier of strength. I should've felt his heartbeat, the rise and fall of his chest, his warmth. Instead, there was nothing. I swallowed the lump in my throat.

Hailey buried her face in her hands. "I can't believe it. I just can't . . ."

I stood there holding my son, drowning in a sea of what-ifs and should-have-beens. The nurse walked in with a clipboard in hand. She was sympathetic and careful with her words when she asked what we wanted to name him. We had already planned so much for our baby boy—a name chosen, a baby shower celebrated.

With Hailey still crying uncontrollably, I told the nurse the name we'd picked out for him months ago. After filling out the paperwork, the nurse asked to take Jacob away. Handing my son's body to her felt like relinquishing a part of my soul. When the nurse left the room, I kissed Hailey on the forehead and stumbled out of there. I made my way past Hailey's parents and rushed through the hospital's automatic doors, my mind a haze of grief.

As I settled into the driver's seat of my Camaro, the dam broke. Tears streamed down my face, each one symbolic of the pieces of my shattered heart. I cried alone, the weight of what we'd lost pressing down on me in the silence. *My future is gone.* The pain was so raw and deep that it threatened to consume me whole.

I STARED OUT THE WINDOW OF MY OFFICE. ORANGE AND gold leaves swirled and twirled in the fall air, dancing across the sidewalk and in the streets. I held two tickets to *The Nutcracker* in my hand, the paper slightly creased from my nervous grip.

As I closed my eyes, the memory of Mia's lilac scent and her soft body pressed against mine taunted me. Even now, I could still taste her on my lips, and fuck me, I wanted more.

You don't date coworkers, remember? I couldn't believe I was even considering it. My gaze drifted to the tickets in my hand. I'd bought them as a peace offering to prove that our friendship was still intact—still strong.

Should I ask her?

Mia had called in sick twice. I understood why. The LA trip had been exhausting, and it had worn me out too. I carefully placed the tickets in my coat pocket and pulled out my cell, thumbing it open to check for new texts. No messages. An unexpected hollowness settled in my gut.

A burst of energy accompanied the abrupt swing of the office door. "Uncle E.T.!" Lindsay, my five-year-old niece, enveloped my legs in a warm embrace. Lifting her into my arms, I showered her cold cheeks with kisses.

I squeezed Lindsay a little tighter, her small frame snug in my embrace. "How's my little Lind-bug?" I cooed, and she giggled against my chest.

How much would Jacob look like her?

Belle, ever the embodiment of sunshine, breezed into the room, her blond hair cascading in waves down the front of her shoulders. "Hey, butthead," she teased with a playful glint in her eyes.

I feigned shock. "Don't say that in front of her," I chided, trying to keep a straight face.

Belle tucked a stray lock of hair behind her ear. "You ready for lunch?" Her casual tone shifted to curiosity. "Where's Mia? I didn't see her in her office."

Lifting Lindsay, I settled her onto my shoulders, her little hands gripping my hair. "You went to see Mia before me?" I asked, mock offense lacing my voice.

Belle shrugged, a mischievous twinkle in her eye. "We like Mia, don't we, Linds?" She winked at Lindsay.

"More than me?" I pretended to be wounded by their betrayal.

Rolling her eyes, Belle shot back, "Don't pretend you don't like her just as much."

I couldn't help but smirk. "She's off today." Letting out a

slow steadying breath, I reminded myself to be patient with Mia.

Belle arched an eyebrow, her hand resting on her hip in a classic pose of sisterly intuition. "What's wrong?" she prodded.

I started down the long hallway, Lindsay still on my shoulders. "What do you mean?" I asked, then tried to steer the conversation toward safer waters. "So . . . our usual diner?"

Belle wasn't easily diverted. She fell into step next to me, a knowing look on her face. "Don't avoid the question. I know when something's bothering you."

Lindsay squirmed too much, so I took her off my shoulders, but continued holding her. "Nothing's wrong, B. Just catching up on work. We got a little behind after our LA trip," I lied, hoping she'd buy it.

Her sidelong glare told me she wasn't convinced. "Liar."

Lindsay glanced between us, her little lips curled up in a smile.

Cornered, I fumbled for words. "I don't know what else to tell you."

"How about the truth?"

Damn. I could never get anything past her. "It's Mia. I'm worried about her, that's all," I admitted, rolling the tension from my shoulders. A part of me was relieved to voice my concern.

Her grin widened. "I knew it had something to do with her. You always seem to be together. Why don't you two get together already?"

"Yeah!" Lindsay chimed in, poking a finger at my face.

I playfully snapped at her finger, making her giggle and pull away. "You know my rule against dating coworkers," I said, though my certainty wavered. "We have a good arrangement." I set Lindsay on the lobby floor.

"Let me guess, you get everything you need except sex. I don't think that's very fair to Mia," she said low enough that Lindsay couldn't hear.

The bad thing was, she was right. But I really did want the sex. *God, how I want it.* Trying to act nonchalant about it, I said, "She hasn't complained."

"Yet," Belle pointed out, stopping to zip up Lindsay's jacket and then wrapping herself in her own coat.

With a huff, I buttoned my jacket. "Mia and I have an understanding," I said, more to convince myself than her. The LA trip had shaken something loose, a realization that maybe our understanding wasn't as clear as I'd thought.

The three of us made our way to the corner diner, immersed in the city's bustling energy. As we entered, the soft chime of the doorbell announced our arrival. The interior was a cozy throwback, with red vinyl booths lining the walls and checkered tiles underfoot.

The aroma of coffee and sizzling bacon filled the air, mingling with the low hum of conversations and soft jazz playing in the background. Friendly staff adorned in retro aprons greeted us with smiles. We settled into a booth, the tabletop dressed in a classic red-and-white-checkered cloth, complete with shiny cutlery and old-school glassware.

I perused the menu, but in the end, I couldn't resist the

allure of my usual go-to: a classic cheeseburger and fries. Meanwhile, Belle shared her plate of fluffy pancakes adorned with a cascade of fresh berries and a dollop of whipped cream with Lindsay.

"How're things at the hospital?" I asked before taking a bite of my burger.

Belle paused. "They moved me to day shift. I get to sleep at night again."

"That's always good." I ate a crispy fry.

"Oh, before I forget, Mom wants me to ask what kind of pie you want on Thanksgiving," she said with a mouthful of food.

My lips curved up. "I don't know. Pumpkin?"

She rolled her eyes. "That's such a generic answer."

"I like what I like."

"Are you bringing Mia?" Belle asked, not making eye contact with me.

I glared. "Why do you ask?"

She grinned. "I was just wondering—"

"Stop prying, Belles." I took another large bite of my burger.

Lindsay picked at her food as she stared out the big window at the passersby.

Belle shot me a severe look. "Just invite her. Mom and Dad asked about her, and she's much better company than the other bimbos you usually bring."

Should I tell her I already invited her? I let out a breath, tilting my head to the ceiling.

"Stop being such a drama queen," she remarked.

"I'll ask her," I replied.

"Good. 'Cause if you don't, I will." A devious smile spread across her face.

And she would too. Belle had managed to get Mia's number at Lucas and Julia's wedding.

I raked my hands down my face and repeated, "I'll ask her."

After lunch, I returned to the solitude of my office, the bustle of the city outside my window a contrast to the quiet stillness inside. I sat at my desk, the laptop open in front of me, but I couldn't concentrate. Mia seemed to have cemented herself at the forefront of my mind. Her lilac scent permanently haunted my senses. I found myself tapping the smooth surface of my desk, a physical manifestation of the restless frustration bubbling inside me.

I stood and walked over to the window, lost in thought, and watched the leaves fall from the trees that lined the sidewalk. Pulling out my phone, I held on to a faint hope for a text from Mia. But the screen, devoid of new messages, only reflected the loneliness of the room. Lindsay's smiling face on the wallpaper was a brief comfort for the emptiness.

With a deep breath, I dialed Mia's number. The tension tightened in my shoulders with each ring. When her voicemail picked up, I hesitated before speaking, my voice revealing more than I intended. "Hey, Sweetness. I just wanted to check on you. Call me back when you get this." I paused. "I miss you." The words had slipped out. Hanging up, I was left with a lingering sense of vulnerability and wondered if I'd crossed a line.

The afternoon dragged on, each minute stretching longer than the last. I probably answered about three emails in my eight-hour shift. Lucas was going to be pissed about that.

When the day finally ended, I drove back to my apartment, leaving behind the confines of the office for the solitude of my personal space. As I stepped inside, the silence consumed me once again.

That evening, as I lounged in the dim glow of my living room, the unexpected buzz of my phone broke the stillness. Mia's voice, weary yet unmistakably warm, filled my ears. I turned down the volume of the TV, giving her my full attention.

I supposed now was as good a time as any to confirm with her. "Thanksgiving is in a few weeks. You're still coming, right?"

There was a brief pause. "I mean, we had a deal," she said.

I smiled. "Good. My whole family is expecting you."

"I see," she murmured.

I couldn't get over the slight rasp in her voice. "Are you okay?" I asked.

"Yeah, I'm fine," she replied, but the simplicity of her words didn't put me at ease.

The darkness of the room seemed to deepen, the moonlight casting shadows across the hardwood floor. "Are you coming into work tomorrow?" I asked, hoping to gauge more from her response.

"I'll be there," she assured me, her sincerity clear even through the phone.

Stop stalling and just ask her. With an exhale, I asked, "Are you doing anything this weekend?"

"No. Why? Do you need me to work?"

Why would she think that? A weight in my chest dragged my heart into my stomach. "No. It's not work. I wanna take you out."

God, why did saying those words feel like pulling teeth?

It seemed she was at a loss for words. She didn't answer for a long moment. "Take me out? Where?"

"It's a surprise." I started to doubt this decision. Resting my free hand on my thigh, I tapped my index finger, waiting for a reply. *She must enjoy torturing me.*

"So . . . just to be clear, this isn't a date."

"No, of course not. It's just a friendly outing." I winced at that last part. *Friendly outing?*

"Okay. What day and time?"

The biggest grin tugged at the corners of my mouth. "Friday at six. I'll pick you up."

I heard shuffling, and then she replied, "Sounds good. I'll be ready."

"Good. I guess I'll see you at work," I said, my words carrying the weight of my growing feelings.

"Okay. Good night, Ethan."

"Good night, Sweetness," I whispered into the phone. I ended the call, but my concern remained. The room fell silent once more, the soft glow of the moon the only witness to the longing that swept through me.

I was stepping into Mia's world, taking her to see *The Nutcracker*. My fingers tapped against the steering wheel of my Camaro. *Why am I so nervous? This isn't a fucking date. We're just hanging out as friends.* Yet here I was, dressed in one of my finest suits, wearing a shiny black pair of Louboutin loafers.

I revved the engine, feeling its familiar power surrounding me as I navigated the New York streets. The city was buzzing with its usual energy, but my mind was solely on Mia.

It took me forty-five minutes to arrive in front of an old red brick apartment building.

I sent Mia a text.

ME

I'm out front.

The front door of the building swung open, and Mia

stepped out into the soft glow of the streetlights. Her gaze met mine through the windshield. She wore a black coat with a pumpkin-orange sweater underneath. I bit my lip at how her dark-wash jeans hugged her curves deliciously. She turned a simple walk to my car into a mesmerizing saunter.

With my heart racing in my chest, I climbed out to open the car door for her.

She raised a brow and stared at me as if I'd done something weird.

I put on one of my trademark smiles. "What?"

"Nothing," she said, giving me a sidelong glance before sinking into the Camaro's well-worn leather seat.

The dusty-pink color on her lips drew my gaze to her mouth. If she only knew how badly I wanted to taste her. Settling in next to her, I started toward the theater.

During the one-hour drive, I kept stealing glances at Mia as the city's glow cast soft light across her face. Every time I looked, my chest tightened a bit more. I was torn between telling her everything and nothing, and I had no idea why.

We rolled up to the theater, a majestic old structure that looked like something straight out of a classic movie. The towering ornate building was draped in the warm golden glow of its vintage marquee, each letter flickering softly. I got lucky, finding parking only a block away. I parallel parked my car, and the engine's steady purr gave way to silence as I killed it. We just sat there, the quiet between us thickening.

Mia angled her body toward me. Something unsettling flashed in her brown eyes. It caught me off guard. Here I was thinking I'd nailed the perfect evening. But the thrill of planning this surprise soured, contorting into uncertainty inside me.

I unfastened my seat belt. "Is something wrong?"

Her gaze drifted to the theater just down the street. "Why are we here?" she asked.

Shit, did I fuck this up? I shifted in my seat toward her. "I bought tickets to see *The Nutcracker*." My eyes never left her face.

She swallowed hard, her throat moving visibly in the dim light. Her head shook gently. "I can't go in there, Ethan."

My brows knitted. "Why?"

"I just can't . . . I don't really wanna talk about it," came her soft reply.

Cars passed us in a blur, their headlights casting fleeting glimmers. I exhaled slowly, disappointment sinking beneath a growing concern for her. The tickets didn't matter. What mattered was the woman next to me, who seemed to be in a silent battle with herself.

I let out a long breath, more frustrated with myself than with her. Buckling up, I murmured, "Okay. Initiating plan B."

"I'm sorry. I know those tickets weren't cheap. I'll pay—"

"No," I cut in, more sharply than I intended. The last thing I wanted was for her to feel guilty or obligated.

She sank back into her seat, eyes downcast, lost in thought.

Just let me in, Mia.

Reaching out, I gently lifted her chin with my index finger, bringing her troubled dark gaze back to mine. "Don't worry about the tickets, Sweetness. I don't care about them. I care about you."

A few heartbeats of silence passed. Slowly, she nodded, her eyes still holding a storm of emotions I didn't understand. But it was enough she knew where my priorities lay.

I need her to feel safe with me.

Another forty-five minutes down the road, I guided the Camaro into a bustling parking lot, the tires crunching over the gravel. Leaves covered everything like an orange-and-gold blanket.

I swung the door of the Camaro open and stepped out. Car horns, faint music, and the low rumble of conversations were muffled in the distance. Zipping up my coat, I braced against the cool air and looked over at Mia. Did she feel the same mix of anticipation and apprehension about what the night had in store for us?

"Where are we?" she asked, stepping next to me.

With a grin, I said, "You'll see."

We started walking through the parking lot toward a large industrial building, Mia's boot heels clicking against the pavement. I stole glances at her, noticing how the crisp autumn breeze brought a flush to her cheeks. We stepped through the front doors. The city's noises faded as I focused on her, waiting for her to piece together where we were.

Her face lit up, like the sun finally winning its battle against the clouds. A smile tugged at the corners of her mouth. The sound of skates blended seamlessly with the gentle tunes drifting from the speakers. Her eyes caught the lively buzz of the ice rink bathed in the soft glow of fairy lights overhead.

"Ice skating?" she asked, a note of surprise in her voice, but there was a sparkle in her eyes that hadn't been there before.

Good sign. Maybe tonight isn't a total fail.

I nodded. "Yeah, you know how?" We walked toward the rink as skaters made their way around.

"It's been a while." She looked me up and down, raising one brow. "You're gonna skate in that?"

Looking down at my designer suit and shoes, I shrugged. "Yeah, and?"

"You're not afraid you'll ruin it?"

"Nope."

I covered the cost of our tickets and skates, and we got to lacing them on without delay. Muscle memory took over. I had my skates on in no time flat.

"Just because you were a big-time hockey player doesn't give you the right to show off," Mia huffed out, wrestling with the laces of her right skate.

"Actually, that's exactly what it means, Sweetness." I watched her struggle for a few more seconds before getting on one knee and holding my hand out. "Here, let me."

A tinge of curiosity crept onto her face, but she obeyed, lifting her skate-clad foot.

I grinned. "Good girl."

Her cheeks turned crimson as she bit her lip.

A corner of my mouth rose. I stared into her eyes, tying her laces with a few jerking motions to make sure they were tight but comfortable. Tucking the excess string into the tongue of her skate, I asked, "How does that feel?"

Her bottom lip slipped from between her pearly whites. "It feels good," she said, her voice barely above a whisper.

My dick went from half-mast to full hard-on with those three words. Maybe it was because I hadn't gotten any in a while.

We made our way to the rink. She stumbled here and there, trying to find her balance on the rental blades. The ice was a bit uneven. Each time she wobbled, I was right there, my hands quick to steady her. Little kids and adults were passing us, but I didn't care. I wouldn't have forgiven myself if she fell and hurt herself.

Maybe this wasn't the greatest idea either.

She steadily skated farther from the wall, gaining balance. "Is there anything else I should know?"

I tucked my hands into my coat pockets, gliding next to her. "About?"

She glanced at me. "Your family. Thanksgiving dinner is coming up quick. I don't really know much about them other than your sister's a doctor."

"Both my parents are retired doctors. They're enjoying life right now," I said as we completed our first circle.

"So, you're the rebel in the family." She shot me a teasing grin. "Was there any pressure for you to follow in their footsteps?"

I shook my head. "Nah, my parents always encouraged me to follow my own path—try new things."

"That's good. They sound like great parents—"

Mia's skate jerked out from under her. My heart leaped into my throat as instinct kicked in. I swooped in behind her, my arms wrapping around her waist in the nick of time, steadying her before she could hit the ice. For a moment, we were caught in this clumsy dance with her back against me. When we found our balance, her body eased against mine, and she rested her head on my chest.

She released a breath. "Thanks," she murmured. "That could've been ugly."

Mia's sweet flowery scent filled my nose. Warmth kindled inside me the moment she leaned into me. *She's letting me be her anchor.*

I chuckled softly, keeping the mood light. "No problem, Sweetness." When she seemed steady on her feet, I stayed close, skating alongside her. "You know, if Thanksgiving goes well with my family, I might just have to bring you to every holiday gathering."

She peered down at her white skates, a smile on her lips. "I'm upping my rates."

Before I could think it through, my hand found hers, and I intertwined our fingers in a gentle reassuring squeeze. "Whatever it costs," I said, meaning every fucking word.

Her gaze dropped to our hands. I second-guessed my move. The last thing I wanted was to make her feel cornered or uneasy. "Is this all right?" I asked, ready to let go if she needed me to.

"It's fine." She averted her gaze.

A little voice inside me kept nagging, suggesting she was just being nice. So, with a slight sense of reluctance, I steered her toward the wall and released her hand. Right on cue, my stomach decided to rumble loud enough for both of us to hear.

She giggled. "Maybe we should get you some food."

"Got a place in mind?" I asked.

Stepping off the ice onto the rubber mats that lined the outside of the rink, she shrugged. "A hot dog sounds good."

The simplicity of her request threw me for a loop. My eyebrows shot up, a grin spreading across my face despite the confusion. "Are you serious?"

One of her eyebrows arched, a playful defiance in her gaze. "Yeah. I know it's not the healthiest, but it's been a while since I've had one."

I chuckled. "Hot dogs it is." We took off our skates and turned them in, shaking off the cold.

Julia had said the best hot dogs in New York were at Manhattan Munchies just a few blocks from the rink. She was probably right. The girl loved her meat.

Mia and I hopped into my car, and I drove the short distance to the tucked-away food stand. As we approached the small window of the wooden shack, the aroma of grilled onions and sizzling meats cut through the fall air. I ordered two hot dogs, which were given to us in a matter of minutes after I paid. We grabbed a few packets of condiments, then stood near an outdoor heater to eat. It was colder than usual that evening. Mia shivered while squeezing ketchup onto her hot dog.

"We can go back to my car and eat." I couldn't believe I was willing to break my own fucking rule for this woman.

She looked at me. "Are you sure?"

"Yeah, come on." I internally cursed myself. *Lucas can never find out about this.*

A few minutes of walking and we were back in my Camaro. I watched Mia's eyes sparkle as she sank her teeth into the hot dog, a smile breaking across her face. She looked so fucking adorable, sitting there in the glow of the streetlight streaming through her window. A drop of ketchup dotted the corner of her mouth. The urge to lean in and lick it clean was overwhelming, but I held back, swiping my tongue over my lower lip.

After we ate, I started the drive back to Mia's place. As I navigated through the bustling streets, my only concern was if she'd had a good time.

It was still early. *Maybe we can watch a movie or something?*

I glanced at her. She was gliding Chapstick over her plump lips. "Did you have fun tonight?" Part of me wanted to ask about *The Nutcracker.*

"I did. And sorry again about those tickets." I was about to prod, but she cut me off. "I'll tell you one day, I promise."

I forced a smile. "Okay." We pulled up to the curb of her apartment building. Turning off the engine, I insisted on walking her up.

"You don't have to do that," she said.

"I want to. You'll be doing me a favor."

She gave me a look, half amused, half exasperated. "How?"

"I'll sleep better knowing you're safe." Before she could argue further, I climbed out of the car to open her door.

She let out a conceding breath. "Fine."

We entered the lobby, the warmth inside a stark contrast to the crisp air outside. The elevator of her apartment building was still broken, so we had to use the stairs. We climbed a few flights until finally stepping onto her floor.

Strolling down the hallway, she stopped at her door, 31A, and crossed her arms, facing me. The corner of her mouth quirked up. "Look, I made it all the way here in one piece."

I rose a brow. "Are you really that annoyed I walked you up?"

She rolled her eyes and began rummaging through her purse. "No." The jingle of her keys filled the silence between us as she turned to unlock the door.

"Don't do that," I said, stepping closer, a mix of teasing and something a bit more serious in my voice.

"Do what?"

In a moment of boldness, I reached out and grabbed her arm, gently turning her to face me. "Don't roll your eyes at me, Sweetness."

Defiance crept onto that beautiful face of hers. "Or what?"

Wrapping one arm around her waist, I cupped her nape with my free hand, pulling her flush against me. When she showed no sign of resistance, I pressed my lips against hers, tasting her sweet cherry Chapstick. Our first kiss, and I was already addicted to her.

"Your lips . . . Fuck, Mia," I growled.

She wrapped her arms around my neck, her mouth consuming mine, our tongues dancing and tangling, eager and desperate. Pressed against each other in the deserted hallway, our passion intensified with each passing second. My lips moved down the curve of her neck.

"What're we doing?" she whispered.

In between leaving kisses on her collarbone, I asked, "You want me to stop?"

She responded by hooking one leg around my waist and grinding her pussy against my hard cock.

"Fuck, Sweetness."

Her lilac scent mixed with my cologne and created an intoxicating aroma that filled the air. My fingers traced the soft dips and curves of her body as I pushed her against the apartment door. God, I wanted more—needed more.

In the heat of our make-out session, a loud and distinct *click* echoed through the hallway. My body tensed, and I quickly placed Mia down, pulling away from her. A tenant exited their apartment. We tried to act nonchalant as he walked past us, but the moment he turned the corner, I caught Mia's gaze.

"Did you see his face?" she whispered, her eyes sparkling.

"Do you think he knew what we were doing?"

She scanned the hallway once more and shrugged. "I don't know."

We both burst into laughter, unable to hold it in any longer. Her laugh was like a melody, a sweet effortless tune that danced through the air, capturing my heart. It was a sound I never wanted to stop hearing.

A few seconds passed until our laughing fit ended. We stood there, staring at each other, smiling.

God, I want her so fucking bad. I'd never wanted anyone like I wanted her, and that should've scared the shit out of me. "I should probably go—"

And figure myself out . . .

She leaned back against her door. "Are you sure?"

My brow furrowed. "What do you mean?"

"Are you sure you should go?"

I moved closer. "Do you want me to stay, Mia?" This wasn't going to end well, but I was physically incapable of saying no to this woman.

She pushed onto her toes, brushing her lips against mine. "I want you to fuck me, Ethan."

My already-hard dick twitched against the zipper of my designer slacks. "We're friends."

"This is just for tonight."

I gazed into her beautiful hazel eyes and studied her. "You're sure?"

She nodded, then turned to unlock the door. Walking into her apartment, she held the door open for me, her silhouette framed by the soft light inside. "You coming?"

This is going to change everything. Turn the fuck around. Walk away. I stood there, frozen, my heart pounding wildly in my chest. Desire for her burned through me. In the end, my body betrayed my mind, and I stepped inside, closing the door.

"Are you sure about this?" I asked, watching her slip her jacket off and hang it in the closet next to the doorway.

She kicked her boots off and looked at me. "I'm sure."

I cupped her face with one hand, my thumb gliding over her velvety lips. "How do you want me?"

A slow grin spread across her face. She lowered to her knees and reached for my belt, unbuckling it. She unbuttoned my pants and pulled the zipper down, her hands working deftly to free my erection from its confines. I felt a rush of cool air on my exposed skin as her hands wrapped around my shaft, gently stroking it. Her gaze never left mine, eyes filled with hazy desire.

My head fell back at the pure ecstasy her touch sparked. "Fuck, Mia," I groaned.

Her lips enveloped the throbbing head, hot and wet. My back pressed against the wall for support as I struggled to control my labored breaths. She took me deeper, her skilled tongue swirling around the tip, sending waves of pleasure through my body.

"This is gonna be over pretty fucking fast if you don't stop," I panted.

That only seemed to spur her on, and she hummed her satisfaction around me. Each caress was like an electric shock, igniting every nerve ending in its wake. I knew I had to take control, so I gently pulled away from her. She released my cock with a pop, the cutest scowl on her face.

Rising gracefully to her feet, she reached out and pulled me close. Body heat radiated through our clothes as our lips met, desperate and passionate. Our tongues battled for dominance. My hand drifted to one of her ass cheeks and squeezed, eliciting a squeal from her.

She pulled away and led me down the short hallway to her bedroom. It wasn't my first time stepping foot in her room. We'd slept in her bed together, but now we were about to step over a boundary I shouldn't cross with her.

She stripped her shirt off and unclasped her bra, revealing the dusty-pink peaks of her puckered nipples. My mouth watered at the temptation. I eagerly assisted her in removing the rest of her clothing, my fingers tingling as they grazed her soft skin.

With a smooth motion, I slipped off my blazer, baring myself to her gaze. She reclined on her forearms, completely naked, and watched me with intense interest as I undressed, every movement slow and deliberate.

"Enjoying the show, Sweetness?" I smirked, removing my slacks and boxers and tossing them off to the side. *Wait . . . Fuck me.* Picking my pants up, I checked the pockets before searching through my wallet.

"Let me guess. No condom?"

"Nope. I never expected this to happen. Do you have any?" I asked, dropping my slacks to the carpeted floor. It was torture staring at Mia in all her beautiful nakedness.

"I'm clean, and I have an IUD."

Is she suggesting what I think she is? I stepped closer and said, "I'm clean too."

"I want to feel you inside me, bare," she said, and god, did that make my cock twitch.

Dropping to my knees in front of her, I spread her legs.

"Not before I get a taste of your pussy." I trailed kisses along her inner thigh, inhaling her scent. My tongue flicked out and slid between her folds. She was like a drug that only affected me, and I wanted all of it.

"Please, Ethan," she panted, twisting the comforter in her fists.

I obliged, plunging my tongue inside her and then swirling it around her clit. She moaned and arched her back, pushing against my mouth. I continued to suck on her, slipping two fingers inside her tight heat. Her hips bucked against my hand as I drove into her harder, faster.

"Oh god, oh god," she chanted.

I raised my head and met her dark hooded gaze. "God has nothing to do with this, Sweetness." It wasn't long before her walls tightened around my fingers as she cried out my name. My cock throbbed painfully at the sight of her coming undone. I couldn't wait any longer; I needed to be inside her.

Her chest rose and fell, a sated look on her gorgeous features.

I climbed on top of her. "Are you sure?"

She groaned. "Yes, just fuck me already."

My eyes narrowed, and I gave her exactly what she wanted. I settled between her legs, slid my cock into her warm, wet pussy, and didn't stop until I was all the way in. "Shit," I hissed. "God, you feel good."

"God has nothing to do with this." She smirked, bucking her hips against me, taking me even deeper.

It took every single ounce of self-control not to come right then. I wanted to savor every moment, every sensation.

She dug her fingernails into my back as I picked up the pace, thrusting into her harder each time.

I leaned down to capture her lips, and Mia moaned into my mouth, her body trembling. *Is she going to come again?* I kissed down her neck, sucking on the sensitive skin and eliciting more sounds of pleasure from her. My hand reached between us to rub circles on her clit. My own need was reaching its breaking point. I rested my forehead against hers, our breaths mingling. "Come on my cock."

She nodded. "I'm almost there."

"Good." The bedframe groaned beneath our writhing bodies as I slipped in and out of her a few more times. I could feel her muscles tensing around me, pulsing. With a final thrust, I released myself inside her with a moan. We rode our orgasms together until I collapsed on top of her, careful to support my weight on her.

We lay there for a few moments before I could pull myself away from her. After I cleaned us both, we collapsed onto the bed together, naked and satisfied. I took Mia into my arms, her back against my chest.

"This is just for tonight, right?" Her voice was raspy with exhaustion.

If that was what she truly wanted, I had no choice but to honor her wishes. Kissing her temple and wrapping her a little tighter in my embrace, I said, "Yeah, whatever you want, Sweetness."

Morning sun filtered through the sheer curtains, shedding light on the remnants of last night's decision. I lay tangled in the sheets, my mind racing faster than my heart. Ethan was still asleep next to me, the rise and fall of his chest a steady reminder of the line we'd crossed. The air was filled with a mix of lilac and bergamot. *And regret?*

I couldn't bring myself to wake him. Instead, I let my eyes roam over the space, over the clothes strewn across the floor. The soft hum of the city was a world away from the cocoon of this room.

Now what?

Regret wasn't quite right for our situation. It was more like fear of losing the foundation we'd built our friendship on. Of not knowing if it could ever be the same. But as light streamed through the bedroom window, casting patterns on the wall, I knew I had to try.

I won't let one night unravel everything we have.

Ethan stirred, his movement pulling me from my thoughts to this complexity that now lay between us.

"Good morning," I whispered. "Last night was . . ."

Amazing. Unforgettable.

He propped himself on one elbow, looking at me, his blue eyes clouded with a mix of emotions. "I know . . ." A corner of his mouth rose. "It was for me too."

"It was just one night." My voice sounded more hopeful than I felt. "It's not gonna be awkward, right?

Ethan ran a hand through his messy hair, a smile on his lips. "No awkwardness. We're good, Sweetness."

Silence stretched between us. I couldn't help but feel a pang of something more, something left unsaid. *But what more is there to say?*

He sat up, and I shamelessly stared at his muscular back. Slipping on his slacks, he asked, "Did you wanna get breakfast?"

I sat up, wrapping the sheet around myself. "I actually have errands to run today."

His shoulders slumped slightly. "Oh . . . okay. Let me just get out of your way, then." He zipped and buttoned his pants.

"It's not that I don't want to get breakfast with you," I started, watching him pull on his shirt.

Ethan's brows knitted. He stopped working the buttons on his shirt. "You were very clear about what you wanted last night. I promise, everything's fine between us."

Despite his reassurance, I couldn't help but think it

wasn't fine. I pushed away the lightheadedness starting to surface. He needed to leave so I could take my meds. "Can I take a rain check?"

He shrugged on his blazer and leaned close, bringing his face inches from mine. "You already know I can't say no to you."

My heart skipped a beat at his words. I stared at him. My brain couldn't process what that meant, and it was worse when he kissed me on my forehead.

"Text me if you need anything."

I gave him the best smile I could muster. "I will."

He walked out of the room. Shortly after, the front door of my apartment rattled, and just like that, he was gone.

THE DAYS LEADING UP TO THANKSGIVING SEEMED TO pass at a glacial pace. I'd made a conscious effort to adhere diligently to my daily routine. I took all my prescribed medications during my quiet hours of the night. I hoped my sluggishness wouldn't be noticeable to Ethan's family.

Julia came through with our girls' night a few days before Thanksgiving. She arrived at my place with a large paper bag bursting with all sorts of junk food. The moment she opened it, the familiar scents of candy and chips wafted through my apartment.

My living room became a cozy haven adorned with blankets and cushions, creating a perfect atmosphere for the much-needed girl time. It was just like the old days, before all the bullshit had happened with my ex, my mom, and *men*. When things were simple and all we had to worry about was getting to dance rehearsals on time. The flickering glow of a rom com set the backdrop for our conversation.

Julia reclined on my worn couch as I brought a bowl of popcorn from the kitchen. "I added extra butter, as requested." I handed it to her and plopped down on the other end, propping my feet next to hers.

She picked a piece of popcorn from the bowl. "Think fast." She tossed it across the length of the couch.

I dove for it and fell off but managed to catch it in my mouth. I sprung to my feet and threw both arms up. "Goal." My headband had fallen over my eyes. We both broke into a fit of giggles.

"That was fucking hilarious," Julia teased.

I pulled the band off and tossed it onto the coffee table.

After our waves of laughter subsided, I sank back into the inviting cushions. The soft upholstery cradled me in comfort. "What's it like being a married woman?"

Julia had a piece of red licorice dangling between her lips. "So far, it's fine. Lucas still annoys me, but I'm my usual bitchy self, so we balance each other out."

I grinned. "Has he said anything about Venom?"

She shook her head. "Not much. He does plan to fly them out here soon." She finished her candy before saying, "By the way, you never updated me on that trip you took with Ethan."

As I exhaled, the memories of our one-night stand came

to the forefront of my mind. The ghost of his mouth on me still haunted me. His hands on my skin, rough and passionate. The feel of his fingers gripping my hips, pulling me closer as he thrust deeper. I shouldn't want more than what I'd asked for that night.

"Nothing happened. We flew there, signed the band, and flew back," I said, avoiding her gaze, hoping my blush didn't give me away.

She studied me, her eyes narrowing slightly. "You can't lie to me."

"What do you think I'm lying about?" I asked, staring at the flat screen and pretending to be invested in the movie.

"I don't believe for one second nothing happened between you and Ethan. You two shared a hotel suite, and I know you've had a crush on him since you met in that Newark bar," she said.

"You mean when Lucas threw his drink on you?" I said, remembering how livid she'd been. She and her rock star husband hadn't started off on the right foot. They'd hated each other in the beginning.

"Don't try to change the subject." Her voice rose an octave.

I threw my head back against the couch cushion and groaned. "Can we drop it?"

"Yeah. But only because I gotta pee." She stood, her movements betraying her concern, and walked into the bathroom down the hall.

I reached for the remote and cranked up the volume on the TV, trying to fill the silence that her departure left. The voices from the rom com were hollow, echoing against the walls of my apartment.

Maybe I should just come out and tell her Ethan and I had sex. But I really wasn't in the mood to play twenty questions with her.

Minutes later, Julia returned, her steps heavier, her expression taut with worry. "What's going on, M?" Her voice was tinged with an edge of anger.

My brows came together. "What?"

She held up my bottle of prescribed medication, her hand trembling. "These are strong drugs."

Shit. I must've left them out. I sat up straighter, a knot forming in my stomach. "Okay. Don't freak out, Jules."

She sat next to me and placed the bottle on the coffee table. "Just tell me what's going on," she implored, her eyes searching mine. "The truth."

I knew there was no easy way to break the news. The words felt like a boulder in my throat. "Remember that pain I was complaining about?"

She nodded slowly, her gaze never leaving mine.

"Well, I finally got it checked." I could feel tears pricking at the corners of my eyes, but I fought them back. "I have cancer," I managed to say, my voice cracking under the strain. Saying it out loud made it real. *Too real.*

Her face paled, eyes widening. For a brief suspended moment, the room fell into absolute silence, so profound it felt as if time itself had stopped. I could hear my own heartbeat, loud and clear, thrumming in my ears. In the stillness, a thousand thoughts raced through my mind—fears about the future, worries about the burden I could become, and a deep-seated longing for things to somehow remain unchanged. Yet I knew with those three words, everything had shifted irreversibly.

"Cancer," she echoed, her voice barely audible. "How long have you known?"

I breathed out, feeling suddenly distant, my fingers nervously intertwined in my lap. "A few weeks now."

"Weeks? Fuck, Mia." Her voice was a mix of hurt and disbelief. "You should've told me when you found out."

I looked down at my hands. "There's a little more. I have to have a tiny procedure done after Thanksgiving." My soul ached from the truth of it.

"Surgery? You should've fucking told me. Surgery is not a tiny procedure, M." Her voice cracked.

I fiddled with a piece of lint on my leggings, avoiding her gaze. "I'm sorry. I didn't want you to worry. I figured I could take care of it before anyone had to know. The doctor said we caught it early."

"That's fucking bullshit." Julia's eyes filled with tears, voice shaking. "I need you healthy. You're supposed to be my children's godmother."

I placed my hand over hers, trying to offer some comfort. "My doctor says I have a high chance of beating this. I'm still going to be there if you ever have kids."

"You promise?" she asked, wiping the wetness away from her cheeks with her sleeve.

Her request lay heavy in my chest. With each breath, I felt like I was stepping off a cliff into the unknown. I might not be able to keep the promise, but I made it anyway. Looking into her eyes, I whispered, "I promise, Jules."

She moved closer, resting her head on my shoulder. The movie continued to play, barely audible. Despite the weight of my confession, a sense of solidarity grew stronger.

Our conversation switched to memories of dancing together, to the many rehearsals we had attended and the shows we'd performed in. It was a much-needed distraction. Spending the night sitting next to my best friend, I found comfort in just being.

IN THE MIDMORNING HOURS OF THANKSGIVING EVE, I folded my clothes and tucked them into my small suitcase, then placed my toiletries bag on top. The usual city sounds of honking horns and distant sirens were replaced by an awkward calmness. Zipping up my suitcase, I looked around my bedroom.

Bathroom products. Three outfits. Two pairs of shoes. After going through my mental checklist, I rolled my bag out to the entryway of the apartment. When Ethan texted me saying he was five minutes away, I made my way down to the lobby.

I stepped outside. The familiar rumble of Ethan's Camaro echoed from up the street. He parked next to the curb, honking the horn.

He popped the trunk and got out. "Hey. You ready to do this?" Taking my suitcase from me, he placed it in the back.

Despite my churning stomach, I nodded. "Yup. Let's do

this." I climbed into the passenger seat, trying to prepare myself for this holiday shindig. But even my meditative breaths weren't helping.

During the initial hour of our journey, we engaged in light conversation about the weather and the new band, Venom. However, the latter part of the ride had gotten quiet. Everything between us seemed to be normal.

Has he already forgotten our one night?

I reclined against the headrest and gazed outside at the passing houses. The painkillers were starting to take effect.

Three hours later, Ethan and I pulled up to his parents' house.

Belle's Mercedes was parked in the driveway. We'd connected when we met last year at Lucas and Julia's wedding reception. She'd opened up about being a single mom and ER doctor and how she hardly had time for friends, much less family.

As soon as we stepped into the huge two-story house, I was greeted by Ethan's sweet Irish mom, Arlene, who walked up to me and gave me a warm tight hug. She reminded me of my mom, and my heart ached at the thought.

"I'm so glad you could make it, Mia." Arlene pulled away, tucking a strand of blond hair behind her ear. "There's my favorite son."

Ethan rolled his eyes, hugging his mom. "Hi, Ma. That's 'cause I'm your only son."

Nolan, Ethan's dad, walked into the foyer from the den. "Hey, you finally made it. How was traffic?"

"Hey, Dad. Same as always," Ethan replied.

Lindsay came flying out of the kitchen, her tiny feet pitter-pattering as she made a beeline for me. I scooped her up, her arms wrapping around my neck. Belle followed at a slower pace, her tired blue eyes giving away just how long her day had been.

"Mimi!" Lindsay screamed, rattling my eardrums, but I didn't mind. She was so adorable. The five-year-old girl cupped my face in her small hands. "Pretty."

I let out a breathy laugh. "No, you're pretty."

Once I put Lindsay down, Belle hugged me. "So glad you didn't leave me to deal with this annoying ass alone." She gestured to Ethan.

"Nice to see you too, punk." Ethan hugged his older sister, nearly squeezing the breath out of her.

Belle managed to free herself from Ethan's hold and looped her arm through mine. She took my suitcase from me. "We're gonna have so much fun."

"I didn't get a chance to tell you," Arlene started as she looked at Ethan. "Hailey and her parents are coming tomorrow. Maybe you two can finally reconcile."

Ethan let out a breath and glanced at me before meeting his mother's gaze again. "I'm . . . with Mia now."

Silence filled the entryway, and I blinked a few times, processing what he'd just said. This was the reason he'd asked me to come. Pulling away from Belle, I made my way up to Ethan and wrapped my arm around his waist. "Yup, we sure are." *Okay, that was a little much.*

Ethan moved, snaking his arms around my waist from behind.

Belle had a smirk on her face. I was pretty sure she'd wanted me and Ethan to date since she'd met me.

Arlene looked from Ethan to me, a smile tugging at the corners of her mouth.

Nolan broke the silence. "When did this come about?"

"It's a recent development," Ethan replied.

Arlene clasped her hands together. "This is wonderful news."

Nolan nodded, flashing a grin my way. "It's about damn time. I knew there was something between you two." He shook an index finger at us.

I felt Ethan's laugh rumble through his chest. "Sure you did, Dad."

"You two can share your old room now," Belle added.

Ethan released me, taking my bag from his sister and shouldering his duffel. "We're gonna get settled."

I started to follow him up the stairs.

"Don't take too long. It's family game night, and I'm in charge of the games," Belle said, a mischievous grin on her lovely features.

"Oh, god," Ethan muttered, dread apparent in his voice. "We won't be long."

As I followed him up the grand staircase, my gaze roamed over the walls lined with family portraits and candid photos. One of them was of Ethan holding his guitar, a microphone in front of him. It looked like he was standing on a stage, singing.

"That was the first talent show I won in high school. My mom snapped that one." He inched closer to the photo. "God, my hair was so grungy."

My lips tilted up. "I think you look cute."

"Well, thanks, Sweetness."

Ethan led me into his room. I had to stop for a second to take it all in. His bedroom was easily bigger than my entire apartment. Late afternoon sun flooded through the tall windows, casting warm light across the massive bed, which took center stage. It was flanked by an elegant armoire and dresser.

"Now that we're alone, I'm sorry for springing that on you," Ethan said, setting our bags next to the dresser.

I sat on the bed, expelling the tension in my body with a breath. "Don't worry about it. That's why I'm here, right?"

His gaze drifted to the plush carpet. He leaned against the dresser, arms crossed. God, he looked so fucking good in those black sweats and gray hoodie. A spark of warmth ignited low in my belly. I clenched my thighs together.

"That's not the *only* reason," he said.

My brow furrowed. "Okay?" My eyes met his blue depths.

"I didn't want *you* to be alone on Thanksgiving."

"How do you know I would've been alone?" I asked, standing and walking toward my suitcase.

He pushed off the dresser and blocked my path. "Your family is in the Philippines, and Julia and Lucas are out of town. Unless you have friends I don't know about, you would've been alone."

I shot him a wry grin. "Fine. Maybe I wanted to be alone."

"So, you don't want to be here?"

Releasing a huff, I said, "No. I do."

He leaned in until our faces were only inches from each other. "Is Mia Cruz admitting that I'm right?" Being this close to him sent waves of heat through my body.

You can't have him. My lips pulled thin as I turned away. "What're you doing, Ethan?"

"I can't get that night out of my head," he admitted.

My mind went blank for a moment. I stared at him. "I don't understand. It's not like it was your first time."

He nodded. "You're right, but it was with you, Sweetness."

Memories of Dad flooded my mind. He was shattered by the loss of my mom. I could still picture him in her old worn recliner; he rarely left it, his dark brown eyes empty and faraway. Days bled into weeks, and he barely moved, barely spoke. The man I once saw as invincible had crumbled right in front of me, and I was powerless to pick up the pieces. Fear of losing him too was suffocating. I never wanted that to happen to Ethan.

He deserves more.

"We don't have to talk about it right now, but I'd like to discuss . . ." He brushed his fingers through his dark hair. "Being with you."

Shaking my head, I said, "We can't be together." An influx of tears began to surface, but I blinked them back.

A knock at the door interrupted Ethan's next words.

"We're going to start the games soon." Belle's voice was muffled.

"Okay," Ethan said, a tinge of annoyance in his tone.

A few seconds passed before I said, "Why don't you head down. I need to freshen up a bit."

"We'll continue this later." He walked out of the room, closing the door behind him.

At least this way I had time to prepare for that difficult conversation. Could I muster the courage to tell him the truth about my situation? If anything, this secret was ruining what remained of our friendship. And I didn't want to lose what we had, but with everything that had happened, maybe it was too late. Had I already fucked it all up?

After I washed my face, I put on some light makeup just so I didn't look so tired. Then I made my way downstairs to join the Miller family in their huge sitting room. The TV was playing a marathon of classic holiday movies, the volume turned low.

Belle started the early evening with charades. Ethan was rather good at it, which was more than I could say for myself. Lindsay had fallen asleep on the love seat next to him. It was the cutest thing ever. I could tell he loved that little girl with his whole heart.

After a few rounds of charades, Arlene said, "I think I'm tired now. This game takes a lot out of you."

I nodded, though lately, living had been exhausting in general.

"Let's move on to the next game, then," Belle said, wearing that same devious smile from earlier. She rushed into the kitchen and emerged a few seconds later with two coconuts. "It's called coconut smoochie. And it's a couples' game."

Ethan's eyes widened. "What?"

"What exactly do we do with those?" Nolan gestured to the coconuts in Belle's hands.

"Start with it between your and your partner's belly. Then try to get it to each other's lips without using your hands." Belle handed me one and passed the other to Nolan.

Arlene stood. "Get up, you old man. This will be the most action we've had all year."

Ethan raked his palm down his face, letting out a sigh. "Too much information, Ma." He got to his feet, careful not to wake Lindsay.

I straightened as well and faced him.

"We don't have to do this." He took the coconut from me.

I shrugged. "Are you scared?"

His eyes narrowed. He placed the coconut on his stomach and pulled me to him, bracing it between our bodies. "Let's see what you got," he challenged.

"We're ready," Arlene said from behind us.

Belle had the biggest smile on her face. "Ready, set, go!"

Arlene and Nolan broke out into laughter after a few minutes. I couldn't see them, but they had to have been struggling.

Ethan and I attempted to roll the rough coconut up our bodies but failed several times.

"Wait. Stay still for a moment," he said, the round hard

thing still braced between our midsections. He grabbed my hips.

Raising an eyebrow, I asked, "What're you doing?"

"I'm gonna need you to trust me."

I nodded. "Okay."

With a determined look, he crouched low, his face coming to my rib cage. He grunted, shifting the coconut between my breasts. The movement caused a good amount of cleavage to pop from my V-neck sweater. His heated gaze went from my face to my tits. "Nice coconuts," he said, voice low enough that only I could hear. "Too bad hands aren't allowed."

My cheeks flushed, and his citrusy bergamot scent enveloped me. "Could you pay attention to the actual coconut?" There was no hiding the grin on my face. "Now what?" I tried not to focus on the electric current between us or how undeniably alluring he was.

He pulled me flush against him, ensuring the coconut couldn't escape from between us. Bending once more, he slid the coconut to the crook of my neck. I felt his nose brush my pulse, and a shiver of pleasure raced down my spine.

"God, you smell good," he whispered.

I hissed, "Stop sniffing me and concentrate."

"I love when you're bossy."

"Technically, you're my boss," I corrected. "Which reminds me. Aren't you breaking one of your rules?"

He squeezed my hips a little tighter. "You're the only one I'd break the rules for."

My cheeks warmed. Releasing a short breath, I said, "Focus, Miller."

Arlene and Nolan were laughing hard at this point, taking Belle's attention away from us. I still couldn't see how far they'd gotten with their coconut.

Ethan's cheek pressed against mine. His lips brushed the delicate shell of my ear as he said, "Get ready to put your mouth on it."

My pussy clenched around nothing at his words, breath hitching as I replied with a shaky exhale, "Okay."

In one smooth motion, I lowered my head and placed my lips on the rough surface of the coconut. To my surprise, Ethan's mouth also found its way onto the opposite side.

I gazed into his eyes, noticing a flicker of heat in his blue-gray irises. His pupils dilated with desire, and I had to tear away from him to resist pressing my lips against his.

"Winners!" Belle pointed to us and somehow managed not to wake Lindsay.

Arlene and Nolan were good sports about losing. We migrated to the dining room afterward, which was a cozy space with dark wooden furniture and soft ambient lighting. Family photos adorned the walls. The table was set with a hearty spread of Irish cuisine: corned beef and cabbage, colcannon, soda bread, and a rich savory stew that filled the air with mouthwatering aromas.

"Everything smells delicious," I said, inhaling deeply while taking a seat next to Ethan. My stomach growled in anticipation. I'd never tried Irish food before, and if I had, I hadn't known it.

Arlene beamed from across the table, dishing generous portions of colcannon. "I'm glad you think so. It's been a while since we all had a proper dinner together."

Ethan reached for the corned beef. "Hope you're hungry. Ma goes all out for these dinners." He winked at me, and my heart fluttered.

"I'm starving." I started to serve myself. As I looked over at Ethan, a soft laugh escaped me. He'd piled his plate high.

Dinner progressed, and the conversation flowed seamlessly. We shared stories and laughter, the bond between us solidifying with each passing moment. Ethan leaned in, his shoulder brushing against mine, and whispered, "I think my family loves you even more now."

A blush warmed my cheeks, but I remained quiet.

"It might be too cold to show her the maze, but you should take her through the greenhouse later," Arlene suggested, a grin on her face.

My brow rose. "You have a maze *and* a greenhouse?"

"Ma has a green thumb," Belle said. "I can't keep a plant alive to save my life."

Ethan chortled. "That's for sure."

Belle tossed a piece of soda bread at him.

"Hey, don't waste food," Ethan said, narrowing his eyes at her.

My lips curved up. Being with Ethan and his family made the worries of my world seem far away. They were replaced by the warmth and comfort of a family meal.

If only moments like this could stretch into eternity.

MIA AND I HELPED MY MOM CLEAR THE TABLE AFTER dinner. We walked out to the charming greenhouse nestled in the fall landscape. The old building was showcased in rustic elegance, its gabled roof covered with orange and gold leaves. Enchanting fairy lights emanated a festive warmth against the cold night.

We stepped inside, and the chilly air was replaced by the scent of damp soil. The lush sanctuary teemed with vibrant greenery that stretched out in every direction.

"This is amazing," Mia murmured beside me, her eyes lighting up with the sweetest wonder. She wandered down an aisle, her movements fluid and graceful. Each plant she stopped to look at seemed to enthrall her. I followed at a distance, mesmerized by her captivated demeanor. Her beauty eclipsed even the most vibrant flowers around us.

I never got into plants the way Mom did, but Mia gave

me a new appreciation for the beauty they held. "I don't know how she keeps up with all of this."

Mia glanced at me. "I'm sure it's a lot of work."

I shrugged. "It's not work if you enjoy it." The faint scent of lilac filled my nose, drawing me closer to her. My mind drifted back to her proximity during coconut smoochie. I could still feel the warmth of her body against mine.

Clearing my throat, I pushed those thoughts down. "By the way, I'm sorry if that game made you uncomfortable."

Mia looked over her shoulder at me. "It didn't. I had fun."

I strode closer. "Belle's a bit extra."

"I mean, she *is* related to you," she teased, turning to face me.

With a grin, I cocked a brow. "What's that supposed to mean?"

Leaning a hip against one of the tables, she crossed her arms. "Come on, Ethan, we both know you're more high-maintenance than a teenage girl, with your name brands and finely tailored suits."

My eyes narrowed, legs eating up the distance between us. "I'll show you high-maintenance." I moved my hands to her sides, initiating a light tickling assault.

Mia squealed as she squirmed, trying to escape my roaming fingers. Her eyes sparkled, and her laughter was like music, filling the space. Her body twisted and contorted. She struggled against my iron grip, determined to break free. She giggled and flailed, but I held her in place, refusing to let go.

"Take it back," I demanded teasingly. In a swift firm

motion, I guided her back until she was pressed against the wall. Holding her hands above her head, I pinned them against the cool surface.

A soft smile graced her lips—those irresistible full lips. My gaze drifted to her deep brown eyes, and it took everything in me not to grab her by the nape and kiss her. "I wanna know why."

"Why what?" Her breath caressed my cheek.

I released her and backed away, resisting my urges with a slow exhale. "Why can't we be together?"

She hugged herself, still standing against the wall. "Can we not do this right now?"

I ran a hand through my hair and exhaled. "If not now, when?"

"I'm in a really complicated place in my life right now, Ethan."

I wanted to call bullshit, but from past experiences, I knew all too well that Mia tended to clam up when she felt pressured, so I said nothing more.

She stared at the floor, clasping her hands. "I don't want to ruin what we have. We've become such good friends, especially after what happened with Kyle. I was really worried I was gonna hate men after that."

I studied her. "Just did what any decent human being would do."

"All those late nights helped more than you'll ever know," she confessed, her fingers fidgeting. "I don't think I ever thanked you properly."

My intentions may not have been entirely selfless at first,

but in time, I realized Mia was everything I wanted to fall in love with. I hadn't wanted to admit it for the longest time; I drove myself mad denying it. A wry smirk played on my lips. "We should get back inside. I can take you through the maze tomorrow, if you want."

"Okay," she said, following me out of the greenhouse.

We entered the house; a dark and silent lull had settled. Everyone had gone to bed. Mia and I ascended the wide staircase, the only audible sound the soft padding of our footsteps. We stepped onto the landing, continuing to my room. I opened the door, and moonlight filtered through the curtains, illuminating the room's timeless charm.

Mia walked toward her suitcase, which sat in front of my old dresser. Something caught her eye. Her gaze lingered on memorabilia and childhood photos until it rested on a picture of me and Hailey—a relic of the past I'd tried to forget.

"Who's that?" she asked.

Memories flooded my mind as I said, "My ex, Hailey."

She tensed, and her expression turned unreadable. Kneeling in front of her suitcase, she rummaged through it, taking out her pajamas and toiletries bag.

"It's a long story," I added.

She stood and leaned against the dresser. "I don't have anywhere to be."

"Fine." I inhaled, then exhaled. "She was my high school sweetheart. It seemed like a perfect match. Hailey's family ran in the same social circles as mine. They still do. Our whole life was planned out. After high school, college. Then marriage." My mind flashed back. "But I got her pregnant not long after we graduated high school." Fuck, I couldn't keep the lump out of my throat.

Mia set her things on the dresser and stepped closer. "You don't have to—"

"No. I want to. We had planned to keep the baby, but the stress of moving and starting college took a toll on us. She went into labor a little earlier than expected. But instead of being a preemie, the baby was stillborn." Tears blurred my vision, but I didn't let them fall.

Compassion filled her face, but she said nothing.

"We were so young. We didn't know how to cope with anything. The guilt and blame tore us apart." It never stopped being difficult to talk about the loss of my child—our child—and the future we never had.

Mia took one final step and wrapped her arms around me. "I'm so sorry, Ethan."

I returned the embrace, pulling her into me. The grief hadn't gotten any easier with time. The what-ifs still gnawed at my insides. I'd forever wonder, *What stage in Jacob's life would he be at?* He'd be ten years old now, going on eleven. The only person besides my family who knew was Lucas, and I'd only given him general details.

Lost in Mia's warmth, I blinked back the tears threatening to fall. We spent a few more seconds in each other's arms, and years of tension seemed to melt off my shoulders. I could've spent forever in her sweet embrace before she pulled away.

I stared at her for what seemed like the millionth time that night. "Thanks. I needed that."

"Any time."

Her gaze drifted to my old guitar sitting in the corner. A grin curved her lips. "Can you play a little for me?"

I smiled. Walking over, I picked up the wooden instrument, dusted it off, and started to tune it by ear. "It's been years since I've played this guitar." We sat next to each other on the bed.

She brushed her delicate fingers over the spruce surface. "I've always wanted to learn. I never had time with ballet and all."

"I could teach you a few chords real quick." Showing off, I played a little riff for her.

Her brows rose. "That's really good." She stared at the instrument, uncertainty in her eyes. "Um . . . sure, I guess."

Positioning myself behind her, I demonstrated how to hold the guitar. "Keep it snug against your body, like this," I instructed, adjusting her posture.

Her hands were tentative, unfamiliar with the strings and frets. "Okay, let's start with a basic chord." I showed her a simple G chord on the fretboard. "Just place your fingers here and here."

Mia tried to mirror my hand placement. I reached over, guiding her fingers into the correct positions. The simple touch sent a jolt through me, sending my mind back to the night we were supposed to forget. Her hands tangled in my hair, her warm body writhing beneath mine, our heavy breaths—

Fuck, focus.

"Good, now strum down from the top string," I directed, watching as she tried to emulate the motion. The first strum was hesitant, but it brought a delighted smile to my face as the sound filled the room.

She grimaced.

"You're a natural," I encouraged, my heart swelling with pride at her small achievement.

She glanced at me, our faces mere inches from each other. "You're being nice. That was horrible." Her eyes drifted to my lips as she bit her own.

A light chuckle rumbled through my chest. "Try it again."

Mia's gaze lingered on my mouth for a moment longer, and then she turned away and adjusted her fingers on the fretboard the way I'd taught her. She strummed the chord perfectly.

"I did it!" she exclaimed, her eyes shining and meeting mine once more.

"You did it," I whispered.

She smiled. "Maybe you should think about performing again."

My eyes drifted to her mouth. "Would you come watch?"

"Of course."

I couldn't resist her any longer. Taking the instrument and leaning it against the bed, I cupped her nape and pulled her lips against mine. She showed no signs of protest, so I deepened the kiss.

Time stopped as our bodies gravitated toward each other. My hands roamed her back, tracing the curves of her body with a hunger that had been suppressed for too fucking long. Mia's fingers tangled in my hair, coaxing me closer, unwilling to let go.

Our chests rose and fell in unison. The barriers between us crumbled, leaving only raw passion in their wake. Laying her on my bed, I hovered above her, my lips trailing delicate kisses along her jawline and down her neck. Each touch elicited a gasp of pleasure from her. My dick throbbed, begging for her warmth—begging to be inside her again.

I settled between her legs and ground my hard cock against her pussy, letting her feel what she was doing to me. A moan escaped her, and I couldn't help but groan my own ecstasy. "Fuck, Mia." I reached beneath her sweater and roamed her soft stomach. Just as my hand skimmed the underside of her breast, she gently pushed me away, her eyes filled with a mixture of desire and something else I couldn't quite figure out.

"I'm sorry. That shouldn't have happened," she said, keeping her palm on my chest.

I climbed off her and sat on the edge of the bed. Her frame quivered ever so slightly, delicately shivering. Her brown eyes held a hint of exhaustion, the sparkle dimmed by the day's spent energy. At least, that was what I assumed.

"Are you okay?" I asked softly, reaching out to caress her cheek.

She moved away from my touch, and I'd be a lying fuck if I said that didn't sting.

Standing, she said, "I'm fine. It's just late. We should get some rest. We've got a long day tomorrow."

I nodded, my own longing mingling with a sense of disappointment. We had been swept away by desire, but Mia's boundaries were important to me.

I met her gaze one final time. "You're right."

She grabbed her things from the dresser and made her way into the bathroom, leaving me alone with the lingering warmth of her touch. As I sat there in the silence, I couldn't deny it any longer—I was falling in love with Mia Cruz.

What if she never feels the same?

A BITTERSWEET ACHE SETTLED INTO MY CHEST WHILE I showered. The thought of dinner with Ethan's family invaded. Echoes of laughter and the warmth of shared moments pressed against me.

I couldn't get the heated look of Ethan's eyes or the way our lips had met out of my mind. His citrusy bergamot scent seemed to linger on my skin, a tantalizing combination.

What we have can't go any further.

I shook my head, and a cascade of water drops fell with each movement. All the tangled threads of my life—my fucked-up circumstances, my unresolved issues—bubbled to the surface. Tears trickled down my cheeks, mingling with droplets of hot water. I couldn't give him the happiness he deserved—not with the weight of my own struggles dragging me down.

After soaping my body and washing my hair, I rinsed off

and stepped out of the shower. The cool air brushed my damp skin as I wrapped myself in a warm, fluffy towel.

My phone lay on the dark marble counter, its screen lit up with a missed call from Julia. I called her back. It rang a few times before she finally answered.

"Hey, babe, how're things going?" she asked.

I slipped my underwear and pajamas on, trying to keep my voice down. "It's going."

"His family giving you a hard time?"

"No, the opposite, in fact. They're perfect." I smiled wistfully, recalling their kindness and hospitality.

"That's good, isn't it?"

I bit my lip. "Yeah, definitely."

In the brief silence, I could sense Julia's concern seeping through the phone. "How're you feeling? I hope you're not pushing yourself."

"I feel fine. The pain hasn't been bad at all," I lied, the words escaping with practiced ease.

"Have you talked to Lucas and Ethan yet?"

"No."

She sighed. "You need to tell them. Sooner rather than later."

I took a seat on the toilet lid. "I know. I'm working up to it."

"Do you know how hard it is keeping this secret from Lucas?"

I inhaled, then blew out. "I'll tell them. Soon."

"I guess that'll have to do for now. Well, I need to go.

Happy early Thanksgiving. Call me if you need anything." Her love and well-wishes seemed to reach through my cell.

The corners of my mouth tilted up. "Happy Thanksgiving, Jules."

After she hung up, I made my way into the bedroom. Ethan was already lying in bed, his back facing me. I plugged my phone into the charger on the bedside table and then slid beneath the blankets. With my back to Ethan, I couldn't stop the doubt from flooding my mind. His presence was a constant reminder of the connection we shared, and despite my resolve, the ache for what we could've been lingered. I stared at the ceiling, the silence filled with unrequited emotions.

Am I making the right choice?

I WOKE UP TO FIND THE SPACE BESIDE ME EMPTY, THE sheets cool where Ethan had been. The sun streamed through the open curtains, flooding the room with a soft glow. I stretched and then pushed the covers off of me, getting out of bed. After freshening up and dressing in my maroon sweaterdress and black ankle boots, I headed downstairs.

The scent of freshly brewed coffee and blueberry muffins filled my nose as I entered the kitchen. Ethan stood next to his mom. He appeared to be helping her prep for the Thanksgiving dinner party.

He looked up from peeling potatoes, smiling. "Morning. Sleep well?"

"I did." As I sat on a barstool at the kitchen island, Arlene turned from the counter, holding out a plate of fresh muffins.

"Good morning, dear. Here, have one of these before Ethan eats them all," she said.

He snatched a muffin from the platter, and Arlene playfully smacked his arm. "Leave some for the others, you rascal."

Ethan held a hand up. "This is my last one."

"Thank you," I said, taking a muffin and biting into it. The burst of sweet blueberries and the warm, soft texture was heavenly. "Oh my god. So good."

"They're addicting. You can't just have one," Ethan said, amusement glistening in his eyes.

"That's just an excuse to be greedy," I teased.

He smirked. "I'm greedy with a lot of things."

My cheeks heated as I stayed quiet and finished the rest of the fresh-baked goodness.

Arlene seemed to miss the innuendo. "You've been helping me for a few hours now, boy. Why don't you take your beautiful girlfriend through the maze? It didn't feel as cold this morning while I was drinking my coffee on the porch."

"Are you sure? There's still a lot to be done," Ethan said, wiping his hands on the white apron he wore.

Arlene practically shooed him away with her hands. "I have everything under control here."

Ethan kissed his mom's cheek before taking off the apron and hanging it up. He turned to me and held out a hand. "Shall we?"

I nodded, lacing my fingers with his. We walked out the back door, stepped down the porch stairs, and strode across the yard to the tall hedge maze. The entrance looked both inviting and slightly daunting.

The crisp autumn air carried the scent of fallen leaves and a hint of woodsmoke, adding to the enchanting atmosphere. Leaves crunched beneath our feet, and an occasional breeze swept through the nearby trees, making the maze feel like a secluded magical world all its own.

Ethan let go of my hand and turned to face me, a playful glint in his eyes. "You wanna play a little game of hide-and-seek?"

I let out a short laugh. "Hide-and-seek?"

His eyes darkened, taking on a stormy intensity that sent shivers down my spine. "Yeah. You hide. I seek."

My heart sped up at the thought of hiding from him, knowing he would be hunting for me—knowing he would catch me. "Okay, you're on."

He stepped back and said, "I'll count to fifty. Better start running, Sweetness."

Without another word, I turned and darted down one of the winding paths. *Damn, I should've worn tennis shoes.* The maze twisted and turned, each corner offering a new hiding spot, a new challenge. Looking over my shoulder, I didn't see or hear Ethan, but that just spurred me forward. He could be anywhere, and I was sure he knew the ins and outs of this maze like the back of his hand.

Hedges towered above me, their dense foliage blocking out the world beyond. I kept running. I rounded another corner as footsteps sounded in the distance.

My breaths came in quick shallow puffs as I ducked behind a tall hedge, trying to steady my racing heart. The air was thick with the scent of earth and leaves, the cool air brushing my flushed cheeks. I shifted backward into the shadows, listening intently for his footsteps.

The crunch of leaves grew louder, closer, and I held my breath, willing myself to stay perfectly still.

"I know you're here somewhere," Ethan called out, low and teasing.

Peeking through a small hole in the hedge, I caught sight of him moving with purpose, his eyes scanning around. My heart thrummed in my chest as I shifted, trying to stay hidden, but a twig snapped beneath my boot.

Fuck . . .

I peered through the hedge again, and he was nowhere to be found.

Where'd he go?

Strong arms wrapped around my waist from behind, pulling me against a hard chest. I let out a surprised squeal, stumbling. He steadied me, his laughter mingling with mine.

"I found you," he whispered, his breath hot against my ear.

His touch was electric, igniting sparks along every nerve ending as he turned me to face him. Our eyes locked in a primal understanding, each wordless exchange building the intensity between us. He captured my lips in a fiery kiss that left me breathless.

His hands roamed over my curves, and I melted into his touch. I wrapped my arms around his neck, wanting him with every fiber of my being. He squeezed my ass cheek, eliciting a low needy moan.

I pushed him away, my fingers trailing down his chest to his belt buckle.

"Are you sure?" he asked, watching me pop the button of his jeans.

"Do you want me to stop?" I asked, hesitating at his zipper.

His blue eyes bored into me. "God no." He removed my hands and unzipped his jeans, releasing his hard ready cock. Our lips met once more in another scorching kiss as I began to stroke him, working him from base to tip.

He pulled the skirt of my sweaterdress to my waist and ran his fingers up between my thighs. I shivered at his electric touch. He carefully pushed aside my underwear, and he massaged my clit with his thumb. Desire pirouetted through me, each turn growing stronger, building like a dancer's crescendo in the spotlight. I clutched his shoulders, not wanting the moment to end.

"Wrap your legs around me," he said, nipping at my ear.

I obeyed, and he carried me over to a stone bench, laying me on it. He brought my ass to the edge before pushing his pants down his muscular thighs. He lined himself up with my core, and I felt the pressure of him entering me.

"Fuck, I love being inside your tight pussy," he said, holding my legs open. When he was all the way in, he stopped.

"What's wrong?" I asked, meeting his gaze.

A corner of his mouth rose. "Nothing." His hands moved to my hips, and he thrust deeper.

The sound of our bodies moving together echoed in the space around us, but we at least tried to stifle our moans. His cock felt so good slipping in and out of me, hitting the right spot every time, bringing me closer to my impending climax.

"Please, Ethan."

He didn't stop. "Please what? Use your words, Sweetness."

"Make me come," I pleaded.

He reached beneath my sweaterdress and under my bra, cupping my breast. "Fuck, I can't say no to you, no matter how hard I try."

Ethan's pace quickened. The vein in his neck pulsed, his breaths becoming shallower with each passing second. I arched my back, meeting each of his powerful thrusts.

Warmth coiled low in my stomach as the walls of my pussy pulsated, tightening around his cock. I brought my hands to my mouth, muffling my cry of ecstasy.

Throwing his head back, Ethan let out a grunt, his hips bucking harder against me. I felt him swell, and then his hot release spilled inside me.

He leaned over and traced soft kisses on my face. "What're you doing to me?" he asked, though I didn't think he expected an answer from me.

Still catching my breath, I said, "We should probably head back to the house."

He brushed his lips over mine one last time before tucking himself into his jeans. He helped me off the bench, his hands steadying me as my legs wobbled. Taking a deep breath, I smoothed out my skirt. We walked back to the house, trying to pretend we hadn't just fucked in the family maze.

WHAT THE HELL WAS I THINKING? IT HADN'T EVEN BEEN twenty-four hours since I'd rejected Ethan, and then I'd let him fuck me in his family's maze. *God, it was so good though. It could be a long while until I'm able to do that again.* Those moments were a temporary escape. I stood in front of the mirror in the bathroom and stared at myself. The vibrations of my phone startled me. I glanced at the flashing screen. The caller ID read *Tatay*.

"Hey, Pop." I put him on speaker and set the phone on the counter. Ethan had gone down to continue helping his mom in the kitchen.

"Happy Thanksgiving, *anak*," Dad said.

I grinned; the festivity in his voice was contagious. "Happy Thanksgiving. How's everything with the family over there?"

In the background, lively music blasted, unmistakably karaoke. It wasn't surprising—Filipinos could turn any hour of the day into a karaoke party, and the familiar sound made me smile. My father spoke Tagalog to someone else before saying, "Oh, *alam mo, nag-eenjoy kami* (Oh, you know, we're having good times)."

"Good, I'm glad."

A knock came from the bedroom door. "Hey, Mia, the guests are starting to arrive," came Ethan's muffled voice.

"Okay, I'll be right out."

"Where are you?" Dad sounded concerned.

"Ethan talked me into spending Thanksgiving with him and his family in Southampton," I replied, running a brush through my dark waves and smoothing out my sweaterdress.

"Oh, that's good, *anak*." The line went silent for a moment, and I wondered if we'd gotten disconnected.

"Before I forget, I booked a flight to come a day before your surgery. I couldn't get any earlier flights due to the holiday," Dad said.

I let out a relieved sigh. "That's fine. I'm just glad you're able to make it."

"So, are you and Ethan dating now?"

I huffed. "No, Pop, we're still just friends. I have to go, but call me later, okay?"

After he agreed, I ended the call and stuffed my cell into the pocket of my sweaterdress, then made my way out of the bedroom. I really wasn't looking forward to this dinner party, but it was too late to back out now.

With a deep inhale and a shaky exhale, I descended the steps into the foyer. Distant voices echoed through the house. Energetic children darted around me. A small boy nearly ran into me, but I sidestepped, avoiding the collision. It looked like they were playing tag.

Where's Ethan? My gaze roamed the living room as Arlene traipsed up to me dressed in a beautiful fitted black dress with matching flats. I was definitely underdressed.

She placed her hand on my back. "There you are, my darlin' girl. I want you to meet a few of our relatives."

Arlene guided me through introductions to her mom and sister, who had flown in from Ireland. Other unfamiliar faces included some of her colleagues, previous patients, and Nolan's family. The rest constituted a mix of neighbors and friends. My gaze found Ethan, engrossed in what seemed like a lively conversation with the woman from that picture in his room, his ex, Hailey. She was still beautiful and wore a long-sleeve blouse, dark-wash jeans, and orange heels. Charm and elegance practically permeated off of her.

A churning in my stomach left me unsure whether my discomfort was from witnessing them together or the first pangs of hunger. I redirected my focus and engaged in a conversation with a longtime neighbor of the Millers. Clare shared heartwarming memories of Ethan growing up, including how considerate he always was, offering to help her with groceries and mowing the lawn.

At five o'clock, Arlene announced that the dinner buffet was ready, and we all formed a line around the massive kitchen island. I eagerly planned to attack the dessert table, which was a few feet from the delicious spread.

Belle stood in front of me as we navigated the line. "So, what do you think?"

My eyebrows wrinkled. I held a white china plate with one hand and used the other to scoop a small serving onto it. "About?"

"Everyone. More people showed up this year." She spooned a glob of mashed potatoes onto her plate.

If I was being honest, this wasn't the type of party I was used to. My family in the Philippines ate with their hands, and they used banana leaves as serving plates. We loved karaoke and were also very loud. "Everyone seems nice." I managed a smile.

The air was thick with conversations about achievements and milestones. Everywhere I turned, there were individuals who had climbed to the peaks of their careers or were enjoying the fruits of their prosperous working lives. Here I was, drifting through it all with a story that would never fit the mold.

My journey could be ending soon.

I glanced across the room, my eyes landing on Ethan and Hailey again. They stood close to each other, laughing. The familiarity in their body language spoke of their shared past. My gaze lingered as I took in the subtle nuances—the way Ethan leaned in a bit, the way Hailey's hand brushed his arm. The pressure in my chest was turning to pain.

I tried to muster a smile, wanting to be happy for him, but the earlier discomfort descended to form a knot in my stomach. His lips, which had been on mine only a few hours ago, curved up in amusement at something she'd said.

Belle glanced at them as we made our way out of the buffet line. "I wouldn't worry too much about that."

I blinked in her direction. "What?"

We proceeded toward the dessert table. Belle stopped halfway there, and her brow rose. "My brother really is into you, Mia. Hailey is just a family friend now."

"They seem really good together," I said, grabbing a plated slice of pumpkin pie.

Belle went for a piece of cherry. "Did he tell you what happened?"

I nodded. "Yeah, it broke my heart."

We moved away from the sweets to place our plates on the high-top table next to a floor-to-ceiling window. The sun was making its final descent over the horizon.

"They were both so young." Belle took a bite of her mashed potatoes. "And they aren't the same people they were in high school."

I pushed my food around the plate with my fork. "Maybe that's why it could work if they tried again." Because I was a sick, complicated mess, and he didn't deserve to be burdened with that.

Belle studied me for a few seconds before saying, "Is everything okay between you two?"

Clearing my throat, I replied, "Yeah, I'm just overthinking everything right now."

Pain exploded in my lower abdomen. *God, not now.* I held my stomach and leaned against the table, taking quick deep breaths.

"Are you okay?" Belle placed her hand on my back.

Not wanting to cause a scene, I fought against the ache

and slowly straightened. "Yeah, I'm fine. It's that time of the month."

She nodded, empathy crossing her face. "Can I get you Tylenol or Midol?"

"No, thanks though. I think I have something in my room."

"Are you sure? I can find you something strong." She winked, but the look of concern stayed on her face.

"Yeah, I'll be fine."

I couldn't shake the intrusive thought of Ethan and Hailey picking up where they'd left off. The steady rhythm of my heart quickened, and an inexplicable tightness gripped my chest.

Battling the sharp pain in my stomach, I threaded my way through the crowd of guests. I walked into the foyer, then up the staircase. A thudding came from the stairway. I grabbed the cold brass doorknob, but before I could turn it, Ethan rushed up to me. Urgency gleamed in his blue eyes.

"Hey, everything okay?" he asked.

I took a moment to tamp down the mounting pain in my body. "I'm not feeling too good." It wasn't a lie.

He stepped closer, our bodies inches apart. His eyes softened. "Did you eat something bad?"

I crossed my arms. "No. I haven't eaten anything."

"Why?"

Rolling my eyes, I let out a measured breath. "What's with the third degree?"

He stood there with a confused look on his face. "Okay, something's wrong, and I'm not leaving until you tell me."

What a stubborn ass. I extended my hand toward the doorknob in an attempt to reclaim some semblance of personal space. But he grabbed me, his fingers wrapping firmly around my wrist.

Despite my instinct to resist, I didn't fight him. "I just need to be left alone," I murmured.

His grip tightened, and his azure eyes filled with unwavering determination. "You're lying. I know you better than that, Sweetness."

The dimly lit hallway seemed to close in on me. Every fiber of my being wanted to retreat, to hide from the intensity of this night, but his attention was anchored in place.

A lump formed in my throat. "I don't think I can stay here any longer." The pain in my chest had lessened.

Ethan glanced behind him at the kids playing on the staircase. He opened the door to his room and pulled me inside, closing it behind him. He crossed his arms and leaned back against the oak surface. "Talk to me."

I needed a reason to leave—to deal with this on my own. "This is your world. I don't belong here."

He sighed and brushed his fingers through his dark hair. "Is this about what happened earlier?"

The confusion in his eyes twisted the silent ache in me. I was offering him a kindness. My choice stood as the lesser evil, a protective measure for him from me. Turning my back to him, I whispered, "No."

His voice neared. "Just tell me what's wrong. I know we can talk this through."

As I drew in a trembling breath, tears welled up in my

eyes. "Go back to your family, Ethan." I turned to meet his gaze.

He stopped in front of me, his citrusy bergamot scent torturing my senses. He scrutinized me in the dim-lit room, where the first streams of moonlight spilled in through the tall windows, casting a gentle glow on the bed.

Ethan stepped even closer. "Is this about Hailey?"

I bit my bottom lip. "You two seem very comfortable with each other. I think she could still have feelings for you."

His brow furrowed. "We're just friends. Everyone here knows I'm with you."

"But we're not together, Ethan." The words came out choked, like my body was physically trying to reject them.

His eyes bored into my soul. "There's something you're not telling me."

I hugged myself, blinking back the tears brimming in my eyes. "I want to go home."

"Please, Mia." He held out a hand, palm up. "Come downstairs. Let me spend Thanksgiving with you." His lips lingered a whisper away from mine.

My fingers tingled with the urge to take his hand, but my mind stopped me, rationalizing the situation. One day he'd realize that I'd done this for him. One day he'd thank me for saving him from the whole situation—from me. "Please. Just let me go."

A slew of emotions washed over his face as he interlaced his fingers on top of his head and took a breath. It looked as though he wanted to argue. Instead, he stepped back. "If that's what you *truly* want, I will." His gaze drifted to the carpeted floor. "I'll let you go." His blue eyes shimmered in the ethereal moonlight, all while my heart fractured into a myriad of splintered fragments.

I released a slow exhale and murmured, "Thank you." The words were laden with the heaviness of finality.

He stuffed his hands into the pockets of his black slacks. "Don't thank me." He walked away, and the door creaked softly as it swung shut upon his exit.

I packed my bag in a hurry and ordered an Uber on my phone as laughter and music drifted through the floor, a vivid reminder of what I was leaving behind.

Making my way down to the foyer, I decided to at least say goodbye to Ethan's mom. She'd been so kind and welcoming to me. Arlene was in the kitchen cleaning the empty platters off the island. She glanced at me, a curious gleam in her blue eyes.

"Mia, is everything all right?" She set the dishes into the huge sink and stared at me, wiping her hands dry with the towel that hung over her shoulder.

"I have a family emergency. Unfortunately, I have to leave, but I want to thank you for your hospitality." I shifted my weight from one leg to the other.

Arlene tsked and said, "I'm sorry to hear that. I hope everything's okay. And it was a pleasure having you, darling." She stepped closer and lowered her voice. "If I'm being totally honest, I think you and Ethan are wonderful for each other."

As though my heart weren't already sinking, it continued its gradual descent into my stomach. Tears started to rise from the pain of wanting someone who deserved better than me. "Please thank your husband for me as well."

Arlene nodded and wrapped her arms around me. I returned the hug the best I could, but if I stayed in her embrace any longer, I'd break. Pulling away, I offered her a reassuring smile, then turned and headed into the foyer and out the front entrance.

The vibrant life inside the house faded as I closed the door behind me, leaving the warmth for cold, quiet solitude. Emptiness consumed me, and each step away from the house felt heavier than the one before it. I waited at the end of the driveway for my ride.

The Uber pulled up, its headlights slicing through the darkness. I paused for a moment, taking in the inviting glow of Ethan's family home. Trying to convince my heart of what my head already knew, I whispered, "It's better this way."

EVERYTHING IN ME SAID, *JUST ACCEPT MIA'S FRIENDSHIP and move on.* But each time I thought of letting go, my heart rebelled. Her laughter, the way her eyes lit up when she talked about her loves, the warmth of her presence—all of it had become the very fabric of my being.

I needed to know what had triggered her to leave. She'd claimed it hadn't been our tryst in the maze. My conflicted emotions prompted me to relive our past conversations for clues. *I don't want to lose her.* But this couldn't keep happening. I wanted to become her everything—if she'd only give me a chance.

I stepped into my dad's dim vacant den, the air heavy with the familiar scent of aged leather and mahogany. In one corner was a fully stocked bar. Walking over, I grabbed a half-empty bottle of whiskey. The liquid poured smoothly into the glass tumbler I'd selected, the amber hue catching the subdued light. With a deep breath, I downed it in one gulp. Warmth spread through me, a momentary distraction from my mess of thoughts.

Belle wandered in through the sliding wooden doors. Her brows rose, eyes scanning the room. "Where's Mia?"

I poured seconds and took a swig. "She left."

Belle rested her hands on her hips. "What happened?"

I released the weight of the evening with an exhale. "I'm not sure. You spoke to her tonight. Did anything seem off?"

My sister chewed on her lip before saying, "She noticed you and Hailey talking. I assured her there was nothing there anymore." Belle tilted her gaze to the wood-paneled ceiling. "She did complain about cramps before going upstairs."

My and Mia's last conversation replayed for the thousandth time. I tried to piece everything together, but it still didn't make sense. I downed the rest of the whiskey without another word.

Belle strolled up next to me, took the bottle from me, and poured herself a shot. She downed it like a pro before slamming the glass onto the wooden counter. "Maybe she just needed a little bit of space. She did look conflicted about something." Belle placed a hand on my shoulder. "I've never seen you like this."

My brows came together as I stared at her. "What do you mean?"

"I mean, whenever Mia was looking away, your eyes were on her like a hawk. Like she was gonna disappear or some shit," Belle mused.

Dammit. I thought I'd been more discreet, but my sister noticed everything.

"Anyway, don't hide out in here too much longer," she said, then walked out, leaving the doors slightly ajar.

I lingered in the den a few minutes more, nursing the remnants of my frustration before rejoining the guests. With a forced smile, I engaged in polite conversation with distant relatives and longtime friends of the family.

As I walked through the kitchen and into the living room, the extravagance of it all hit me like a wave. It was like a scene straight out of a glossy magazine, everyone around me basking in their own sense of success and status. Glancing around, I could see why Mia might have felt out of place here. This wasn't her scene at all. For her, it was about real connections, not superficial interactions. And if I was being honest with myself, this wasn't me anymore either.

An hour later, the house quietly buzzed with the aftermath of the festivities. Mom, Dad, and Belle were saying goodbye to the final guests in the foyer. I wandered into the kitchen and found Hailey clearing the last of the dishes.

I leaned against the doorframe, watching for a moment. Her movements were precise as she placed the plates into the sink and wiped down the counters. "Looks like you still know your way around," I said.

She turned to me, a platter in hand, her expression softening. "Of course." Studying me for a long moment, she asked, "Is everything okay? You just kind of left midsentence earlier."

"Yeah, everything's fine," I replied.

She continued to stare, drying her hands and then

crossing her arms. "I know it's been a while, but I can still tell when something's off with you."

Letting out a sharp breath, I remained silent. *Would it be weird to talk to my ex-girlfriend about Mia?*

As if reading my mind, Hailey said, "Is it your girlfriend?"

"She's not my girlfriend." The words tasted bitter on my tongue. I pushed off the doorframe and started helping, putting plastic containers of leftovers in the fridge.

Hailey frowned, confusion apparent on her face. "But you told everyone she was."

"Wishful thinking," I muttered.

She tapped her finger on the counter a few times. "Why did you lie?"

I placed the last of the food into the fridge and faced her. "To stop my parents from meddling. They've been trying to set me up with someone ever since *our* breakup."

"I take it Mia went along with it for you," Hailey said.

Walking up next to her, I squeezed out a dishcloth and began wiping down the large counters in small circular motions. "Yeah, I promised to do 50 percent of her workload if she did."

Hailey let out a laugh. "Where is she? Did she go to bed already?"

I shook my head. "No. She left."

"What happened?"

"I'm not entirely sure," I said, replaying Mia's words in my mind. *Please. Just let me go.*

After Hailey rinsed the last dish, she started soaping up the sink. "You don't have an inkling of an idea?"

"No."

"Come on. Just think about it for a second," she said.

I rinsed off the cloth and hung it on the towel rack. "I did, and I am. I've been racking my brain trying to figure out why the hell she keeps pushing me away. I don't know if she's afraid of getting hurt again or what." Bracing my hands on the edge of the marble counter, I continued, "If only she knew I'd be the only one hurting here." I inhaled deeply, swallowing the lump in my throat. "I think I love her, Hailey."

My words lingered in the space between us, raw and heavy. The realization hit me full force, and saying it out loud had only solidified it.

Hailey's gaze shifted to the white tiles of the kitchen floor. She remained silent and looked as though she was mulling over my little outburst. Finally, upon her exhale, she said, "You and I both know how complicated love can be. Maybe she's scared, or maybe she's going through something she's not ready to tell you about. Maybe you just need to be there for her and wait."

I let out a shaky breath. "I feel like she's slipping away, and I'm powerless to stop it."

"Sometimes the strongest love comes from the willingness to wait for it." Hailey squeezed my shoulder, offering a reassuring smile.

Mom walked into the kitchen, her lips curving up. "You

two didn't have to do the last of the cleaning. I could've done it."

"It's only fair. You did do all the cooking," I said as Hailey dropped her hand to her side.

Mom kissed my cheek. "My sweet boy."

"Everything was delicious, Arlene," Hailey said. "I should probably get going."

"I'm glad you could make it tonight." Mom wrapped her arms around Hailey. "You take care of yourself, and don't be a stranger."

Hailey turned, giving me a brief hug. "I hope it all works out for you, Ethan. I really do," she whispered into my ear, then made her way out of the kitchen.

Mom stood there in the middle of the kitchen, staring at me. "Have you heard from Mia?"

I shook my head. "No."

"I hope everything's okay." There was no mistaking the maternal concern on her face.

"Me too," I said, resisting the urge to check my text messages.

"She really is a wonderful girl. You did good," she said.

It had all felt very real to me, but I didn't have the heart to tell Mom it was all a lie.

THE NEXT MORNING, DAD WALKED ME OUT TO THE OLD Camaro. The crisp scent of dew and damp leaves enveloped the surroundings. I unlocked the trunk of the car and opened it.

Dad handed me the small laptop bag he carried. "It's unfortunate Mia had to leave early."

I tossed my duffel in and slammed the trunk closed. "I'm sure she's fine," I reassured him, a conviction in my tone that mirrored the hope I harbored for her well-being.

He crossed his arms, his jacket swishing with the motion. "What about you, son?"

Moving toward the front of the Camaro, I began brushing away some of the freshly fallen leaves from the windshield. "What about me?" I asked, a perplexed furrow creasing my brow.

Dad helped me with the other half. "You just seem different."

"How?"

He dusted his hands off. "For a moment, I saw that happy, carefree boy you used to be."

I mimicked him. "Is that good?"

A light chuckle escaped him. "I think so. You should keep her around."

"Who?" I teased, feigning ignorance.

"You know who," Dad replied, briefly embracing me before retracing his steps back toward the house.

I settled into the driver's seat of the car and turned the key in the ignition. The engine roared to life. Shifting into reverse, I navigated the driveway and started the long drive home. The midmorning sun hid behind white clouds. Maybe I hadn't really changed. It could be I was always like this and Mia had just helped bring it out of me again.

Once I arrived at my penthouse, I sat on the sofa, still clad in the outerwear that shielded the autumn chill. *Don't be a chickenshit. Just call her.* I pulled out my phone, unlocked the screen, and thumbed through the contacts. I stared at Mia's number on the screen for a few seconds before finally tapping that intimidating green icon. I activated the speaker, and the rhythmic tones of the dialing sequence echoed through the empty room.

"Your call has been forwarded to voicemail . . ."

I let out a heavy sigh and hung up.

Did Lucas know anything? I was pretty sure he would've told me. There was one person who most likely knew everything that was happening with Mia. I navigated through my contacts once more, scrolling until I found Julia's number. With a long inhale and slow exhale, I called her, crossing my fingers for an answer. The phone rang for what seemed like a lifetime.

Children's voices infiltrated the call, their cheerful laughter and talking creating a momentary diversion. The clamor subsided and was replaced by calmness. Julia's voice emerged, breaking through the remnants of the playful symphony. "Hello. Ethan?"

I stood and began to pace the length of my dim living room. "Hey, Jules. Did I catch you at a bad time?"

"No, just between classes. What's up?"

"How's married life?" I asked, cringing as soon as the words left my mouth.

She deadpanned, "Really? You called to ask about my married life? Cut the shit."

How was I supposed to explain what was going on between me and Mia? I couldn't just outright tell Julia that I'd fucked her best friend. Twice. I let out a breath. "I'm sure Mia told you about spending Thanksgiving at my parents' house, right?"

"Yeah," Julia said, drawing out the word. "How'd it go?"

I remained quiet, trying to find the right words.

"What happened, Ethan?" It came out as more of a demand than a question.

I didn't want to tell Julia that I was falling in love with her best friend—not before I could tell Mia. "Something just . . . feels off about her."

The line went silent for a long moment. Julia knew something, but she wouldn't give away Mia's secrets.

"Have you asked her?"

"Yeah, but she's gotten fucking good at deflecting." I plopped down and sank into the sofa.

Julia let out a soft laugh. "Can't blame her for that. She learned from the best."

I chortled. "Not sure that's something I should be proud of."

Her next words dripped with a blend of sorrow and something else I couldn't put my finger on. "It's not my place to tell you, Ethan. I'm sorry."

The gravity of the situation became palpable, and desperation seeped into my tone. "Is it serious?"

Her voice trembled as she said, "I can't say."

Frustration churned in my stomach, but I understood why she couldn't tell me. I would've done the same for Lucas. "I get it, Jules. I'll let you get back."

We said our goodbyes, and I sat there, the unanswered question constricting my chest. My leg began to bounce restlessly. I tapped my thigh with an index finger in rhythm with my pulse.

Fuck it. Getting to my feet, I hurried into my private elevator with renewed determination.

AFTER THE FORTY-MINUTE CAR RIDE, I CLIMBED THE few flights of stairs to Mia's. I stood in front of Mia's apartment door, catching my breath. My knuckles rapped against the solid wood, each knock resonating with a mix of anticipation and apprehension. The door swung open, revealing my beautiful, sweet Mia. My eyes met her brown ones. With raised brows, she stood there bundled in a thick sweater and leggings, as if she sought refuge from more than just the autumn chill. The circles under her eyes seemed more prominent, and her complexion was dull.

"Ethan," she rasped. "What're you doing here?"

I entered her apartment uninvited, walking past her into the small living room. "You can't keep pushing me away."

She shut the door and crossed her arms, facing me. "You shouldn't be here."

"Did I do something wrong?" I stepped closer, but she backed away. God, that stung.

She squeezed her eyes shut and shook her head. "No. You didn't do anything. It's me."

"Are you really using that line on me?" I half joked.

"It's true." She was too calm about this—too unbothered. Did she really not give a fuck about this?

I followed her into the kitchen. "So, that's it, then?"

She reached for a glass in one of the chipped white-painted cupboards and filled it with water from the tap. She took a gulp, placed the cup onto the linoleum counter, and faced me as she inhaled. "Trust me, Ethan. Letting go of me is the best thing you can do for yourself right now." She leaned against the edge.

"What're you talking about?" I didn't falter. "Why're you saying things like that?"

Her face remained neutral. "You mean nothing to me," she said, but her voice trembled.

Her words were like a slap to the face. I studied her. Desperation crept into her eyes, almost as though she would say anything to get me to leave.

"I don't fucking believe you," I said.

Her nostrils flared. "What do you want from me?" She walked past me into the living room.

"How about the fucking truth for once?" I stayed on her heels. "You have no idea how much I've been racking my brain. I was so worried that I called Julia."

She glared at me. "You had no right. What did she tell you?"

"Nothing. She refused to answer any of my questions." I kept my distance this time.

Her eyes became glossy. "Get out," she whispered.

I stood my ground. "No. Not until we talk about this—about us."

Her chest heaved as she stepped toward me, pointing a finger at the door. "There is no us, Ethan. Just go!"

I didn't move, no matter how much her words pierced me. "Please, Mia . . ."

Her five-foot-three self tried to push me toward the door. I stumbled a few times but didn't budge for the most part. Grasping her wrists, I steadied her, locking eyes with the dull brown that mirrored her underlying turmoil. Her breathing quickened, and she swayed.

The room seemed to shrink, suffocating us both as we stood there, locked in a battle of wills. Her entire being seemed to tremble with the same emotions I was grappling with: fear, frustration, longing.

Her eyes roamed mine, searching for something—perhaps a glimmer of understanding or forgiveness. Weariness danced within the depths of her gaze.

My brow furrowed. I released my grip on her wrists, letting my hands fall to my sides. "Please, Sweetness, let me in."

She stared at me, sweat on her forehead, breaths alarmingly shallow. Her knees buckled, and she collapsed.

In an instant, I rushed forward, catching her before she hit the floor. "Mia?" Fear gripped my insides as I cradled her in my arms. Her skin was so cold. This wasn't the first time she'd fainted. *Maybe I should call 911.* I slipped my phone out of my pocket. The screen lit up, and just as I was about to call an ambulance, her chest rose upon a deep inhale and her eyes flickered open.

I held her close, breathing in her lilac scent. "Fuck, Mia, you scared the shit outta me." She pulled away, and I helped her into a sitting position. "Can I get you water?"

Holding her palm to her forehead, she nodded. "Please."

After I guided her to the sofa, I went into the kitchen and refilled her glass from earlier. She was resting her head back on the cushions when I walked back into the room and handed it to her.

"Thanks." She took a small swig and set it on the coffee table.

I settled next to her. She was still alarmingly pale.

"Well, that was embarrassing." Her gaze met mine, lips tilting up.

I couldn't believe she was trying to make light of what had just happened. Something told me this wasn't just about skipping a meal. Shaking my head, I said, "No. You don't get to do that."

"Do what?"

"You don't get to pretend like that's normal. And don't tell me it's because you didn't eat." I started to pace in front of the TV, which was playing one of her favorite reality shows.

"Pretending is all I fucking have at this point." The anger in her voice was apparent.

I interlaced my hands on top of my head, tilting my gaze to the textured white ceiling. "Please tell me what's going on with you. Do you want me to get on my knees and beg? I will."

She fixated on the flat screen for a few seconds as if searching for the right words. After what seemed like forever, she finally looked at me and said, "I have stage I ovarian cancer."

My gaze snapped to her, brows rising. I took a deep breath, filling my lungs completely before slowly letting it out, as if I could somehow release the shock that had gripped me.

What can I possibly say to ease the weight of this truth? There were no words that could make this better, no words to undo the reality of what she was facing. I sank to my knees in front of her. This was uncharted territory for me, but I knew one thing: I couldn't lose her. I wouldn't let her go through this without me.

I placed my hand over hers and gently squeezed. Searching through the many questions plaguing my mind, I asked, "So, what's next?"

"I have a small procedure scheduled this week." Her tired eyes met mine, a flicker of determination behind them. "Don't worry about me. My doctor said I have a high chance of remission."

Small procedure. Those words felt like a cruel understatement, a facade meant to shield me from the reality of what she was facing. I didn't want to believe this was happening, that she had to endure this at all. The thought of her in that sterile environment, surrounded by cold machinery and clinical lights, twisted something in my gut.

"This isn't your problem," she said, her voice low but lacking conviction. "You should probably go." She pushed to her feet and started for the door.

I followed. "Are you okay to be alone?"

"I'll be fine. I'm a grown woman." She unlocked and opened the door.

"I know that." I could tell she needed space, and to be honest, I needed a little time to process everything. "Please call me if you need *anything.*"

She nodded. "I will."

I stepped out of the apartment into the hallway. Taking my time, I made sure she closed and locked the door. Everything about this situation had left me numb. Nothing in the world mattered anymore.

Not a goddamn thing.

The world around me faded into a blur as I made it out of the building, city lights flickering like distant stars against the night sky. Each breath I took was heavy, filled with the weight of my unspoken fears. The air was thick with the scent of exhaust, a reminder of life continuing on while mine was suspended in time.

As I approached my car, the metal gleamed under the streetlights. I climbed in, the black leather seats cool to the touch, and the purr of the engine broke the silence. I drove on autopilot, lost in a haze of worry and dread, the cityscape blurring past like a bright canvas smeared with shadows.

Before I knew it, I was stepping off the elevator into the cold silence of my penthouse. My legs buckled, no longer able to support the weight of the truth I was carrying. I found myself on my knees on the chilly marble floor, the surface pressing unforgivingly against my shaking body. My hand instinctively went to my chest, trying in vain to ease the relentless tearing of my heart.

Mia—my sweet Mia—was fighting a silent enemy that was slowly eating away at her with each passing day. How long had she been going through this? Had she been masking her pain all this time, right under my fucking nose?

"God, I'm such an idiot." I had grilled her, interrogated her, treated her like she was hiding some criminal secret. All the while, she was in battle, coming to work, putting on a brave face as if everything were fine. Tears stung my eyes, but I fought them back fiercely. It was Mia enduring this struggle to survive. But for me, I could lose everything I'd ever needed.

Dragging myself off the floor, I slumped onto the sofa. What could I possibly do?

A suffocating weight settled in my chest, each breath becoming a laborious effort. My thoughts churned like a violent sea. It was as if I were submerged, struggling against the currents of my mind, unable to break the surface for a much-needed gasp of air. My surroundings closed in around me. The ache in my heart intensified, and I clenched my fists, trying to stop everything.

Mia's presence was threaded through every corner of my world in a way I'd never allowed anyone else—not even Hailey. I was unshakeable in my certainty that I had to be there for her, to stand by her in this fight.

If there's a chance I could lose her, I need to spend as much of her life with her as I can.

No hesitations, no doubts.

I'm all in.

Tuesday rolled around. The dinner Julia had planned loomed over me. With each passing hour, unease twisted my stomach a little tighter. Lucas was the last person I needed to tell.

That evening, I sat with Julia and Lucas in their modern dining room. The table was set impeccably, and the light from the abstract chandelier cast a gentle glow that usually put me at ease, but tonight it just highlighted the flutter of nerves inside me.

I caught myself taking tiny sips of water, each one an attempt to steady the anxious energy bubbling within. My eyes were drawn repeatedly to the window, to the expansive view of New York City. The bright lights blurred into one another, forming a dizzying mosaic.

I forced myself to focus on Lucas and what he was talking about workwise—something about Coachella and Venom.

"I wanna find out if Gale would be interested in being one of the guitarists. I think she'd fit in well with them." Lucas looked at me and asked, "Do you think you and Ethan could talk to her?"

Julia chimed in, "I would talk to her myself, but I don't want her to feel pressured."

"It'll give you more time with Ethan too." Lucas waggled his brows.

Julia rolled her eyes.

As much as I wanted to keep this conversation light, I inhaled a deep breath and said, "There's something I've been meaning to tell you, Lucas."

He finished chewing his food before placing his fork on the plate. "Okay. Shoot." He glanced at the look of concern on Julia's face.

The room fell into silence, as though even the walls were absorbing this wretched tension. The rhythmic ticking of the clock on the wall punctuated the quiet.

"I've been . . ." I glanced at Julia, and she nodded reassuringly. "I've been diagnosed with ovarian cancer." The words tasted bitter.

Another hush settled over the room. Julia's hand found mine in a gesture of unwavering support. Her eyes glistened with unshed tears, expressing a depth of empathy and concern that resonated through our shared history.

Lucas maintained a steady gaze. He leaned back in his chair and let out a long breath. "We're here for you, Mia. Whatever you need."

A surge of gratitude welled within me. The emotional

weight of my revelation lingered, but I found solace in the warmth emanating from my best friend and boss.

"Thank you." I wiped the wetness from my cheeks. "My surgery is in two days. My dad's flying in tomorrow."

Lucas nodded. "Don't worry about anything at work. I'll have Ethan pick up your workload."

That wasn't what I wanted. The surgery would take a toll on my body, but I didn't want to just give up and let someone else do my job. *Especially not Ethan.* I needed to at least be able to try, even if it meant pushing myself a little. "Let me at least do my admin tasks."

Julia and Lucas exchanged concerned glances. "Are you sure that's a good idea? Maybe you should focus on recovering," Julia pleaded with me.

But I couldn't ignore the rebellious urge inside me. "I can at least answer emails and set up appointments from home," I insisted.

Lucas leaned in closer, a stern expression on his face. "We'll see how you're feeling first. I think either way, I'm gonna hire a temp or two."

I blew out a conceding breath. "Fine. Thank you both. Seriously. It feels good to finally tell you." Even though Julia had already known.

The energy at the dinner table lightened with cheerful chatter after that. But as much as I tried to push it away, my problems lingered in the back of my mind, making it difficult to fully enjoy these moments.

THE NEXT EVENING CAME QUICKLY, AND SOON THERE was a knock on my apartment door. I rushed to answer it and immediately sank into my dad's warm embrace. It wasn't until then that I realized how much I needed him here. He'd always seemed to be the stronger one of us, unshakeable in any storm.

After he rolled his suitcase in, we sat at my small kitchen table.

"It's so good to see you, *anak*." He placed his warm hand on mine. "And you look well considering . . ."

The corners of my mouth lifted. "Thanks, Pop."

"So, catch me up on things."

I rubbed the back of my neck. "Life has been . . . *baliw* (crazy)." While waiting for his reply, I found myself doing pointe exercises beneath the table. My toes gracefully arched and relaxed, a habit that always grounded me.

"*Paano ito naging baliw* (how has it been crazy)?"

I switched to English; my Tagalog wasn't as good as I wanted it to be. "I feel like I've been failing at everything. My job, my relationships. I'm even failing at being sick."

Dad let out a long exhale. "It may seem like that now, but you can only do your best with the cards you're dealt."

"I feel like folding some days."

He squeezed my hand. "I'll never let you do that, *anak*." His eyes glistened.

Shit. I probably shouldn't have said that out loud. Returning his gesture, I said, "I'm sorry. I'm just so tired."

As though reading my mind, he said, "Why do you feel like you always have to do things by yourself? You have so many people in your corner."

"I know." Deflecting the topic to something other than my situation, I asked about my grandma.

"Lola was admitted to the hospital again. She's been having heart problems, but she's stable now," Pop said, leaning back in his chair.

The main reason he'd gone back to the Philippines was to take care of his mom, my *lola*. Guilt tightened my chest. "Is she gonna be okay?"

He nodded and pulled his hand away. "Yeah, she'll be fine. I hired a caretaker for her." A brief silence ensued before he asked, "What time is your surgery tomorrow?"

"Eight in the morning. Dr. Colton said it shouldn't take more than a few hours."

Dad glanced at the time on his phone. "We should probably get to sleep, then."

I retrieved a pillow, sheet, and blanket from my small linen closet and helped him make the couch as comfortable as possible. "I really should invest in a futon," I mused.

"This is fine, Mia-bear." He spread the pink-and-gray blanket over the cushions. "How has Ethan been?"

Damn. I was hoping Dad wouldn't ask about him. "Fine. He's just been working, I think."

"Does he know?"

"I told him a few days ago. We haven't talked since." I

tried to keep the bitterness out of my voice. What had I expected? For him to stick around? Who was I kidding?

"Give him time. This isn't exactly an ideal situation," Dad said.

I merely nodded.

"Good night, *anak. Mahal kita.*" He stretched his arms toward me.

I hugged him good night, then made my way into the bathroom down the hall. Turning on the hot water, I waited for steam to rise from the bathtub. Under the shower's warm embrace, each drop of water felt like it was cleansing more than just the physical. It was washing away the turmoil within me, layer by layer. Finally stepping out, I confronted the mirror veiled by the lingering mist. I stared at myself through a new lens, obscured yet clearer in some intangible way.

Give him time.

When I walked out in my bathrobe, a faint glow from the living room told me Dad was watching TV. I padded into my room and threw on pineapple pajamas. Just as I plugged my phone into the charger, it started to vibrate. A video call from Ethan.

I quickly took the towel off my head, hair still damp. Then I sat on the bed and answered it. His handsome smiling face appeared on the small screen.

"Hey," was all I could get out.

"Hey, how are you?" he asked. It looked like he might be lying in his bed . . . or a bed.

Why would he call me from someone else's bed? I leaned back against my headboard. "I've been better."

He stared at me, an amused gleam in his eyes. "Yeah, sorry. I don't know why I asked that."

"Did you need the password for the LV Productions email or something?" I asked, trying to move this awkward conversation forward.

His brow furrowed. "No. I called to check on *you*, Sweetness. I heard your surgery's tomorrow."

I nodded, holding the phone in front of my face. A lump formed in my throat as I bit my lip. Despite the great odds, that small chance of failure terrified me.

He sat up, leaning against his own headboard. "Everything's gonna be okay."

"Yeah, I know. A walk in the park." I said it as though it were common knowledge.

"Exactly." He smiled, but somehow, I knew it was forced. "I have a lot of work to catch up on at the office, but I'll stop by later."

"My dad's here," I said, a hint of warning in my tone.

He shrugged. "So? I'm pretty sure he likes me."

If he only knew. I rolled my eyes. "You can visit if you want."

A corner of his mouth rose. "Great. I'll see you after your surgery, then."

I got off the phone with him, dried my hair, and sank beneath the plush covers of my bed.

Everything's gonna be okay. I so wanted Ethan to be right.

I AWOKE BEFORE SUNRISE, THE EARLY-MORNING darkness pressing in around me. My heart was caught in a vise of fear and uncertainty. I dressed in comfortable loungewear, my movements slow and deliberate.

Walking into the kitchen, I found Dad sitting at the table waiting for me. He gave me a small smile that didn't quite reach his eyes. "The cab should be here in five minutes."

It had been over twenty-four hours since the last time I'd digested anything. With the way my stomach churned, I wasn't sure I could keep anything down. "Let's get going, then."

Dad shouldered my overnight bag, leading the way down to the lobby. We stepped outside into the cool morning air, the city still enveloped in the quiet of dawn.

Minutes later, a yellow taxi pulled up to the curb, its engine humming softly. We climbed in, and I gave the driver our destination. The buildings zipped past in a blur, yet I was wrapped in a bubble of stillness.

Dad's presence was a comforting anchor. He reached over and squeezed my hand, his touch warm and reassuring. "Everything's going to be okay, *anak*."

Thoughts, feelings, and memories tangled together in a chaotic ballet, each vying to take center stage in the whirlwind of my mind. I couldn't seem to focus on just one, so I let them pirouette and collide, hoping that some kind of clarity would emerge.

Dad and the driver stayed silent throughout the whole ride, and I was grateful for it. Silence was exactly what I needed.

The taxi pulled up to the front of the hospital. My heart raced, pounding so fiercely I thought it might escape my chest. After Dad paid the driver, we stepped onto the sidewalk, the autumn chill barely registering. I stopped in front of the sliding doors, drawing in a steady breath before walking inside.

The moment I crossed the threshold, the unmistakable sterile scent swept over me, transporting me back to a time I'd hoped to never relive. Each inhale was laced with memories—sitting in these very hallways, the fear, the hope, all of it mixed together during my mom's battle. I found it strange how a smell could throw me back so completely, how it could make my heart ache with the loss I'd tried to bury.

"Mia." Julia stood in the hospital lobby. She walked up to me and wrapped her arms around me.

My brows rose. "What're you doing here?"

She pulled away and tucked a strand of dark hair behind her ear. "I had to be here for my best friend. Hey, Mr. Cruz." She gave my dad a brief hug.

I shot her my sincerest smile. "Thank you, Jules."

Checking in was seamless, and soon a nurse was leading me back, guiding me toward the pre-op room. The quiet, almost serene atmosphere of the hospital's interior was miles apart from the bustling city outside. This world moved at a different pace, measured by the soft footsteps of nurses and the murmur of hushed conversations.

I stepped into the room and sat on the bed, my gaze sweeping over the medical equipment. My nerves spiraled, but I couldn't let the fear consume me. Instead, I redirected my attention, letting my feet fall into the rhythm of pointe exercises. Each stretch and curl of my toes brought me back to myself, stirring the resilience that had been a part of me for as long as I could remember.

The young nurse who'd guided me here began her dance around the space, prepping for the procedure. She walked over with a warm, genuine smile.

"I don't think I introduced myself. I'm Emma," she said.

"Hi," I managed, but my grin felt more like a tight line than an expression of joy.

"Don't worry, dear." Emma's voice was soothing, a temporary balm on my frayed nerves. "You're in good hands."

I nodded, trying to steady my trembling hands. "I know . . . It's just hard not to be nervous."

"It's completely normal to feel that way."

Her words were meant to comfort me, but the risks of the surgery still lingered in my mind like a dark cloud I couldn't shake.

Emma asked me a barrage of questions, jotting down my answers on her tablet. Her presence became a rock I clung to amid the violent sea of worries. All too soon, she was handing me a hospital gown.

"It's time to get changed," she said, her tone gentle.

Alone in the bathroom, the act of swapping my clothes for the hospital gown felt like shedding my last layer of protection, leaving me exposed and vulnerable. I stepped back into the room, and Emma handed me a warm blanket. "This will keep you warm."

I murmured a quiet thank-you while draping it around myself, letting it serve as a tiny barrier against the cold space. I shuffled to the bed and slipped under the crisp sheets.

Emma began affixing the leads onto my skin, each sensor a cold bite against the cozy embrace of the blanket.

"Little pinch." Her hands were gentle and precise as she inserted the IV access.

Resting my head against the pillow, I tried to anchor myself in the moment, to steady my thoughts with deep measured breaths.

Emma noticed. "That's it. Just focus on your breathing, Mia. It's going to be okay." She held my hand and gave it a squeeze.

The beeping of the machines and the sound of my

heartbeat were my focal points, yet my mind raced with what-ifs.

"What if something goes wrong?" The question slipped.

Emma's warm brown eyes met my gaze. "You're in very capable hands," she assured me again.

Slicing through the haze of fear, the truth of my situation came into focus—the constant ache, the endless months of suffering in discomfort, the cancer. This fight was for the life I still had left, for a future beyond the shadows of pain. Holding on to this thought, I mustered the courage to confront what lay ahead. I could place my trust in the skilled hands ready to lead me through.

The door swung open, and in walked Dr. Colton. He greeted me with a sincerity that reached his eyes.

"Good morning, Mia." His voice was soft. Calm. "You ready?"

I managed a nod.

With his team arrayed behind him like a quiet force of support, Dr. Colton went over the procedure again. Each word, each step, was laid out with clarity and care, grounding me to the moment, to the here and now.

"You're going to do great," he said.

The journey to the surgery room was a blur, my mind caught between fear and hope. Inside, lights loomed overhead as I was moved to the operating table, the center of this meticulously prepared stage. The flurry of activity around me was distant, buffered by Dr. Colton's steady presence at my side.

His hand in mine, his voice a constant murmur of

reassurance, was the last clear sensation before a mask was fitted over my face, my world quickly narrowing.

"Count backward from ten," the anesthesiologist said, a gentle command that felt like stepping off a ledge into the unknown.

"Ten . . . nine . . . eight . . . seven . . . six . . ." My voice wavered, trailing off into a calm oblivion.

Awareness slowly crept into the edges of my mind. It wasn't pain that welcomed me back, but rather a dull throbbing discomfort that pulsed through my body. My eyelids were like lead, stubbornly resisting my efforts to lift them. The clean, sharp scent of the hospital cut through the haze left by the anesthesia, a reminder of where I was. The room was awash in a soft diffused light, gently coaxing me back to reality.

"Welcome back, Mia," came a comforting voice.

Emma. Shifting my head, I squinted, finding her familiar face looming over me. She offered me a smile, a beacon of calm in the confusion that enveloped me.

"How do you feel?" Her voice was laced with genuine concern as she adjusted my blanket.

"Like I've been hit by a semitruck," I rasped, the words feeling thick and clumsy in my mouth.

Emma chuckled softly. "That's to be expected. But you

did great. Dr. Colton will come in soon to talk to you about how everything went."

True to her word, it wasn't long before the doctor appeared at my bedside. "The operation went very well. We were able to successfully remove the cancer without any complications."

I gave a small nod, letting his words sink in. It felt like I'd been holding my breath forever, waiting for this very assurance. Hearing him say it out loud soothed my worries, which had been a constant burden leading up to the surgery.

"Thank you," I whispered. "When can I go home?"

"We'll keep you under observation for a little while longer, just to make sure there are no immediate postoperative issues," Dr. Colton explained. "But if everything continues to go as smoothly as it has, you could be home by tomorrow."

Home. The word filled me with a mix of longing and apprehension. The recovery road ahead would be its own challenge, but for now, the hurdle of this procedure was behind me.

"Thank you, for everything," I said, tears welling up in my eyes.

"You're welcome, Mia. We'll do everything we can to make sure your recovery is smooth. I'll check on you again later, but if you need anything at all, don't hesitate to ask Emma." He gave her a nod before walking out of the room.

Emma busied herself with checking my vitals and making notes on her tablet. The comfort of her routine attentiveness grounded me. "It looks like you'll be stuck with me for a while longer."

"Thank you," I said, my voice stronger now.

She smiled. "You just focus on getting better, okay?"

"Okay," I agreed, settling back against the pillows, the gentle beeping of the monitor a steady reminder of the life that flowed within me.

I'm still here, Mama—I made it through act one.

THE OFFICE WAS AN EMPTY SHELL WITHOUT MIA'S vibrant presence. Her laugh and the click-clack of her heels on the tile floors were noticeably absent. Every time I checked my phone and found no messages, that undeniable ache in my chest intensified, reminding me just how much I missed her.

Fuck. My fingers twitched with the memory of tracing the soft curves of Mia's body. Every inch of her skin had seemed familiar and precious. I could still feel the warmth of being inside her. Our mingled moans of ecstasy echoed in my mind. God, I wanted more of her—all of her. If she would have me.

My cell vibrated in my pocket, shaking me from my thoughts. It was Julia. I answered, putting her on speaker.

"Hey, Ethan."

Heart in my throat, I greeted her back and asked, "How'd it go? Is she okay?"

"She's in recovery. They're going to keep her for a night to monitor her, but the procedure went smoothly," Julia said.

I let out a breath, rolling the tension from my shoulders. "Thank God."

"She should be home tomorrow, but I'll let you know if anything changes."

"Thanks, Jules. I thought I was gonna go insane waiting," I mused, trying to lighten the mood.

"She's gonna be just fine, Ethan," Julia assured me once more. We said our goodbyes, and I returned to standing alone with my thoughts in the empty office.

There was only one place I could get my mind off of this for a while.

LATER THAT EVENING, I WENT BACK TO MY PLACE AND packed my acoustic guitar. I drove to a hotspot called Bar Nine that held open mic nights.

A couple of hours later, I was walking into the lounge's dim ambiance. The gentle buzz of conversations mingled with the occasional clink of glasses. Amid the eclectic furniture and the warmth of the room, I stared at the empty stage.

"Well, if it isn't Ethan Miller," a familiar voice called to me from behind.

I faced the woman, offering a smile. "Hey, Gwyn. You have a spot for me tonight?"

She curled her fingers and looked at her red-painted nails. "We have a pretty full roster, but I think I can work you in."

"Thanks, beautiful. I appreciate you." I winked at her.

"The least you could do is buy me a drink." She tucked a strand of wavy auburn hair behind her ear and rested a hand on her hip.

I sighed and followed her to the mahogany bar top. I ordered a whiskey and Coke, and she called for a Long Island from the bartender.

She studied me, taking a sip from her glass. "I haven't seen you in months. What have you been up to?"

I'd known Gwyn for years, since before I'd started managing No Blood, No Alibi, so I was pretty comfortable talking to her. "Lucas and I have been building our clientele for his new label."

"I heard about his retirement and marriage to that dancer from his music video. That unsettled the masses for a good while," she said before taking another swig. "Even with your busy schedule as manager and scout, you seemed to always make time to come play for us."

Fuck. She's onto me. I downed my drink, then inhaled. "I've just been working hard to pick up clients for Lucas."

Suspicion crept onto her features. "I'm gonna pretend to believe that. Only because I have to go MC now." She drank the rest of her Long Island, slammed the glass down, and then, before she walked away, said, "We'll continue this later."

I grinned. "Looking forward to it."

The lounge played host to a couple of performers, each leaving their own unique stamp on the evening. First, there was a guy with a raspy voice, his acoustic guitar cradled like a lover in his arms. The stage lights cast his face in shadow, adding a layer of mystique to his performance.

After him, a woman took the stage, her presence almost ethereal. She had a voice that could only be described as liquid silver, flowing effortlessly through a range of ballads that spoke of love's delicate dance. Accompanying herself on a piano, her touch was gentle and deliberate. Her hair fell in soft blond waves around her shoulders, catching the light in a way that made her seem otherworldly.

By the time I took the stage, the bar was filled with an energy that was both electric and expectant, a challenge I was ready to meet. I stepped onto the wooden stage and into the light, ready to bare my heart in the only way I knew how. I hugged my guitar, its polished wood a reassurance beneath my fingertips. My music filled the room, and my voice was a conduit for all the emotions I couldn't express.

After my performance, Gwyn approached with two tumblers in hand filled with amber liquid. She handed me one. "You really poured it all out there."

I thanked her for the drink. "Yeah, guess I did."

She nodded, her eyes never leaving mine as she sipped the liquor. "So, who is she?"

My brow furrowed. "What?"

"The woman you were singing about. No one sings Ed Sheeran like that without someone in mind," she said, an amused smirk on her face.

She was a determined creature. She'd get it out of me sooner or later. I let out a conceding sigh, averting my gaze. "Her name is Mia."

A corner of Gwyn's mouth rose. "Pretty name."

My eyes snapped to her. "Even more beautiful, the woman herself."

"So, what's the problem?" Gwyn asked, swirling the amber liquid around in her tumbler before taking a swig.

I didn't feel like summing everything up in that moment. "It's complicated."

She studied me. "And what about your roster of eager partners?"

Shaking my head, I replied, "It's gone. I don't want that anymore."

Gwyn raised a sculpted brow. "Really? Is this Mia it for you, then?"

I couldn't deny the pull I felt toward Mia, but there was so much uncertainty, obstacles that seemed impossible to get around. I wanted her to be sure—to know without a doubt. But life didn't offer those kinds of guarantees. I was only sure of one thing: *she's worth the risk.*

"Maybe." Downing the rest of the whiskey, I placed it on the bar. "It was nice seeing you, Gwyn."

"Likewise. Don't be a stranger," she said.

I gave her a two-fingered salute, then walked away, my guitar case in hand. I stepped into the night, and the sounds of the city wrapped around me. Standing on the sidewalk, I realized that no amount of music could fill the void Mia left.

As I unlocked the car door, the interior lights flickered on. I slid into the driver seat.

Mia needed all the support she could get, and I needed to prove to her that I was in this for the long haul, that I wasn't going anywhere. The reality of what I was contemplating settled over me. I needed to be with her, to let her know I was ready to take this step forward. If she would just let me.

I TRAIPSED THROUGH THE FRONT DOOR OF MY apartment with Dad's assistance, the familiar scent of eucalyptus enveloping me. The muted chatter of neighbors and the occasional thud of footsteps from above hinted at the quiet rhythm of the evening settling in. Inside, the apartment felt like a cocoon, a serene escape I desperately needed after my hospital stay. Dad helped me clean my stitches before he fell asleep on the couch, his gentle snores filling the living room. I didn't blame him. We'd both had a long couple of days, and he hadn't even had the chance to recover from his jet lag.

I changed into my favorite pink pineapple pajama pants and a white cami and sank into the comfort of my bed. The sounds from the TV show playing in the living room started to lull me to sleep. A knock at the front door startled me. Dr. Colton had told me I could walk around, so I carefully made my way to the door. I opened it to find Ethan's smiling face on the other side, a bag full of groceries cradled in one arm.

He looked so fucking good in his gray hoodie and black sweatpants. Despite my current condition, my body still wanted him in every way. A simple "hey" was all I could get out.

"Hey, sorry I didn't call. Did I wake you?" he asked, looking over at the couch where my dad slept.

Shaking my head, I gestured for him to come in. "No."

He walked past me and started for the kitchen. I trailed behind him, wondering what goodies were in the brown paper bag. He placed it on the small island and just stared at me for a long while.

I looked down at myself, and my eyes widened. I crossed my arms, cheeks warming. *Shit, no bra.*

His gaze drifted to the incision site on the right of my stomach just below my belly button. I knew he could see the gauze and tape there through my thin cami.

"Does it hurt?" he asked, stepping closer.

"Only a little. I can't make any sudden movements, obviously. No strenuous exercises." I placed my hand on the counter, savoring the cold laminate against my skin.

"Can I see?"

My brow furrowed. I hadn't expected him to make that request, but Ethan had always been a curious one. "There's not much to see." I raised my shirt, stopping just below my breasts.

He bent down until his face was level with my stomach.

Placing his hands on my hips, he stared. "Will it leave a big scar?"

I shook my head, my senses too occupied, reveling in his touch.

With slow, meticulous movements, Ethan pressed his mouth above the taped gauze. His lips were warm against my cool skin despite the dressing separating us. He lingered there, the gesture melting my heart.

Pulling away, he looked up at me. His blue eyes had turned gray in the fluorescence of my small kitchen. "I'm glad the procedure went smoothly."

My lips quirked up as I whispered, "Me too."

He straightened, releasing me. "You want a late-night snack? I bought ingredients to make gourmet grilled cheese."

I let out a short laugh. "Sure. What makes it gourmet?"

"The fact I'm cooking it." He smirked and winked at me.

Rolling my eyes, I said, "Wow, corny much?"

His gaze penetrated me. "Only for you, Sweetness."

I tore my gaze away from him, looking at the bag of groceries. "So, what can I help with?" I started to take items out of the brown paper bag, but he stopped me, grabbing my forearm.

"Go rest. I'll bring it to you when I'm done." He twisted my arm so that my palm faced him, and then he kissed the pulse in my wrist.

My cheeks heated. "Okay." The word came out breathy. When he released me, I strolled out of the kitchen, past my snoring dad, back to my room. I slipped beneath the cool covers, letting out a sigh. How much more of Ethan's kindness could I take before I finally gave in?

I can't allow myself to love him.

Dad's snores seemed to get louder. I didn't mind; he was catching up on some much-needed rest. I wasn't as tired as I'd expected to be.

Glancing at my laptop on my bedside table, I wondered how full the LV Productions inbox had gotten. I placed the computer on my lap and decided a quick look wouldn't hurt. It wasn't as though I had anything else to do.

A few more minutes passed before Ethan stood in my doorway, a plate of grilled cheese in one hand and a glass of water in the other.

He walked into the room and made his way to my side of the bed. "You better not be working."

I bit my lip. "It's not like I have anything better to do."

Ethan placed the glass on my bedside table, then took my laptop from me, closing it and putting it on the dresser. "Lucas hired a temp to fill in while you're out. The admin work won't pile up."

I released a slow breath and nodded. I'd forgotten that little detail, but I still wanted to be somewhat useful during my recovery.

He handed me the plate. "Eat up, beautiful."

Taking it, I thanked him and bit into the warm gooey sandwich. "Oh my god," I moaned. "This is so good."

He grinned and climbed next to me on the bed, making himself right at home.

Shit. The last time we were in this room together was when we—

I pushed the thought away.

"I'm glad my cooking can make you moan like that," he said, smirking.

Dammit, he's way too flirty tonight.

"If I'd known grilled cheese would have that effect on you, I would've made it sooner," he purred.

I let out a giggle, trying to keep my food in my mouth. After chewing and swallowing, I said, "I didn't even know it would have this effect on me."

"Glad I could help you discover that about yourself." He stretched his long legs out in front of him, crossing one ankle over the other. "I'd like to assist you more in that area."

My brows came together. I took the last bite of the sandwich and started licking my fingers. "What do you mean?"

He pursed his lips as though debating his next words. "I wanna help you discover more about yourself in every way possible."

Was he being serious or suggestive? "Define *every way.*"

Ethan placed his hand on my thigh, and even through the comforter and my fleece pajamas, I could feel the heat between us.

"I wanna explore every bit of you, Sweetness. Really take my time to savor you." His fingertips drifted up my forearm to my bicep, goose bumps sprouting in their wake.

It didn't get any clearer than that. "I wish I weren't in such a fragile state," I murmured.

He chuckled, taking the empty plate from me, and then interlaced his fingers with mine. "I'm gonna tell you something, but I want you to know I don't expect you to respond."

I nodded, glancing down at our hands and how perfectly they fit together. "Okay."

His broad chest rose upon his inhale, and then he said, "Being with you in this way has always been enough for me."

I stared at him, my brain unable to form a response. It seemed my efforts to spare him from heartache were failing, but maybe that wasn't such a bad thing.

Ethan leaned over and placed a gentle kiss on my forehead. "Get some sleep. I'll see you tomorrow." He was gone before I could fully comprehend what he'd been trying to say.

Lying flat on my back, I replayed his words over and over.

Being with you in this way has always been enough for me.

EACH DAY THAT PASSED POSTSURGERY, I TRIED NOT TO rely on Dad or Ethan. They did their best to make sure I didn't get out of bed too often. I'd snuck around trying to do some things myself, clinging to any semblance of my temporarily lost independence.

But even though I had so much support from my dad and

friends, the ache for my mom remained imprinted on my heart. She would've known what to say, how to make this seem like any other hurdle we'd clear together. In the midst of healing physically, I found my heart yearning for the comfort only she could give me.

A week had passed in the blink of an eye. Christmas and New Year's were approaching quickly. One evening, after Ethan left, Dad brought me a dinner tray they'd prepared. Dad sat at my bedside with a concerned look in his dark eyes. The savory scent of chicken adobo filled my nose as I stared at him, spoon in hand.

"I taught Ethan how to make adobo. He had to go to a show," Dad said.

"Something wrong, Pop?" I asked.

He glanced at his clasped hands in his lap. "It seems Lola's condition took a turn. The caretaker said she collapsed today. She's been admitted to the hospital for more tests."

I was afraid something like this would happen. I couldn't keep him from his mother. "You should go back."

He shook his head. "I can't—"

"You can, Pop." I placed my hand over his. "I'll be fine. I have Julia, Lucas, and Ethan."

Tears brimmed in his eyes. "How did I get so lucky to have such an amazing daughter?"

My lips curved up, and I shrugged. "*Mahal kita*, Pop."

He stood and pressed a kiss to my forehead. "*Mahal kita din*, Mia-bear." Then he walked out of the room, and I couldn't keep the tears from falling.

It didn't take long for Dad to book a flight. He left for the

Philippines Friday night, leaving me alone with Ethan. As soon as Dad had hugged me goodbye and stepped out the door, a wave of sorrow had washed over me. But knowing that Ethan was here for me kept the worst of it at bay.

Ethan slipped into the routine effortlessly. Oftentimes, he sat beside me on the bed working on his laptop while I slept or watched the small flat screen that sat on my dresser. The rhythmic tapping of his fingers on the keyboard was a comforting sound, oddly enough.

One evening, as he watched a reality show with me, his black-framed glasses perched low on the bridge of his nose, my heart swelled. Here was this strong, capable man, indulging in my guilty pleasure without complaint.

My focus drifted back to the screen. "You know, you're here more than Julia these days. I have half a mind to give you my spare key."

"If that's something you'd feel comfortable with, it would make things much easier," he said, glancing at me.

I hadn't expected that response from him. My brow rose. "Really?"

He nodded. "Only if you're comfortable with it."

I didn't need to think about it. Giving Ethan a key felt like the natural thing to do. "If you want it, I'll give it to you."

He stared at me, his eyes sparkling. "Oh, I want it."

God, I hadn't meant for it to sound so suggestive. Heat flooded my cheeks.

He leaned closer. "Give it to me, Sweetness."

The urge to kiss him was strong, but I didn't want to disturb my stitches. He seemed to sense that and moved so that he was hovering a few inches above my body. His breath was hot on my cheeks. He slid his hand up my nape, lingering there. I pressed my lips against his, and it was as though my body knew him. He pushed his tongue into my mouth and moaned. His hand on the back of my neck trembled. He was holding back.

Before I could get my hands beneath his T-shirt, he pulled away. "We should stop. I want to be careful of your stitches."

My fingers fell away from the hem of his shirt. I inhaled and nodded. "You're right."

He carefully climbed off me and took back his spot next to me on the bed. How could I possibly watch this show with the worst lady boner ever?

Damn these stitches.

Day by day, I found myself standing more on my own, needing less help from Julia and Ethan. Even though I didn't need him as much, Ethan still made it a point to come over *every single day*. Most nights he'd fall asleep on the bed next to me. And somehow, several changes of clothes had ended up at my apartment.

Julia visited a few days before I started my chemo treatment. Together, we transformed my apartment into a sanctuary. In my small kitchen, we unloaded bags of groceries, filling the fridge with a colorful array of produce. The hum of the refrigerator and the clinking of cans resonated as we organized everything.

"I'm sorry I can't go with you Monday, but I'll visit as soon as my last class ends," Julia said, placing snack bags of veggie chips into the cabinet.

"It's fine. The doctor said I probably won't feel any side

effects until later," I replied, trying to make the upcoming uncertainty seem less important somehow.

Julia leaned against the island, staring at me. "Are you scared?"

Terrified was an understatement, but I summoned a facade of strength for her. For myself. "Nope. You know me, I always roll with the punches." A half-hearted grin played on my lips.

She pushed off the counter and pulled me into a tight embrace, her voice shaky. "I know. And I admire the hell out of you for that." She backed away, and her eyes bored into mine. "Everything will be fine."

Her words hung in the air, a mantra of hope. Assurance. Yet beneath the surface, I sensed the fragility of her own conviction. I nodded, my silence speaking volumes about the swirling emotions inside me.

The knock on the door broke the quiet. Unsure of who it could be, I answered it. There stood Ethan, carrying a big suitcase and duffel. My eyebrows rose.

"Um . . . what's this?" I gestured to his luggage.

"I wanna be here for everything, Mia." He stepped closer but didn't cross the threshold. "If you'll have me, I'd like to move in." He stood there, waiting for my answer.

"This is *not* what I meant when I gave you my spare key." I glanced back at Julia, who was standing in the doorway of the kitchen, nodding in approval. I didn't need Ethan to move in with me. That was far from what I needed. Crossing my arms, I replied, "Sorry, but no."

His brow furrowed. "It's like I live here anyway. The only time I go home is for clothes. I'm either here or at the office." He pursed his lips as though thinking of what to say next.

Julia stomped into the living room. "Would you stop being so fucking stubborn and accept the man's help?"

I glared at her. "Whose side are you on?"

She huffed, placing a hand on her hip. "Yours, but you're being stupid. What would've happened if Ethan hadn't been there the night you passed out?"

Dammit, I hate when she's right. My chest rose and fell on a contemplative breath.

Turning to Ethan, I made room for him to step inside. A grin tugged at the corners of his mouth as he strode in, hauling his bags.

"Fine," I said, closing the door behind him and locking it. "But this is just temporary."

Ethan set his luggage down next to the couch, stretching his arms briefly before heading straight for the kitchen. I heard the sound of cabinets opening and pans being pulled out. Peeking in, I found him already chopping vegetables with surprising ease. "You don't have to do that," I said, moving closer. "I can help."

He glanced up with a small smile. "I've got this covered," he said, his tone calm but firm, making it clear he wasn't about to let me lift a finger.

I turned to Julia and grabbed her hand, pulling her eagerly into my room and shutting the door behind us with a soft click. My heart raced as I turned to face her, my long dark waves falling in disarray over my shoulders. "What the fuck, Jules."

She grinned like a child who had just been caught sneaking cookies from the jar. "What's wrong, M? I thought you two were *just friends*." Her tone was mocking.

My body tensed; I was conflicted between wanting to tell her the truth and keeping my secret. Her finger pointed at me like a spotlight ready to expose me.

I collapsed onto my bed with a groan. "We *are* friends."

She didn't back down, sitting next to me and waiting patiently for the truth to come out.

Julia's death glare had always terrified me. I couldn't hold it in any longer. "Fine. Something's been going on between me and Ethan. Okay?"

The words were heavy and shameful as they left my mouth. I could still sense his soft lips, his firm body pressed against me. Instead of the expected response of excitement or judgment, there was only silence.

"Say something," I pleaded.

But all she offered was a hesitant, "I don't know."

It wasn't reassuring at all. My doubts and fears came rushing back in full force. Did Ethan really care about me, or was this just another game to him?

Is this going to be just like Kyle?

"Well, if nothing else, you could have some good sex." She waggled her eyebrows.

That was an understatement. I smiled. "Friends with benefits? That never ends well."

But part of me couldn't help but be tempted by the idea

of a welcome distraction from everything else preventing me from living my life. I paced back and forth, torn between my desires and my fears.

She stood from the bed, her soft footsteps echoing as she made her way over to me. Her hand gently steadied me. "Just try not to overthink it too much, okay, babe?"

I nodded, knowing that was easier said than done.

She glanced at her watch. "I should get going," she said, then headed out of my room. I trailed behind her.

After Julia bid farewell to Ethan with a warm hug, she slipped on her boots and bundled up in her coat. I hugged her tightly one last time, then watched her leave through the door, locking it behind her.

It's just the two of us now. I rolled the tension from my shoulders and tried to steady my ragged breaths, but my nerves were getting the best of me. I couldn't shake the feeling that something was off. Different.

I walked into the kitchen and watched Ethan navigate around the space. The savory scent of marinara filled my nose. On the stove, pans sizzled and a pot boiled. The sounds of his home cooking were like a relaxing melody.

The aroma was comforting, and I couldn't help but feel a sense of gratitude for his unexpected presence. It was more than just the food; his decision to leave the luxury of a New York City penthouse and move into my humble Brooklyn nest to support me through my treatment was truly, deeply, madly touching.

Was that something a "friend" would do? Julia would've done it in a heartbeat if she didn't have her ballet studio and a new husband to manage, but this was Ethan. I didn't quite know where we stood in our confusing relationship. We hadn't put a label on anything, and I wasn't sure I could do that.

I reached into the fridge, and my fingers closed around the slender neck of a bottled water. I pulled it off the shelf, shut the door, and stared at him.

"What about work?" I asked.

He didn't look away from his cooking. "Lucas told me to take as much time as I need."

My brow rose. "How much time off did you take?"

"Enough." He tasted the sauce and muttered, "Needs more salt."

"Can you be more specific?" I unscrewed the cap and took a swig.

His gaze met mine. "Don't worry, I'm still gonna work from my laptop. And Venom should be arriving in New York soon. So, Lucas wants me to play chauffeur." He turned back to his cooking.

I left it at that. Stepping closer, I looked at the red sauce he was making. I crossed my arms. "Did you make marinara from scratch?"

"Doesn't everyone?" He took the boiling pot of pasta off the fire and drained it into the sink.

I placed the plastic bottle on the counter. "You're quite the cook."

He winked at me. "I'm no gourmet chef, but I have my signature dishes."

I studied him. "Can I ask you something?"

He glanced at me again and tilted his head. "Yeah. Shoot."

"We're friends, right?"

Ethan retrieved two plates from the cupboard and set them on the island next to me. He winked at me. "Maybe."

I cocked an eyebrow. "What does that even mean?"

He closed the distance between us, his confident smirk growing with each calculated step. The dim lighting in the kitchen cast shadows over his face and made his eyes appear almost black as they bored into mine. He backed me against the counter, his strong body trapping me against its cool surface. Without a word, he leaned in and captured my lips with his, igniting a fire in my core. My fingers dug into the edge of the white laminate, but I couldn't bring myself to push him away. Not this time.

As his touch grew more urgent, a rush of desire washed over me, consuming all rational thought. But amid the overwhelming pleasure, a nagging doubt crept into my mind. Was this just lust or something deeper?

With each glide of his cool hands across my skin, my body arched and moved as if responding to the choreography of his touch, like a dancer drawn to the pull of the music. His skilled fingertips moved from my waist to my hips, tracing every curve and sending shivers down my spine. He lifted me by the backs of my thighs and set me on the counter, spreading my legs. A soft moan escaped my lips, muffled by the intensity of the moment.

His grip on me tightened, sending tingles through me as his lips worked against mine. I could feel the hardness of his cock through my thin leggings, each movement sending sparks of pleasure through me. Time stood still as we lost ourselves in this intoxicating dance.

He broke the kiss, his heavy breaths mingling with mine. His eyes, darker with desire, flickered with a hint of amusement as he surveyed my flushed face. "We should eat," he said, pulling away, his hands lingering on me before he scooped me up and set me down.

That did not answer my question. I inhaled deeply, attempting to steady myself before I sat at the table, my hands trembling from the intensity of our brief moment. Ethan brought two steaming plates of spaghetti over, and the rich aroma of garlic and tomatoes filled my nose. I took a bite. It was impossible to deny the perfection in each strand of pasta and every flavorful mouthful.

He sat across from me and cleared his throat as though we didn't just have the most passionate make-out session ever. "So, your first treatment is Monday, right?" His gaze remained fixed on his plate, the twirl of spaghetti capturing his attention.

"Yeah," I mumbled, a weight settling in my chest.

"I read about the side effects." He finally looked up.

I pursed my lips. "It's a doozy, huh?"

Ethan pushed his food around with his fork as though searching for the right words. The soft clinks of utensils against porcelain filled the space. Finally, he broke the quiet. "How're you feeling?"

I raised a brow and considered his question. "Like, physically? Mentally?"

He shrugged. "All of the above?"

I didn't want to burden the moment with unnecessary weight. I dropped my fork onto my plate, and a corner of my mouth rose. "It feels like a horror movie."

"Well, you know horror movies eventually end." Ethan's attempt at reassurance brought a warmth to the conversation, a genuine desire to provide comfort.

"They also have horrible endings." I grinned, a touch of humor masking my underlying anxiety.

Ethan smirked in response. "True. That was a terrible analogy. But the beautiful girl always survives."

My shoulders rose in a half-hearted shrug. "Am I the beautiful girl or just the first one to scream?"

He canted his head and smiled. "Sorry, Sweetness, you're the heroine in my story."

The air between us was heavy. Dense. Like a thick fog that refused to lift. The hindrance of my impending treatments weighed me down, adding to the already-suffocating silence. With an uncertain future hanging in the balance, I was torn between my own desires and what Ethan deserved.

I THOUGHT I WAS PREPARED MENTALLY AND emotionally, but as Ethan and I strode through the white hallways of the medical center, doubts crept in. Each step felt like a march toward the unknown. The fluorescent lights only added to the sterile atmosphere. I clung to Ethan's silent support, walking through the clinical expanse.

My mind raced with all the potential side effects: fatigue, hair loss, sores in my mouth and throat, diarrhea, constipation, nausea, and vomiting. The list seemed endless, each possibility more dreadful than the last.

Standing in line at the front desk, I couldn't help but notice the other patients in the waiting room. Some were distracted with magazines or quiet conversations, while others simply sat in silence.

When it was my turn, I handed over my ID and emergency contact information. Vulnerability constricted my chest with each keystroke the receptionist made. This piece of paper held important details about me and who to call in case of complications. It was a reminder of how much control I'd already lost to this disease.

Fuck cancer.

The receptionist handed my info back and told me I'd be called soon. We settled into a cozy corner of the room. The space was softly lit and inviting, far removed from the sterile chill one might expect. Our surroundings hummed with the quiet strength of shared hopes and silent prayers.

I leaned my head against Ethan's shoulder, breathing in his scent and taking comfort in his warm presence beside me. Time seemed to stand still in this place, where every second felt like an hour.

He placed a hand on my thigh and squeezed. "You okay?"

I glanced at him and offered an assuring smile. "I know we just got here, but I'm ready to go home."

His blue eyes were full of comforting concern. "We will, Sweetness. You need this though."

Averting my gaze, I let out a heavy sigh. *He's right. I wish I didn't though.*

The nurse called my name an hour later, and we followed her down a maze of corridors to a small room filled with medical equipment. My heart raced as she expertly drew blood, a routine procedure that always made me cringe at the sharp sting of the needle.

Afterward, we made our way to the infusion floor, where machines beeped rhythmically and healthcare professionals moved about in hushed tones. Cherie, the young but experienced RN, tied the tourniquet around my arm, located a vein, and inserted the IV for the chemotherapy, popping free the band around my arm. Despite her youthful appearance, her proficiency put me at ease.

Once it was in place, I settled into a plush leather recliner, draped with a cozy fleece blanket Ethan had brought from home. It was his attempt to bring a touch of familiarity to the clinical atmosphere. Colorful chaos unfolded from the reality show that blared from the TV on the far wall.

I sat there hooked up to the IV, noticing the way Cherie kept looking at Ethan, who sat in the seat next to me, engaged in a book. It was clear she mistook him for my boyfriend, but in that moment, explaining the mix-up was too much effort. I had bigger things on my mind as I prepared for my treatment and braced myself for the inevitable side effects.

Ethan looked so fucking sexy in his black-framed reading glasses. I averted my gaze before he could notice.

"What're you reading?" God, my arm itched, but I resisted the urge to scratch, taking deep breaths.

He closed the book, keeping a finger between the pages he'd been reading. "It's a coming-of-age story by Haruki Murakami."

"So, you can sing and play the guitar, and you're a bookworm?" I glanced at the IV in my itchy arm. "Didn't know you were so well-rounded."

He grinned, pushing his glasses up the bridge of his nose. "Thanks. I think?"

I grinned.

"I used to read all the time."

"Why'd you stop?"

He paused as though weighing his answer. "Life got too busy."

I let out a slow exhale and rested my head against the recliner. "I know what that's like."

"There's more to me than you think, Sweetness."

Damn. Was he offended? "Yeah. I'm starting to see that."

When he'd opened up about the heartbreaking story of Hailey's miscarriage, a deep ache had erupted inside me. There'd been raw pain in his voice and vulnerability in his tear-filled eyes as he described the profound loss they had faced. The room had been suffused with his grief, and it had wrapped around me like a tangible cloak of sorrow.

In those moments, a realization had hit me. Ethan and I shared a common thread of loss. We were both navigating the turbulent waters of unresolved grief.

Hours passed, and my body grew heavy and sluggish. The medication finished dripping into my veins. Cherie had checked on me regularly, her soothing voice reassuring me that this was a normal reaction. She expertly flushed my IV and adjusted my blanket while I tried to distract myself with the reality show.

A short time later, she gave me the all clear to leave. Ethan drove us home, the streetlights illuminating the darkness of the evening in a blur.

Normalcy quickly evaporated in the stillness of night. The effects hit me like a tidal wave. My body was burning from the inside out, my stomach roiling with nausea. The warmth of the bed suddenly suffocated me, and I stumbled to the bathroom, barely able to stand. Falling to my knees in front of the toilet, I hurled, praying for relief as chills shook my body uncontrollably. The soft light from the nightlight did nothing to ease the turmoil gripping me.

Gentle hands pulled my hair away from my face. The persistent heaving continued, my stomach revolting against the invisible assailant. Pain coiled tighter and tighter, an unbearable knot that seemed to squeeze the breath out of me with each retch. Dizziness accompanied the ordeal, a disorienting sensation that added to my overall misery.

Leaning against the toilet seat for support, I felt the queasiness intensify, and a low moan escaped my lips. "This sucks ass . . ."

"What do you need?" Ethan rasped.

Shaking my head, I managed a weak smile. "Nothing, thanks though. Just go back to sleep."

"Oh no, you're not getting rid of me that easily, Sweetness." His hands gently gathered my hair once more, lightly tugging the strands.

"What're you doing?"

"Braiding your hair."

My brows rose, but before I could say anything, another wave of nausea hit me. At this point, I was throwing up bile.

Ethan tied off the end and said, "I'll be right back."

With a nod, I muttered into the bowl, "I'll be here."

In what felt like the blink of an eye, he was back, a bottle of water in hand. "We need to keep you hydrated," he said, unscrewing the cap with that signature calm concern. He tilted the bottle toward my lips.

Closing my eyes, I took slow, deliberate sips, trying to steady myself. "You sure you wanna be here for this?"

His hand moved in soothing circles on my back. "I don't wanna be anywhere else."

I scoffed and managed a faint grin. "You're such a liar."

He kissed the top of my head. "I could never lie to you."

THE INITIAL WEEK UNFOLDED WITH A RELENTLESS cascade of challenges, each day bringing its own set of struggles. Nausea was a constant, making it nearly impossible to keep anything down.

Thank God for saltine crackers and nausea meds.

The persistent fatigue gripped me with unrelenting force, casting a heavy veil over my waking hours. Sleep became both a refuge and a necessity, the weariness demanding relief in the form of countless naps.

Julia provided support, juggling her busy life to be by my side whenever possible. But Ethan had become the real MVP in my routine, helping me manage daily tasks hindered by treatments and side effects. With their unwavering presence, the burdens of the illness lightened, giving me strength to face each day.

I wanted to go back to the time when I was self-reliant, when I didn't need anyone else for my basic survival. It quickly became clear that wasn't going to happen anytime soon. And with that realization came the acceptance that I needed them.

At least for now.

"We're here!" a small familiar voice echoed from the living room. My lips curved up as I shuffled in to see Belle standing in the entryway with Lindsay.

Amid the chemo's draining side effects—it was all a fog— I recalled Ethan mentioning something about Belle. She was going to drop Lindsay with us so she could cover a night shift at the hospital.

Lindsay, bundled up in her bright pink jacket, her blond curls bouncing with each step, beamed up at me with her big blue eyes. "Mimi!" she squealed, running up to me.

I bent down and opened my arms just in time for Lindsay to crash into me. We nearly toppled over together. It was good I was feeling fairly strong at the moment.

"Hey there, little ladybug," I greeted her, trying to lift her into a hug, but my strength failed me. Instead, I decided to stay kneeling at her level, hoping no one noticed.

Belle grinned, handing Ethan a small fuchsia backpack adorned with colorful cartoon characters. "She's been talking about building a fort with Uncle E.T. all day." Her eyes flickered with a hint of teasing.

I laughed, knowing Ethan's fondness for Lindsay and his slightly awkward but endearing way with kids.

Lindsay nodded. "Can we, can we, can we? Please?" She wriggled away from my arms and ran toward Ethan. He scooped her up, a smile spreading across his face.

"Yeah, if it's okay with Mia," he said, his voice filled with genuine excitement.

I grinned. "Let's do it."

Belle watched Ethan and Lindsay with a fond smile. "I'll leave you to it, then. Thank you both for doing this. I really appreciate it."

Holding Lindsay with one arm, he said, "No problem. We're gonna have a great time, aren't we?"

Lindsay's enthusiastic squeal filled the room as Belle said her goodbyes and left, closing the door behind her.

Ethan set Lindsay down. She immediately settled onto the floor in front of the TV and began rummaging through her bag. In a matter of minutes, she was surrounded by toys, coloring supplies, and drawings.

I caught a glimpse of one. "You're a good artist, Linds."

She smiled wide. "Thanks, Mimi."

"Who are the people in that picture?" I asked, pointing to the paper nearest her.

She picked it up and gestured to each stick figure character. "That's Granny, that's Papa." She peered at me to make sure I was paying attention.

I nodded for her to go on.

She dragged a finger to the other four and named each of them. "Mommy, me, Uncle E.T., and you, Mimi!"

My heart swelled. I clutched my chest, struggling to keep my overwhelming elation and gratitude at bay.

Ethan wrapped an arm around my waist and pulled me close. He placed a gentle kiss on my temple before saying to Lindsay, "That's a beautiful picture, Lind-bug."

Blinking back tears, I stepped out of his hold. "I'll grab some blankets for the fort."

"Do you need help?" he asked, his brow furrowed in apprehension.

"I'm not *that* incompetent." I crossed my arms.

Stepping closer, he said, "I didn't say you were."

It had been difficult for me to rely on him so much these past few weeks, but I hadn't blamed him. At least, I didn't think I had. "I'll be right back."

"Okay, Sweetness." Ethan studied me for another second before kneeling next to Lindsay, joining her in the colorful world of creativity. With each stroke of her crayon, her imagination breathed life onto the pages of her coloring book. She giggled as Ethan playfully imitated the sounds of the characters she drew, their laughter intertwining in a harmonious symphony that echoed throughout the cozy apartment.

I strolled into my room and went into my closet to retrieve my three biggest blankets. I was filled with joy at being able to experience Ethan and Lindsay's bond, yet I felt heartache for myself. Their closeness only served to highlight my fears of being inadequate for Ethan's future; it was a reminder of why I couldn't let myself be with him.

Lindsay helped Ethan build the fort while I sat on the

couch. It seemed retrieving the blankets from my closet had fatigued me. Once they finished, I joined them inside the small space. The little girl's excitement was contagious, and I allowed myself to be swept up in it.

An hour or so later, Lindsay was asleep in Ethan's strong arms. Watching him with her had broken something in me. He needed to be a father. Knowing that I might never be able to give him what was best, I could not continue to allow him to make any more sacrifices, even if it meant facing the painful truth of my own limitations.

THE WEEKS WERE A BLUR, MY DAYS CONSUMED BY THE monotonous routine of treatments. Christmas and New Year's passed in the blink of an eye, but I couldn't feel the holiday spirit like everyone else. It was like living in another world, one where joy and celebration were just dreams amid dismal memories.

I stepped out of the shower and was enveloped by the warm steam and comforting scent of lavender. I couldn't help but be reminded of the simple pleasures I used to take for granted before my illness took over. The lingering scent of my flowery shampoo only added to the nostalgia.

I slid on my favorite pineapple pajamas, then was careful not to make a sound as I crept into the living room. Ethan sat slumped on the couch, his face washed in the soft blue glow of the television. I curled up next to him, my eyes trained on his profile as he stared blankly at the screen, lost in thought.

A heaviness settled in my chest as I watched him like this. His usually relaxed features were now etched with lines of weariness, evidence of all the hours he'd spent stressing over me. He had given up so much for me—his time, his energy, maybe even his own peace of mind. Guilt and gratitude warred within me, wrapping around my heart like a brick wall.

How much more is he going to sacrifice for me? The muted colors of our surroundings mirrored my conflicted emotions. I wanted him here, which was completely selfish.

His gaze shifted from the TV to me, a faint grin teasing at his lips. But behind his friendly facade, I could see the concern in his eyes. It was always there, lingering beneath the surface. "You look cute," he complimented before turning back to the flat screen.

A small smile tugged at the corners of my mouth. But deep down, I knew he was just being polite. He'd been by my side every day during my treatment, never taking a break from this suffocating apartment and me. "You should take a night off," I blurted out.

His piercing gray-blue eyes met my tired ones, confusion evident in his expression. "What?"

"Go on a date or hang out with Lucas." I fiddled with the hem of my pajama top.

Ethan lowered the volume and turned to face me fully. "What's this about, Sweetness?"

I picked at the lint on my Christmas socks. "You haven't gone out or done anything besides take care of me."

He shrugged. "I knew what I was signing up for."

I shook my head. "Please. Go out and live a little. For both of us."

Ethan studied me. "What's going on in that head of yours?"

With an annoyed sigh, I said, "You've been stuck here every day for a month. A couple hours of breathing room won't hurt either of us."

He tilted his head, squinting. "You sure you'll be okay?"

Crossing my arms, I said, "I'm pretty sure I can handle a few hours without you. Besides, Julia said she'll be by later."

His mouth opened and closed a few times, a subtle dance of uncertainty playing on his features. The lines around his eyes tightened and revealed the flicker of worry he could never hide from me.

"Is everything okay?" he asked.

I met his gaze, struggling to maintain my composure. "I'm fine."

His eyes searched mine, probing for the truth behind my words. "You just seem kind of distant lately."

"I'm just trying to survive all of this, Ethan," I said, frustration seeping into my words.

"Is there anything I can do to help?"

"I'll figure it out. I just need a little space," I replied, trying to push away the thoughts that had been haunting me.

"I care about you, Mia." He reached out to touch my

arm, but I flinched away from his fingers. "I understand how much pain you're in, and I just want to help."

My walls began to crumble. I choked back my tears. "You can't understand. No one can," I sobbed, feeling helpless and alone. "I can't be what you need right now."

His gaze softened. "I may not understand, but I want to try," he said, his voice filled with genuine concern. "Why are you not willing to try for me?"

"I just . . . need some space."

Ethan's expression shifted, a mix of hurt and determination flashing across his face. He took a deep breath, his shoulders sagging slightly. "Fine." He started toward the door only to stop midway. "I wish you cared to know how long I've been waiting for us."

"Then stop waiting, Ethan." The words almost caught in my throat, but I forced them out. I dragged myself out of the room.

Seconds later, I heard the door open, then slam shut, rattling in its frame. Burying my face in my hands, I struggled to hold back my sobs. The apartment closed in on me, suffocating as tears streamed down my cheeks, the weight of my words pressing heavily against my heart.

Not being there for Mia during her fight was something I wrestled with daily. She used to dance like the world couldn't contain her spirit. Seeing her in that bar in Newark over a year ago—it had hit me like a bolt of lightning. I was just looking for an escape from the grind, but then there she was, magnetic and impossible to ignore.

Somehow, I'd allowed doubt to slip through a crack in my resolve. It wrapped around my heart and squeezed tight. I was all too familiar with loss. But the thought of losing Mia? That was a different kind of hell. *She just needs space.* But I couldn't see my world without *her.*

I pushed those thoughts down, as deep as they would go, because she needed *me.* She needed me to believe in a future where she would dance again, where Cancer was just a zodiac sign. I needed to carry that hope for her when she might not want to anymore.

Cradled in the black leather seat of my old Camaro, I

navigated a less busy street through the city. The engine's soft rumble created a steady rhythm, serving as a sort of soothing melody to the thoughts playing on repeat in my mind.

I called Lucas, hoping like hell he could help me figure this shit out. We met at an upscale lounge on the outskirts of the city. The rich aroma of fine whiskey, aged leather, and mahogany surrounded us as we settled onto plush barstools, the ambiance both opulent and heavy.

"So . . . we just gonna sit here and drink?" he asked after I downed my first shot, a knowing smile playing at his lips.

I took a sip of my second drink, savoring the warmth of the top-shelf whiskey as it spread through me. "What if we do?"

He shrugged. "I don't know. Guess I'm cool with that."

Silence lingered between us, and muted conversations and gentle jazz music buzzed.

"How's Mia doing?" he asked.

"She's . . . surviving," I said after taking another sip.

He released a slow breath. "Come on, Ethan. What's going on?"

"I understand what she's going through. I know she's in pain, and I know what the chemo is doing to her body. It's just . . . I never thought of how hard it would truly be." I ran my fingers through my hair.

Lucas chuckled. "You sound like an asshole, you know that?"

I could always count on him to be honest.

"She never asked you for help in the first place," he continued.

I glanced at him, wondering how—

These girls tell each other everything, I realized.

"I know," I said, "but I couldn't just let her deal with this alone. Her dad had to leave."

"Have you ever asked yourself why?" Lucas peered into his tumbler and gently shook the ice around.

My brow furrowed. "Why what?"

The bartender came and refilled our drinks before Lucas said, "Why couldn't you let her do this on her own? We both know how much she needs her independence."

Shit. He was trying to get me to own up to what was going on between me and Mia. "I . . . care about her. We're . . . friends." That last word left a bitter taste in my mouth.

Lucas stared at me, his eyes searching mine for the truth. "Are you sure about that?"

"Am I sure I care about her or that we're friends?"

His shoulder rose. "Both."

"When it comes to her, I haven't been sure about anything," I muttered. That was probably the whiskey talking.

He cocked a brow. "What do you mean by that?"

"I don't know, man." Downing my tumbler, I called for another.

"Is there anything you *do* know?" he asked.

There was no point in lying to him. "I can't imagine my life without her."

"You ever think about what that means?" He turned, swiveling his barstool toward me.

"All the fucking time, man."

He tossed the last of his whiskey back and asked, "What're you gonna do about it?"

I shrugged. "I don't fucking know. She won't let me do anything. We haven't put a label on anything, and I'm not sure she wants to."

He tilted his head. "What do *you* want?"

Dammit. A lump rose in my throat, and my eyes blurred with tears, but I had no right to let them fall. "I want her to live through this. I want her to have a long happy life." My eyes drifted to my empty glass. "And I want it all to be with me. I love her. And it scares the shit out of me."

Lucas slammed his palm onto the bar top, startling the old man sitting next to us. He whispered an apology before turning back to me. "Finally. God, that was like pulling teeth."

I rolled my eyes.

"What're you gonna do about it?" he asked, pushing his empty tumbler away.

The bartender stopped by and asked if we wanted refills. Lucas shook his head, but I decided one more wouldn't hurt. After my glass was filled, I said, "Now isn't a good time."

"Will there ever be a good time? What if—God forbid— you don't get the chance to tell her?"

Fuck . . . I can't let that happen. Brushing my fingers through my hair, I murmured, "You're right."

He shot me a smug grin. "I know."

"I think marriage has made you smarter," I teased.

"It's all Julia."

My best friend and his wife were sickeningly cute despite the way they'd met. I was glad they'd found their happiness.

"Don't forget to pick Venom up from the airport tomorrow," he reminded me, his tone casual but carrying an underlying note of authority.

I glanced at my Apple Watch. The digital display showed the date and time. "Is that tomorrow?" I asked, feigning surprise, although I knew damn well it was.

His eyes narrowed, a hint of annoyance flickering in them. "Don't be an asshole. Take the SUV—you know where the keys are."

Straightening in my seat, I gave him a mock salute. "You got it, Boss."

He chortled.

My cell buzzed. I expected to see a text from Mia, but when I checked, it wasn't her.

HAILEY

Hey, it was nice reconnecting with you at your parents'. I know this is a long shot, but I wanted to let you know Jacob has a headstone now. Hope you're doing well.

My chest tightened. I had never visited his grave. I sat there frozen, and the words on my cell screen blurred as a wave of guilt and sorrow crashed into me. I'd let so much time pass without honoring Jacob's memory. The loss ate away at my heart and threatened to shred me.

With each sip of alcohol, the taste became increasingly bitter, but I couldn't stop drinking. The whiskey burned my throat, heat spreading through my body. I wanted to be numb, entirely.

The noise and chatter only served to amplify my feelings of isolation. Mia's laugh echoed through my mind, bringing with it memories of days before her illness, spent on her couch watching our favorite Netflix show without a care in the world. My heart ached for those moments again as I sat on the barstool, now on my fifth glass. *Or maybe it's my sixth?*

Longing surged through my veins but was quickly followed by the sharp fear of being rejected by the one woman I couldn't live without. It was like standing on a cliff's edge over a tumultuous ocean, the waves enticing and terrifying all at once. I found myself grappling with these opposing feelings, empty tumbler in hand.

Lucas interrupted my thoughts. "That's enough of this, man. The girls are gonna kick my ass if I bring you back shit-faced."

"Think it's a little too late for that," I slurred.

It was well past midnight, the clock's hands inching toward one, casting a ghostly glow in my small apartment. The nocturnal symphony of the city melded with the faint dialogue of some rom com playing on TV, the scenes flickering unheeded. Julia had dozed off beside me on the couch.

I jumped at the knock on the front door, causing Julia to jolt awake. I pushed off the couch to answer it, finding Lucas with a barely conscious Ethan propped against the doorframe.

"Special delivery," Lucas joked, a corner of his mouth twitching up.

I stepped out of the way, and Lucas heaved Ethan inside, the scent of alcohol filling my nose.

"Seriously, Mia, what's in this guy's diet?" Lucas joked.

An unbidden laugh bubbled up in me.

Julia jumped up before Lucas dropped Ethan onto the

couch with a flair of dramatic humor. "Hey, Sunshine, have a nice nap?" he teased his wife.

Julia, quite disheveled, rested her hands on her hips. "What the hell did you do?" she demanded, suspicion in her narrowed eyes.

Lucas raised his hands in mock surrender. "For once, this isn't my fault." He pulled a phone out of his coat pocket and set it on the coffee table. "Here's his phone; he almost left it in the bathroom. Might want to spray Lysol on it."

Julia side-eyed her husband before turning to me. "Are you gonna be okay with him like this?"

I nodded, my eyes lingering on Ethan's prone form. "Yeah, I'll be fine."

After goodbye hugs were exchanged, Lucas and Julia left. I draped a blanket over Ethan and started for my room.

The whole coffee table vibrated. Ethan's cell screen lit up with a text. I shouldn't have looked, but I did.

ALICE

Hey sexy, I miss you. 😉

It was a gut punch I couldn't dodge, and it sent a sharp twisting pain straight through my heart.

Did he hook up with her tonight? Tears clouded my eyes, but I fought them fiercely. In the fleeting dance of our moments together, Ethan was like a mirage—elusive and never fully mine. Each lingering touch and tender kiss seemed to hold the promise of more. They may have just been sparks in the night, beautiful but brief. And in a bid to protect my heart, I tried to believe they'd meant nothing.

We'd never put a label on whatever we were. A voice in my head scolded me for caring so much. But here I was, ensnared by this desire that refused to subside. It burrowed deep, casting shadows of doubt over every whispered word, every stolen moment that I'd fooled myself into believing I could compartmentalize.

Ethan's voice pulled me away from my thoughts.

Curiosity piqued, I leaned closer.

"I can't lose . . ."

"Lose what?" I asked.

Ethan's eyes fluttered open, revealing the stormy hues of his gaze. "You, Sweetness," he rasped.

His breath carried the faint trace of my favorite whiskey, blending subtly with the citrusy undertones of his musky cologne. He claimed my lips with his, and I tasted the faint bitterness of it mixed with the sweetness of my cherry-flavored Chapstick. Our mouths moved together in a slow sensual dance. His touch was gentle, leading me closer to his body with a sense of purpose. The heat from his fingertips sent shivers down my spine.

I forced myself away from him. Each step was like my soul being torn in two. Every kiss and touch with Ethan deepened what I felt for him, making it harder to deny what was growing between us. I didn't dare look back as I made my way to my room, the door clicking shut behind me. In the solitude, I dragged trembling hands down my face and tried to remember why we couldn't be together.

Waking up was agony; my lower back rebelled against every move I made. Snatching the pills and water from my nightstand, I downed them with a silent plea for them to work fast. As I lay back down, Ethan's kiss from last night warmed my lips.

His whisper-soft caress had left an impression that echoed through me, his presence a constant imprint on my skin. His touch, soft and wanting, haunted me. This was the same Ethan known for his casual hookups, a guy who avoided attachments. *I probably shouldn't think much of it.*

That text from Alice invaded my thoughts, adding fuel to my already-burning jealousy.

A knock on the door snapped me back to reality. "Are you decent?" Ethan's voice was muffled.

I cleared my throat. "Come in."

He walked in, and fuck me. What was it that made guys in gray sweatpants so fucking hot? He stood awkwardly by the doorway, almost as if he was afraid to come any closer. God, I wasn't contagious. His dark hair appeared damp, like he'd just stepped out of the shower. He stared at the carpet for a long moment. "I'm sorry about last night."

Crossing my arms, I asked, "Why'd you drink so much?"

His lips quirked up. "You told me to take the night off."

I rolled my eyes. "I suppose I set myself up for that."

He pursed his lips.

"So . . . is there anything else?" I picked at the lint on my comforter.

"I don't know. *Is there anything else?*"

My gaze locked with his, and I couldn't help but wonder if he even remembered the kiss. Was it just another fleeting moment? Part of me wanted to ask him about it, to validate my feelings, but the other part feared the answer. In the end, I simply shook my head and let the subject drop. It was easier to pretend than to face potential heartache.

"How're you feeling today?" He stepped closer.

"I'm good. I was about to get up and make breakfast." I tossed the covers off and heaved my legs over the edge of the bed.

God, I feel so weak today.

He helped me stand. "Well, what do you want? I can make it."

"It's fine. I feel strong enough to make my own breakfast today." I tried to keep the annoyance out of my voice. He was just trying to be helpful, and I almost wished he wouldn't.

"Are you sure?" He walked the short distance to the kitchen with me.

"Yes. Stop hovering. Go watch TV or something." I waved him away.

Ethan gave a conceding huff. "Call me if you need anything." He made his way to the living room.

I can do this. It's just breakfast.

Standing for this long was already making me dizzy, but I was determined to do this for myself. By myself. I settled on oatmeal, placing the bowl into the microwave. The walk across the kitchen had left me lightheaded. I leaned against the small kitchen island, willing myself to get through this. There were a million people in the world who could make their own breakfast.

The final beep pierced through the quiet kitchen, signaling my meal was finally ready. My stomach grumbled with anticipation as I reached for the dish without a second thought. In my haste, I burned my fingers on the scalding-hot bowl and dropped it onto the linoleum with a loud crash.

"Fuck," I cursed under my breath, relieved that I had narrowly avoided having the dish land on my feet. I bent down to clean up the broken pieces and cut my thumb on a sharp shard. "Shit," I hissed through gritted teeth.

Ethan rushed in, concern etched on his face. "Are you okay?" He quickly crouched down beside me and extended a hand, helping me straighten.

Wincing, I grabbed a nearby towel and hastily wrapped it around my bleeding thumb, blood staining the pristine white fabric. A sharp sting pulsed through my hand. "I'm fine, just distracted," I muttered.

With careful and deliberate movements, Ethan disposed of the sharp broken pieces. The glinting fragments sparkled in the light as they fell into the trash bin near the doorway. He grabbed a broom and began sweeping up the smaller shards that littered the floor.

I watched him, clutching my injury against my chest, tears brimming in my eyes. The pain wasn't from the cut, but from a deep despair that had been crushing my heart for weeks. Even making breakfast was becoming an impossible task.

Ethan finished cleaning, then washed his hands in the sink. I stood there, still holding pressure on my throbbing thumb, defeated.

After he dried his hands, he said, "Here, let me see."

I let him gently unwrap the crimson-stained towel. He examined the small gash, his brow furrowed in concentration.

"The bleeding slowed. Where's your first aid kit?"

"Under the bathroom sink." I sniffled, trying to stifle the remnants of tears.

He left in quick strides, disappearing for just a moment before reemerging with a familiar white box. He opened it, took out the necessary supplies, and started to clean the cut.

"Talk to me," he urged, his voice a soothing cadence amid my own self-pity. The peroxide mingled with his bergamot scent as he focused on tending the wound.

I suppressed the knot forming in my throat and looked away, avoiding his blue eyes. I'd thought I could be strong throughout this treatment, yet here I was a few weeks in, fighting against the icy weariness threatening to seep into my bones. With each day that passed, my facade was cracking, my walls crumbling.

"There." His voice was low and soothing.

"Thanks." I attempted to step away from him, but he maintained his position.

His arms caged me in, hands gripping the edge of the

countertop. "Not so fast. Tell me what's going on in that head of yours."

I glanced down at the veins in his forearms and bit my lip. "It's stupid."

"You never say anything stupid," he said, crouching down to my level, his gaze meeting mine.

Heat spread across my face. "I just . . . wanted to do something for myself for once." I avoided eye contact, fiddling with the hem of my oversize sweatshirt.

His brows came together. "You are doing something for yourself. You're going through this treatment." His stormy eyes flicked to my lips. "You're not letting this fucking disease win."

"I guess . . ."

His strong arms wrapped around me, drawing me closer. With one hand, he cupped my face, running his thumb over my cheekbone before tucking a strand of hair behind my ear. His lips, warm and pliant, pressed against mine. My eyelids lowered, and I could feel the roughness of his unshaven chin grazing my skin, sending shivers down my spine. My heart raced wildly as I surrendered to him. I didn't know if this lightheadedness was from his kiss or the meds I'd taken.

The thought of Alice's text was like a cold splash of water, jolting me back to reality. I pushed against Ethan's chest, distancing myself from the temptation of his lips. "You really need to stop doing that," I murmured, frustration coating my voice.

He stepped back, something like confusion etched across his features. "I'm sorry. It won't happen again," he promised in a low tone. But as he turned away, a look of determination flashed across his face. "Actually, no. I'm not sorry."

I shook my head. "You can't be serious. We both know you don't do relationships."

He stood firm, arms crossed. "It's not that I *can't* do relationships. I just choose not to."

A breath escaped my lips. "What're you trying to do here? This . . . Us . . . It wasn't meant to happen. Not now, not ever." I retreated to the opposite side of the kitchen island, putting distance between us.

He leaned against the counter, his gaze unwavering. "How can you say that, Mia? You know damn well this is different."

I raised a skeptical eyebrow. "Is it? Because your history suggests otherwise."

A hint of hurt flickered in his eyes before being replaced by determination once again. He shook his head. "Is that how it's gonna be? You're really gonna judge me on my past?"

What was I even saying? Inhaling, I regained my composure. "We need to keep things as they are. It's better that way."

"Mia—"

I cut him off, turning away from his piercing stare. "No, Ethan. I need you to accept this." Fuck, my eyes started to blur, but I blinked back the tears.

He hesitated for a moment before finally conceding with a soft resigned exhale. "If that's what you want."

I glanced over my shoulder at him, my heart aching with

conflicted feelings. I cared for him—maybe I even loved him. Nothing could change between us. "Yes. It's the way it has to be."

He nodded slowly. "Okay."

"Okay." Despite my confident nod, nagging doubt screamed inside me. *Is this truly the best decision?* My heart roared in rebellion, but my mind said yes. I was a walking countdown, and saving him from inevitable heartbreak was the best I could give him.

He cleared his throat. "Do you think you'll be okay here? I have to pick Venom up from the airport."

I nodded. "I'll be fine."

He studied me for a few seconds. "Okay. Call me if you need anything. I'll probably be gone most of the afternoon."

The kitchen grew heavy as Ethan stood in the doorway, the tension palpable between us. His eyes held a mixture of regret and something else—something I couldn't allow myself to acknowledge. Without a word, he turned and walked out. The soft sound of the front door opening and closing moments later settled like a final note in the silence that followed.

I stood in the middle of the empty room, my feet rooted to the floor. Ethan's words echoed in my mind. *If that's what you want.* Closing my eyes, I focused on my breathing. Everything around me was shifting as though the ground had suddenly been yanked away. I was falling, trying to find something, anything, to hold on to.

CHAPTER 25

Ethan

JFK AIRPORT WAS A BUSTLING METROPOLIS, A CONSTANT flow of people moving to and fro. The air was filled with the scent of coffee and excitement as signs advertised flights and car rentals. Amid the chaotic swarm, I spotted Venom huddled together near the baggage claim. Their bodies were slumped with fatigue, their faces etched with exhaustion.

Gia straightened and waved at me, her black combat boots stomping against the floor. Her shoulder-length dark hair contrasted with her ripped purple fishnet tights, which drew attention from the more conservative passersby. She smirked at their disapproving glances.

Liv flaunted a sleek black dress that hugged every curve, paired with skyscraper heels that added to her statuesque appearance. Krissy's free-spirited bohemian look contrasted sharply with Liv's. Sam, the most laid-back of the group, completed their eclectic dynamic with her beanie and plaid shirt.

"Good morning, ladies. How was the flight?" I called out, approaching them, trying to sound as welcoming as possible.

"Hey, Ethan. It was fine. Long," Gia said, about to shoulder her duffel.

"Here, let me get that for you." She handed her bag over to me. "Lucas asked me to give you all the grand tour. You ready?"

Liv chimed in, "Yes, please get me out of here."

Krissy flashed me a flirty grin. "Lead the way."

Sam, quiet until now, looked around. "I can't believe we're actually here."

I led them through the terminal, their anticipation radiating from their every gesture and smile. We made our way through the automatic doors. The girls' excited laughter and chatter echoed over the bustling streets, blending with the constant hum of traffic and the occasional honking. I gestured toward the black SUV, its shiny exterior reflecting the towering skyscrapers. They climbed into the vehicle, their eyes filled with awe as they observed the never-ending activity all around.

Settling into the driver's seat, I suggested, "You have to see Times Square while you're here."

Gia leaned forward with excitement. "Is it true that it's like daylight there, even at night?"

"You'll see," I replied, starting the engine. "First, let's get a taste of Manhattan."

I navigated through the streets as Venom admired the sights. It would've been a welcome distraction if my thoughts weren't preoccupied by Mia. My soul ached to be with her, but our fears were at odds with our hearts.

Refocusing on the task at hand, I pointed out iconic landmarks to the girls and couldn't help but feel envious of their refreshing excitement at the newness. They had no idea about this cutthroat industry, and I struggled with the weight of responsibility to guide them toward success in this media jungle.

After a bit of sightseeing, I drove us to LV Productions. As soon as we crossed the threshold into the studio, a wave of energy pulsed through the air, like electricity crackling and buzzing all around us. The walls were adorned with posters and photos of famous musicians. Among them were the members of No Blood, No Alibi.

Gia strode in after me and let out a low whistle. "Damn . . ." She peered through a glass window into the spacious recording booth.

Krissy followed, equally awed.

I couldn't help but grin at their reactions. "Welcome to LV Productions."

Sam's eyes sparkled at the sight of all the instruments in the room. "This is so cool."

Liv's gaze swept over the space. "I can't wait to get started."

I gestured to the state-of-the-art mixer; its sleek knobs and buttons glinted under the dim studio lights. "This is where we'll master your music. Lucas has plans for you all to collaborate with some award-winning sound engineers."

The main door opened, and in strolled Lucas, an

enthused smile on his face. After greeting him in my usual smart-ass way, I made introductions between him and the girls. I could tell that their minds were whirling with thoughts about working with such an established figure in the music industry.

Gia tilted her head as she glanced at me. "Hey, where's Mia?"

My heart sank, and my muscles tensed. I didn't know what to tell her or how to explain the situation. "She—"

"Mia's taking some time off for health reasons," Lucas said, knowing I didn't want to go into detail about it.

"Is she okay?" Liv asked.

I managed a smile and replied, "Yeah. She's fine."

"Why don't you girls get set up?" Lucas gestured to the booth door. Once all the members of Venom were inside, he turned to me. "So?"

My brow wrinkled. "So what?"

"Did you get to talk to Mia about how you feel?"

Crossing my arms, I let out a breath. "I tried. It didn't go so well."

He started to mess with some of the controls on one of the panels. "What happened?"

My chest tightened just thinking about the last conversation I'd had with Mia. "She doesn't want anything more."

"Did she tell you why?"

"No. Then again, I never asked."

He sat down and stared at me. "Mia and Julia are a lot alike, you know."

I sat back against the edge of the table. "How so?"

"They're both stubborn as fuck and don't like to ask for help."

Massaging the space between my eyes, I asked, "What's your point?"

He leaned forward, resting his forearms on his thighs. "I know everything's a shit show right now, but you can't give up on her."

"How do you know I'm gonna give up on her?"

"I don't. What I do know is that Mia Cruz is the best fucking thing to ever happen to you. And despite all the fucked-up shit that's happening right now, I've never seen you more fulfilled—happy even," he said.

I tucked my hands into my pockets, swallowing the lump in my throat. "She really is the fucking best."

He nodded and met my gaze. "So, don't give up on her. Now, get out of here. I've got work to do." A corner of his mouth rose. "Tell Mia I say hi."

"Thanks, man. I will." After saying my goodbyes to Venom, I excused myself from the studio and made my way down the long hallway. I stepped outside into the brisk New York air with a newfound hope.

I pulled my cell from my black jacket, and Alice's message stared back at me, a reminder of a chapter in my life I was trying hard to close. As I scrolled through my phone, thoughts of Mia intermingled with Alice's seductive digital words. *Did Mia see this? Is this why she was so adamant about our friendship?* The uncertainty gnawed at me.

Then there was Hailey's message, like a flashing neon

sign I couldn't ignore. It was time to face the music. Before I could fully commit to whatever was happening between me and Mia, I had to make peace with every single aspect of my past. Starting with my son.

UNDER AN OVERCAST SKY, I FOUND MYSELF AT THE EDGE of the windswept cemetery, guided by the directions in Hailey's text. The winter's chill bit at my cheeks as I trudged through the grounds, the icy grass cracking beneath my shoes.

Approaching the designated area, I found a figure standing in quiet solitude before a gravestone. It wasn't until I drew closer that I recognized Hailey. She turned, her face lighting up with a gentle smile as our eyes met.

Hailey closed the distance between us, her arms wrapping around me in a warm embrace. "I'm glad you're here," she whispered, her voice muffled against my coat.

I returned the hug. "How long have you been here?"

"Not too long. Maybe ten minutes or so," she replied, stepping back to stand beside the grave marked *Jacob Miller* —our baby's final resting place.

I shuffled next to her, the ground crunching beneath my sneakers. The headstone was simple, and the realization hit me like a tsunami. "You gave him my last name," I murmured, a mix of surprise and sorrow in my voice.

Hailey nodded, her gaze fixed on the grave. "It seemed right, considering the future we had planned."

As I stood there, memories flooded back, each one a reminder of the loss we shared. I glanced at Hailey, her face a canvas of grief and maturity. It struck me how much we had both changed, grown.

Maybe things could be different now. I couldn't shake this guilt gnawing at my stomach, like I was betraying Mia by simply being here with someone else.

"I'm sorry it took so long to do this," Hailey started, hugging herself. "I didn't want to do it because . . ."

I canted my head, studying her glassy blue eyes.

"Then it would make his death real," she choked out.

This was a lot of fucking emotion for one day. I wrapped my arms around her and pulled her into an embrace. "We both needed time," I whispered into her hair.

She clung to me, her tears soaking into my coat. We stood there, holding each other, the weight of the past mingling with the faint hope of the future.

"I'm sorry for how everything turned out after. I should've been better . . ." *Fuck, this is difficult.*

She stepped away from me. "We were so young. We didn't know how to handle anything. The best thing we can do for ourselves now is heal."

Blinking back tears, I asked, "How do I do that?"

Hailey stared at me. "I can't answer that, Ethan." Her eyes drifted back to our son's headstone. "I'm glad you came. Maybe we can get coffee sometime."

With my hands buried in my pockets, I said, "Yeah, that sounds good."

"I know you have a lot going on right now, so just call or text me." She leaned in and left a lingering kiss on my cheek, warm and familiar. "I'll see you later, Ethan."

"See you."

As I watched her walk away, her figure gradually blending into the distance, a sense of relief washed over me. A part of me that had been locked away, tangled in the memories of our shared past, had started to unfurl. It was a good step forward.

Left alone in the cemetery, I stood before Jacob's grave, and the world around me paused. Wind whispered through the barren trees, limbs brushing against one another, soft and steady.

"Hey, Jacob. I'm sorry it's taken me this long to visit you. A lot has happened." I cleared my throat. "I wish I could've known you." The words tumbled out, awkward and heavy. The chill stung my eyes, or maybe it was the onset of tears. "Your mom is incredible. You would've loved her. Things didn't work out between us after you . . ."

My breath formed a cloud in the cold air. "I guess I'm just trying to find my way, trying to make sense of how things happened—why they happened." I looked around at the other graves, each a story, a life, a set of dreams and sorrows.

I knelt, brushing the ice off the headstone before tracing the letters of his name. "You know, I was really looking forward to being your dad. I wanted to be there for your first steps, your first words, teach you to ride a bike, watch you grow up." Tears blurred my vision. "I've been living with someone, which is a big deal for me. She's awesome." I straightened, sticking my hands into my pockets. "I'm pretty sure I'm in love with her."

I swallowed the lump in my throat and wiped the wetness from my cheeks with my sleeve. "Be at peace, Jacob, and know you're always a part of me. I promise to *always* carry you in my heart." I took one last glance at his headstone. "I love you, son." I turned to leave, my chest aching with my acceptance of the past. It was a tentative step toward a future that was still so uncertain.

CHAPTER 26

Ethan

I STEPPED INTO MIA'S APARTMENT AND WAS GREETED BY the dimly lit living room, which was shrouded in shadows dancing in sync with the flickering TV light. After hanging my coat on a hook in the entryway, I kicked off my shoes and placed them neatly on the rack by the door.

Mia lay asleep on the couch, her hair in a tousled mess, surrounded by scattered used tissues. My gaze settled on the screen, where a woman, so much like Mia, spoke with palpable affection. My eyes widened. *Mia's mother?*

How had I been so wrapped up in my own issues, so blind to Mia's deeper struggles? As I watched the candid home video, her mother's words, "That was a beautiful performance. You always do so well, Mia-bear," resonated with pride. Mia was dressed in a ballet costume and looked to be in her late teens. Her mom was holding the camera.

Exhaling slowly, I covered Mia with her favorite

pineapple fleece blanket with a newfound understanding. A quiet moan escaped her as she turned onto her side, still lost in sleep.

"I hope you never stop dancing," Mia's mom said. I switched the TV off, plunging the room into darkness. But she had stopped, though she had at least taught when she worked for Julia. I knew why though. It was the same reason I hadn't gone to Jacob's grave.

Making my way into the kitchen, I retrieved a glass from the cupboard and filled it with water from the tap. I took a long drink, my thoughts churning. There was so much distance between me and Mia, and I didn't know if I could bridge that gap.

I strolled back into the living room, glass in hand, and stared at my sleeping Mia. "I'm not gonna give up on us."

THE NEXT MORNING'S LIGHT BARELY PIERCED THROUGH the blinds. Despite the heaviness in my mind, cooking breakfast offered a brief escape. The rhythmic clinking of utensils and the sizzle of eggs in the skillet filled the quiet kitchen with a soothing sound.

I approached Mia, who was still lying on the couch. "Want some breakfast?" I set the plate of eggs and toast on the coffee table in front of her.

She pushed into a sitting position. "Thank you." She

grabbed the plate and fork and started eating. "What time did you get home?"

"Just after nine."

"How did everything go with Venom?"

"They're excited. Gia asked about you," I said, keeping my tone light. "Lucas told them you took time off for health reasons."

She nodded in approval. "I'll have to thank him for that later. I'm glad things went well with the band."

"Yeah, they're ecstatic to be here."

The conversation drifted to my visit to the cemetery and my unexpected encounter with Hailey. "She asked me out for coffee," I confessed.

"That's good," Mia replied, her gaze shifting away. "Maybe you should try to work things out with her."

I studied her. "How can you say that after the conversation we had the other day?"

She bit her lip, brow furrowing. "I don't know. I'm just trying to help you move on."

"Well, don't. It's pissing me off." She appeared to be taking this whole thing a lot better than me. "I can't do this right now."

Mia's voice was barely audible. "Will things ever be normal again between us?"

Fighting to keep my emotions in check, I said, "Give it time." The bitterness in my voice surprised even me.

Needing space, I walked into the kitchen and started to pace. I needed to respect Mia's wishes to keep things platonic, to safeguard our friendship. But the truth was, my feelings for her weren't something I could simply switch off.

My fingers raked through my hair. I was unable to ignore what was growing stronger each day. At the same time, pushing Mia away was a risk I couldn't take.

The last thing I want is to lose her completely.

Every day since our little squabble was like carrying an anvil around my neck. Leaning against the bathroom sink, I tried to catch my breath. My shower had drained me. I closed my eyes and willed strength to return to me. *I just need to make it to my room.*

Stepping out of the steam-filled bathroom in my loungewear, I tripped over my feet and bumped into Ethan. He caught me, wrapping his arms around me and pulling me into his hard bare chest.

God, what timing . . . My stomach fluttered as I pushed away from him, my cool palm making contact with the heat of his skin. "Sorry."

"Are you okay?" he asked, steadying me.

I nodded, my fingers brushing through his smattering of dark chest hair.

A low groan escaped him as his hand fell over mine,

stopping me. "Don't start something you can't finish, Sweetness." The corner of his mouth rose.

Fuck me. My cheeks warmed, and I stepped away, dropping my hand to my side. "Again, sorry."

Before I could walk away, he said, "I'm meeting Hailey for coffee today." His voice had a hesitancy so unlike the confident Ethan I knew.

"Oh. That's . . . good," I managed to say, plastering on a grin.

He averted his blue gaze. "Yeah. I guess. Need anything before I go?"

"No, I'm fine. Julia's coming over." The effort to keep my smile was physically draining me.

He just nodded.

I finished the short distance into my room and closed the door behind me, leaning heavily against it. Ethan deserved someone who could give him a *full* life. But the thought of him with someone else was like a knife twisting in my heart. As I slid down the door, my hand instinctively drifted to my chest, where it felt like a thousand tiny needles were piercing. *God, I'm so tired of hurting.*

The sound of the apartment door opening and closing echoed through the space. He was gone. Tears threatened to spill, but I fought them back, taking deep measured breaths.

Why, out of everyone, did I have to fall for Ethan?

Julia and I settled onto the couch in my living room. On screen, an action flick played, its gunshots and explosions too loud for me to think. Exactly what I needed.

Her words sliced through the noise of the movie. "Do you ever miss dancing?" she asked, the simplicity of her question hitting me with unexpected force. It was as if she had just picked an old lock inside me, unleashing a torrent of memories I'd tried my best to keep buried.

I lowered the volume of the TV. "Yeah, I do." Admitting it was like acknowledging a secret desire that'd been suppressed for too long. The scent of rosin, the feel of pointe shoes, the euphoria of applause—it all came rushing back, sweet yet painful.

"You should consider getting back into it." Her eyes reflected her wistful reminiscence.

I was caught in a mix of good times from before and the aches that seemed to fill my days since. My mind was racing, torn between the happiness I'd once known and the pain that had become too familiar.

"I don't know. It's complicated," I managed to say. Visions of my mother, her supportive smiles, and the gaping void left by her absence swirled in my mind.

Julia reached out, her hand warm and steadying. "I know it's hard. But what happened—how it happened—wasn't your fault." Her words were meant to comfort, but they stung like lime juice in a raw wound.

"I wasn't there for her, Jules. It fucks me up every time I think about it. I was supposed to be there, not relishing the admiration of people I didn't even know." The tears I continuously held back spilled over. Missing my mother's final moments lingered, tainting all my memories thereafter.

Julia enveloped me in her arms. "Mama Cruz loved you. She wouldn't have wanted you to give up your joy," she said, her voice cutting through my fog of sorrow.

"You don't think I know that? I know she would've been proud of that performance. She wouldn't have missed it for the world. That's why I should've been there for *her*. She was dying," I choked out. The weight of my remorse was overwhelming.

"I'm sorry I brought this up, M. I didn't mean to upset you. It's just . . . You're such an amazing ballerina, and I bet you still have it," Julia said as her hand drew soothing circles on my back.

I let out a heavy breath while tears streamed down my cheeks. "I'll think about it," I murmured, more to her than to myself.

She kissed my temple. "I'm sorry, babe."

I wiped the wetness away with the sleeve of my sweatshirt. "It's okay. I thought time would make it easier, but it still feels so fucking fresh." The room seemed to close in on me.

She looked at me. "You know I'm here for you, right?"

With a nod, I replied, "Yeah, I know. Thank you."

Silence filled the space as her gaze roamed the apartment. "Where's Ethan?"

"He's out with his high school sweetheart." I turned back to the movie, my voice flat, trying to mask the hurt that lingered just beneath the surface.

"When did that come about?"

"Thanksgiving, I think. They have this whole history. I think they might get back together," I said with a shrug, feigning indifference. Of course, I was just talking out of my ass.

"You'd be okay with that?" she asked, her voice rising an octave.

"Yeah, why wouldn't I be?" I kept my eyes glued to the screen, putting up a barrier against the questions I didn't want to answer. Ethan deserved happiness, and I couldn't give him the kind of happiness he needed.

"Despite what you said about you and him being 'just friends,' I see what's going on between you two," she said, her observation too astute.

"What do you think you've seen?" I started playing with a loose thread on my blanket, pulling at it as if unraveling my own tangled emotions.

She was silent for a heartbeat. "Remember when you said you'd do anything to have Kyle look at you the way Lucas looks at me?"

I nodded. "Right before we walked in on the bastard fucking Laiyla."

Julia's dark eyes met mine. "Ethan stares at you like that all the time. And I love you, Mia, but you're fucking it up."

Swallowing, I blinked away more tears threatening to fall down my cheeks. Words caught in my throat, so I merely shrugged.

"Seriously, babe. What the fuck are you doing?" Her voice was a mix of frustration and concern.

I shook my head. "He wants things I may never be able to give him. Plus, you know he's a fuckboy just like Kyle." *That last part isn't entirely true.*

She chortled. "I don't think a fuckboy would move in with someone and help her through cancer treatments. His feelings for you run deep, and maybe it's you. You need to get your head out of your ass."

I shut my eyes, sinking deeper into the cushions, seeking refuge in their softness. "It's better this way."

Her voice rose like a wave crashing against the shore of my denial. "You are *not* making anything better where he's concerned."

I turned to face her, noticing how the soft light caught in her dark eyes, making them shimmer. "What if all I have to give him isn't enough?"

"Then you kick his ass out, and I'll move in to take care of you," she mused, her words an attempt at lightening the mood.

My lips curved into a grin that didn't quite reach my eyes. "It's not that simple, Jules," I whispered.

"It's not that complicated either," she replied, her hand resting on my thigh.

I inhaled, then exhaled slowly, the act a small attempt at finding my calm. Peace. "I'll try talking to him. I just . . . don't know if I can handle being thrown away again."

"If he's smart, he'll know better," she said.

Julia left after the movie ended, its last scenes just a jumble of noise and movement that I'd hardly noticed. I found myself alone, the quiet of the apartment amplifying the void. Curled up on my bed, wrapped in the comfort of my thick blanket, I let my thoughts drift.

What am I going to say to Ethan? Part of me wondered if facing rejection head-on was what I needed, a way to cut through the uncertainty so I could start moving forward. The night stretched out before me, full of so many possibilities, each wrestling for a place in the quiet depths of my weary heart.

As I walked through Central Park with Hailey, my mind wandered miles away, tangled up in thoughts of Mia. Memories and fantasies converged, from the good times we'd had before her cancer to the struggles we were experiencing now, looping in my head like a haunting melody.

"Ethan?" Hailey's voice snapped me back to reality. Her eyes were filled with concern, a stark contrast to the vibrant sunset painting the sky in shades of orange and purple.

I blinked, once, twice, three times. "Huh? Yeah, sorry. What were you saying?"

She was idly spinning the sleeve around her coffee cup, her breath mingling with the steam in the cool early evening air. "You told me everything that's happened since Thanksgiving, but you never said if you worked things out with Mia."

Shaking my head, I replied, "It seems we've gone backward."

Her brows came together. "What do you mean?"

"Things are just really complicated right now," I said.

"How so?"

I couldn't look her in the eye and also didn't have it in me to answer her.

Nodding slowly, she said, "I know it's strange to talk with your ex about this, but indulge me for a second."

Silence again.

She took a deep breath and then asked, "Do you love her?"

Her question hit me like a freight train. I stopped and stared at the ground. "I do. But it's not that simple."

"Love never is." She placed her hand on my arm. "If you love her, fight for her."

If only it were that easy. My frustration bubbled. "It's not just about wanting to be with her. It's about what she's going through, what she needs. I don't wanna add to her burden."

Her eyes softened. "Sometimes being there for someone, even when it's hard, is exactly what they need."

Tilting my head toward the sky, I said, "I don't know what to do anymore."

"You continue to show her how much she means to you —every day, in every way you can. Be there, even when she tries to push you away. Especially then."

She was right. And she'd only confirmed what Lucas had told me in the studio. *Don't give up on her.*

Hailey smiled, a bittersweet expression on her face. "Mia's lucky to have you. Just remember to take care of yourself for her."

"Thanks. I think I really needed that pep talk," I said in an attempt to lighten the mood.

She chuckled softly. "It's nice to see you learning from your mistakes. Despite everything we've gone through, I do want you to find your happiness, Ethan."

I grinned. "Thanks, and I want the same for you too."

The cool air brushed against my cheeks as we resumed our walk through the park. I glanced at the trees, their bare branches reaching up to the sky. I was ready to get back to Mia and fight for her. No matter how complicated things got, no matter how many times she tried to push me away, I wasn't going to give up.

I stood in front of Mia's apartment door, my mind swirling with words that needed to be said. Taking a deep breath, I pushed the door open, the familiar creak sounding louder than ever in the silence.

The living room was bathed in soft dim light, the outside world trying to peek through the sheer white curtains. Streetlights cast dancing shadows across the carpeted floor, giving the space a surreal feel, like a scene pulled straight from an old noir film.

My stomach churned, and my heart pounded against my

rib cage as my gaze scanned the room. "Mia?" Only the distant muffled sounds of New York answered.

I took in the scattered cushions on the couch and the half-read book on the coffee table. Then my eyes landed on Mia lying motionless on the floor. A chill raced through me at the sight of her pale face half hidden by her hair, the moonlight casting a ghostly hue over her still form.

Panic surged through me, and I rushed to her side, my footsteps sounding unnaturally loud on the carpeted floor. "No, no, no, Mia?" My voice trembled as I cradled her limp body with one arm. "Mia, wake up!"

Fumbling with my phone—my fingers were clumsy—I dialed those three dreaded numbers. "I need an ambulance." I stammered our address into the phone, my throat tight, chest constricting. "She's unconscious." The dispatcher asked me if she was breathing. I brought my ear to her chest. "Her breaths are shallow."

"I have an ambulance ten minutes away, sir," she said, her voice calm.

"Okay, thank you." I hung up, and the coldness of Mia's hand sent a shiver down my spine. "Hold on. Don't leave me. Not like this." My voice broke. I wasn't a religious man, not by any means, but in my panicked despair, I prayed, "Please, God, don't take her from me."

As soon as the paramedics burst in, the room erupted into a frenzy of activity. Their movements were quick and precise, cutting through the stillness with urgency. The clatter of their equipment echoed against the walls. I stepped away from Mia to give them space to work.

"Sir, can you tell us what happened?" one of the paramedics kneeling beside Mia asked, his voice steady.

I struggled to find my voice. "I found her like this. She's a cancer patient."

The other paramedic, a woman with a calm, focused demeanor, began assessing Mia. "We're going to take good care of her. What's her name?" she asked.

"Mia Cruz," I replied, my gaze fixed on the gentle placement of an oxygen mask over Mia's face.

"Are you her boyfriend?"

Her question, simple yet profound, caught me off guard.

"Yes," I found myself saying, feeling the weight of that admission settle in. The idea of fully embracing that role, of publicly acknowledging my deep, complicated feelings for Mia, sent an unexpected jolt through me.

The first paramedic turned to me. "Has she been undergoing treatment recently?"

"Yes." I continued to answer their questions about her condition.

They prepared Mia for transport, and I just stood there. I couldn't imagine my life without her—didn't want to. One of the paramedics suggested I pack her a change of clothes. I tossed fleece leggings, a sweater, winter jacket, and fur lined boots into a small duffel. Every second felt like an eternity as I followed them out of the apartment. They wheeled Mia on the stretcher.

The icy air hit me the moment I stepped through the lobby doors. Shivering, I zipped up my winter coat. We hopped into the ambulance that was parked out front. The city lights blurred past as the driver put the pedal to the metal, merging into a vibrant river of traffic that seemed to flow with my own racing thoughts. The siren cut through the night. I held on to hope, to the belief that Mia still had time, here, with me.

I woke up slowly, my eyes opening to the dimly lit confines of a hospital room, the sharp scent of disinfectant filling my lungs. The walls, painted a drab beige, were decorated with generic artwork that did little to lift the sterile atmosphere. Ethan was slumped in a chair next to my bed, his steady breathing creating a soft rhythm in the room's silence. The monitor beside me cast a pale light over his handsome features.

The sheets were overly crisp, almost abrasive against my skin, their coolness a contrast to the simmering fear inside me. The last thing I remembered was a dizzying sensation, the room spinning wildly before I succumbed to darkness.

I shifted, and Ethan's eyes snapped open, instantly locking on to mine. Apparent relief washed over his face. "Hey, you're awake." His voice was a gentle whisper.

Even though my stomach was doing flips, I forced a wry smile. "Hey."

He took my hand in his. "You scared me, Sweetness," he said, his gaze seeming to reach the depths of my soul.

"I'm sorry," I whispered back.

He flashed me a comforting smile. "Dr. Colton should be back soon."

The silence that followed was heavy. It stretched on endlessly until Dr. Colton entered the room, his footsteps echoing on the linoleum floor. "Good morning, Mia. How're you feeling?" he asked.

"I feel fine." And my version of "fine" was only minor pain.

He nodded, pulling up a chair beside me. "We've reviewed your scans, and unfortunately..." He let out a long breath before continuing. "It appears we didn't get all of the cancerous tissue. It's spreading. You're going to need a radical hysterectomy."

My brow furrowed as I tried to comprehend what he'd just said. "Could you explain what that involves?" I asked, trying to keep my voice steady.

"Of course," Dr. Colton said, his tone shifting to a more clinical cadence. "It's the removal of the uterus, the cervix and the tissue around it, and the upper part of the vagina. Given the location of the growth, this surgery is necessary to ensure we remove all of the cancerous tissue. I'm so sorry, Mia. I thought we could put this off for a couple years."

Ethan squeezed my hand, his worry evident even in his silence.

I still couldn't fully process what the doctor had said. "And after?" I asked.

"You'll need to stay in the hospital for a few days for monitoring. Recovery time varies. Typically, patients resume normal activities within six weeks. However, you'll need to avoid strenuous activities for a while longer," Dr. Colton explained.

"Will she need to continue her chemo treatments?" Ethan chimed in.

"We'll reassess after surgery, but given Mia's situation, adjuvant therapy might be recommended to reduce the risk of recurrence," Dr. Colton replied.

I didn't want to ask the next question, but I had to be sure. "And . . . children?"

Dr. Colton's expression softened. "I'm afraid this means you won't be able to conceive. I know this is a lot to take in, and we have support services available to help you through this."

It all started to hit me at once, and tears welled up in my eyes.

Dr. Colton stood, his professional demeanor giving way to a more empathetic tone. "We'll need to schedule the surgery soon, but please know, Mia, you're not alone in this. We'll be here every step of the way." he said, his pen scratching against the tablet. "I'm sorry to keep you. You and your boyfriend probably want to get home."

"He's not my boyfriend," I blurted out instinctively. I glanced at Ethan, half expecting to see a flash of hurt or surprise, but his expression remained unreadable. Composed.

"My apologies," Dr. Colton said. He looked at Ethan for a moment, and then he walked out.

I didn't know how I should feel. Ethan remained next to me, holding my hand. After a nurse came in and removed my IV and gave me my discharge instructions, he helped me to my feet, his arm offering support as I wobbled. Dressing in my own clothes felt strange, the fabric scratchy against my skin. We strode through the hospital's emergency room exit, the sliding doors hissing closed behind us. The city welcomed us back with distant honking and the muffled chatter of people passing by. Brisk air bit at my cheeks, a contrast to the hospital's regulated warmth.

"I don't wanna go home yet," I said, still standing in front of the hospital.

"Central Park is just across the way. Are you sure you feel up to it?"

I huffed, zipping my winter jacket all the way up. "I'm not some porcelain doll. I'll be fine."

He said nothing and let me take the lead. About fifteen minutes later, we were walking through the park. It was like a serene painting with its bare trees swaying in the cold breeze, their branches etched sharply against the sky.

We found a secluded bench near a frozen pond, its surface a smooth mirror reflecting the snow-covered trees and overcast sky. The muffled sounds of the city were replaced by the subdued symphony of the park: the distant laughter of children, the rustle of small animals in the underbrush, the occasional chirp of a bird braving the New York winter.

The bench's cold seeped through me, mirroring the numbness in my heart. Nearby, a mother was chasing her little one around. Their laughter rang through the air, filled with life and joy, reminding me of all the possibilities that now seemed out of my reach.

Ethan remained standing a few feet from me. "Talk to me, Sweetness."

Julia's remark about the way he stared at me leaped to the forefront of my mind like a grand jeté. Shaking my head, I said, "Stop looking at me like that."

He frowned. "How am I looking at you?"

I averted my gaze. "I don't deserve that look."

"No. You deserve more." He paced in front of me, brushing his fingers through his hair. "I'm just gonna come out and say it. I love you, Mia."

Love? My heart skipped a beat. *He doesn't mean it.*

Ethan moved closer. "Did you hear me, Sweetness? I love—"

I held up my hand, palm facing him. "Stop. It isn't love."

He sat next to me, frustration evident on his handsome features. "What do you think it is, then?"

"Pity," I said firmly.

He looked surprised, almost offended. "I think I know what love is."

"Do you?" My voice was laced with skepticism.

"What's that supposed to mean?" he asked, a frown creasing his brow.

"How about we go through the list of women, starting with Alice?" I challenged him.

"Not this again," he muttered, looking down at his clasped hands, then back at me. "No one holds a candle to you. Not even close." He inhaled a deep breath. "When I first met you, I was sure I'd found a true friend, but somewhere along the way, everything changed. It's hard to pinpoint the exact moment. It could've been at my parents' house when we spent Thanksgiving with them. It could've been before that. All I know is I fell hard for you."

I just stared at him, breathless. Wordless.

His blue eyes bored into me. "I love the way you take care of everyone despite your own struggles. I love your resilience and ability to move forward, even when life keeps knocking you down. The more time I spend with you, the more I realize how fucking amazing you are, Mia."

I swallowed the lump threatening to rise in my throat. "I don't think you understand what this surgery means."

"It doesn't change how I feel about you," he insisted.

"How can you say that? This changes everything." My vision started to blur. He tried to pull me in for a hug, but I placed my hand on his chest, pushing him away. "I don't want your pity, Ethan."

He straightened. "Dammit, it's not fucking pity. Why can't you see that?"

My next words came out without a single thought. "I want you to move out."

He stood and stepped backward. At this point, the wrinkle in his brow seemed permanent. "You don't mean that."

I stood and turned away, tears stinging my eyes as the

cold winter air bit at my skin. "I do mean it." My voice was steady, even though every word felt like a shard of glass. "You need to move on. We both do."

"You're not thinking straight. This . . . This isn't you."

"It is me," I shot back, facing him. "This is me being realistic. I'm not the same person I was before all this, and I can't be who you want me to be."

He moved closer, his eyes searching mine. "I don't want you to be anything other than who you are. I love you for you, not for what you can give me."

"You say that now." My chest tightened. "I can't give you the future you deserve. The family, the kids . . . all of it. It's not fair to you." I blinked back my tears, keeping the rising tide of emotions at bay.

Ethan reached out, but I stepped away, putting even more distance between us.

"This isn't about some fucking ideal future. We can make our own path, our own happiness. It doesn't have to look a certain way," he said.

I shook my head, a bitter laugh escaping my lips. "So, what? We play house? Pretend everything's normal?"

"It's not pretend," Ethan said, his voice rising slightly. "It's about accepting and adapting. We can find a way. We can make this work." His blue eyes were glossy, a sheen of unshed tears reflecting the midmorning sunlight.

I wrapped my arms around myself, feeling a deep aching chill. "I can't ask you to give up your desire for a family of your own."

"*You* are all the family I need, Sweetness," he insisted.

I gazed into his eyes, seeing the earnestness, the love, but also the pain I was causing him. "I want you to move out," I repeated.

Ethan's shoulders slumped, his expression one of defeat. "If that's what you want."

"It's what I need," I whispered, the finality of my words hanging in the air like a closing red curtain.

The silence stretched between us, broken only by the distant sounds of the city and the muted laughter from the nearby playground. Finally, Ethan nodded in silent acceptance of my decision.

We left the park, our steps slow, the distance between us growing with each stride. The ride back to my apartment was quiet, a tangible void filled with unspoken thoughts and the echoes of a conversation that had changed everything.

THE CAB ROLLED TO A STOP OUTSIDE MY APARTMENT building, the familiar rumble of its engine a comforting but now bittersweet reminder of our time together.

Ethan glanced at me, his blue eyes holding a storm of emotions. "I'll come back for my things later." His voice was strained. "I just need some time to clear my head."

I nodded and, without saying another word, stepped out of the car. The cool air brushed against my cheeks. I closed the car door, and the taxi driver pulled away, the engine's fading rumble mirroring the growing distance between us.

Once back in my apartment, the quiet hit me like a hurricane. It wrapped around me like a suffocating blanket. I grabbed a spoon and a carton of cookie dough ice cream, then slumped onto the couch. Its soft worn cushions were a small comfort in the emptiness that filled me.

My phone rang, saving me from the stillness I was drowning in. I answered without checking who it was. "Hello?"

"Mia-bear," came my dad's voice, warm and tinged with worry. "Everything okay? Ethan messaged me and told me you'd passed out."

Of course he told my dad. Letting out a breath, I went through a play-by-play of everything that had happened, including what Dr. Colton had said about the hysterectomy. When all was said, Pop remained silent for a long moment.

"I should've never left," he said.

"Lola needed you. I wasn't about to make you choose."

He exhaled, the sound heavy with guilt and sorrow. "I wish there were something I could do to make this easier for you. I wish I could just take it all away."

"I'm scared, Daddy. I don't want to die," I admitted, my voice barely above a whisper. "I don't know if I can get through this."

"You can—you *will*," he said. "I'm going to buy a plane ticket tonight. I'll be there for your surgery."

I let out a relief-filled breath. "Thank you, Pop. *Mahal kita.*"

"I love you too. You'll get through this. You're strong."

There was a brief silence before he went on. "But you know what I miss most about you, *anak*?"

I shifted on the couch, feeling the cushions mold around my body. "What's that?"

"Your smile. There was a time when that smile never left your face."

After eating another spoonful of ice cream, I asked, "And when was that?"

"When you were a dancer," he reminded me gently.

As soon as he said that word, my spoon hovered motionless over the ice cream carton, the sweetness suddenly unappealing, cloying even. I set the spoon down, a sigh escaping me. Why did everyone have to keep reminding me? "I don't think that's true," I forced out, trying to sound nonchalant. "Just a lot has changed since then."

"We both know that's not true. You should start again," he prodded.

I set the ice cream down on the coffee table, feeling a chill that spread into my heart. "It's not as easy as you think." The memory of my mother's death after my performance still haunted me.

"She wouldn't want to see you like this, Mia-bear," he said softly.

Tears began to stream down my face. "I should've been there, and I wasn't. And I can't—I won't ever forgive myself," I choked out, the pain raw in my voice.

Dad's voice shook slightly. "She never wanted you to put your life on hold. She wanted you to live it. And that's what you haven't been doing. It's what you need to keep doing."

"You don't think I'm trying?" I whispered.

"I know you're trying. Maybe it's time for you to stop *trying* to find your happiness. Go out there and live it. Mama would never fault you for that," he encouraged.

I wiped the wetness off my cheeks, tasting the saltiness on my lips. Dad had a way of saying what I needed to hear, even when I didn't want to.

"Please, Mia. Try to start dancing again, even if it's just for yourself," he urged, his voice laced with a pain different from mine.

I could try. For him. "Okay," I managed to say.

Dad and I exchanged a few more words, his voice a steady presence on the other end of the line. When I ended the call, every emotion flowed through me. Fear had become a constant, but now it mingled with a sense of gratitude. Dad's promise to be there, to face this with me, was a small but significant comfort.

I found the strength to put away the ice cream. Walking into my room, I rummaged through my closet, moving aside clothes and boxes that were like memories from someone else's life. At the very back were my old pointe shoes, a little dusty and worn, but still holding the spirit of dance. They were relics of a past life, one where music and movement were my refuge.

I picked up my phone, hesitating for a moment. One text to Julia was the first step on my long, uncertain journey. I hoped she wouldn't mind opening up the studio on her off day.

My fingers hovered over the screen before I finally typed out the message.

ME

Can we meet at the studio tomorrow? I need to . . . try something.

JULIA

Of course. What time?

As I stared at her message, a mix of apprehension and determination swirled inside me.

ME

9 a.m.

JULIA

Sounds good. I'll see you then!

I sat on the edge of the bed, the ballet shoes in my lap. Their familiar texture, the frayed ribbons—it brought back a flood of memories. The stage, the sound of my feet gliding across the floor, the applause. And then the crushing news about Mom . . . It all blended into a bittersweet symphony that had been my life.

I took a taxi to Julia's studio the next morning, the leather seat cool beneath me. My neatly packed ballet gear rested next to me. The hum of the city was a constant reminder of life's forward motion. The question of whether I wanted to move with it or stay stagnant plagued me. Dad's words from last night replayed in my mind. *Maybe it's time for you to stop trying to find your happiness. Go out there and live it.*

The cab rolled to a stop, and I paid the driver before stepping out into the crisp air. The familiar red-brick building stood tall and dignified, guarding all the hard work and sweat left within its walls. The usual buzz of activity was absent, leaving the parking lot eerily quiet.

I pushed the studio door open, and the familiar scent of wood polish mixed with a hint of floral perfume hit me. It was comforting and overwhelming all at once. The large mirrors and barre welcomed me back into their embrace despite my long absence.

Julia was dressed in her dance attire, but her usual pointe shoes were replaced by black sneakers. She locked the door behind us, her eyes scanning me carefully. "Hey, babe. How're you feeling today?" she asked, her voice tinged with a mix of concern and something else I couldn't quite place.

Dropping my duffel with a definitive thud, I unraveled the tangled threads of the past day's events, my shared moments with Ethan spilling out in a cathartic release.

"Dammit, M . . . I really wish you would've called me. That was probably a lot to process." She wrapped her arms around me, pulling me against her.

My heart tugged at the thought of the imminent surgery. "It was."

Julia stepped back as her eyes narrowed on my duffel. A slow smile spread across her face. "Wait. What's going on here?"

"I wanna try dancing again," I said.

She tilted her head. "Really? Are you sure you feel strong enough? I don't want you passing out on me."

"Yes," I said, more firmly this time, a sense of resolve growing inside me. "So, can you put on one of those classical songs we used to warm up to?"

Julia stared at me for a few seconds longer, and then without a word, she made her way to the sound system. I took this chance to change into my ballet attire—a ritual that felt both nostalgic and new. As I pulled on the familiar embrace of my pink leotard, wrapped the sheer skirt around my waist, and tied the ribbons of my pointe shoes, a dormant part of me stirred to life. Each piece of attire, each fragment of my past, pieced me back together, calling to the dancer I'd once been. I was reclaiming my identity, a reemergence of the joy and passion dance had once brought to my life.

Julia was waiting by the mirrors, a small black remote in her hand and an amused, affectionate look on her face. "Wow . . . You look like a ballerina," she teased, a playful glint in her eyes.

I rolled my eyes but couldn't help the small smile that formed. "Shut up," I replied, the banter easing some of my tension.

She stepped closer, her demeanor turning serious as she took my hand. "Are you sure you wanna do this?" Her gaze searched mine.

I nodded, a surge of something like courage coursing through me. "It's time."

She backed away and pressed a button on the remote. The hauntingly beautiful notes of "Clair de Lune" filled the room, the piano's melody enveloping me like an old friend. I froze, memories flooding back—my last performance, the call about my mom.

"Mia," Julia said, staring at me, worry apparent on her face. "Maybe you should sit down for a sec."

Tears were streaming down my cheeks, and I quickly wiped them away. "No. I need to do this. Start the song over," I said, my voice stronger than I felt.

She inhaled and nodded, restarting the track.

I let the music's rhythm seep into me, initiating my

movements. There was a hint of awkwardness, a rustiness from too much time away from my art. But as I continued, fluidity began to replace stiffness—my body started to remember. I started to remember.

The studio transitioned from a place of harsh memories into a space of comfort and belonging. This was my escape, separating me from the fears and uncertainties that had been clouding my life. With each note, I grew more confident. Expressive. I was Mia, a dancer, alive with every pirouette, every petit jeté.

When the music stopped, I was breathless, a mix of exhilaration and sorrow swirling within me. Julia was there in an instant, wrapping me in a warm reassuring hug. I leaned into her, my lips curving up.

"You did it," she said, her voice muffled against my shoulder. "I'm so proud of you."

I laughed despite the lingering tears. "That probably looked like shit."

Pulling back, she shook her head. "No, you were beautiful. You still have it, babe." She retrieved a white towel from a nearby cabinet and handed it to me.

I wiped my face. "Thanks."

She had a curious smile on her face. "What made you decide to do this?"

I didn't know where to begin with that question. "My dad basically told me I'm happier when I dance. He told me to stop trying . . ."

Julia listened, her face a picture of understanding, of patience. "So, what about Ethan?"

Interlacing my fingers on top of my head, I paced a few feet from her. "What about him?"

She stared at the wooden floor as though she was having an internal argument with herself. "I promised Lucas I'd stay out of it and wouldn't say anything."

I cocked an eyebrow and crossed my arms. "But?"

"Ethan called Lucas last night and told him everything that's been going on between you two."

I couldn't blame Ethan for going to his best friend with this. My brow furrowed. "And?"

"And Lucas has never seen Ethan like this before. So defeated and lost." Her studious gaze met mine.

"He's already been through so much, and he's given up a lot to be there for my treatments, including his penthouse."

"Doesn't that say something about how he feels?" she asked.

"I don't want to be another thing he needs to worry about." More tears surfaced, and I couldn't stop them from falling down my cheeks.

"Isn't that what people do when they truly care about each other? They stand by each other, no matter how tough it gets," Julia reasoned, moving closer. "Don't discredit his feelings. He's not staying because he feels obligated or out of pity. He's staying because he wants to. He cares. Because he loves you."

Could I allow myself to trust in the sincerity of his actions? The weight of his kindness pressed against the walls I'd built around my heart, urging me to reconsider what I deemed impossible. "It's just hard to accept that someone could be that selfless, especially for me."

Julia smiled, taking my hands in hers. "You're worth it, Mia Cruz. More than you'll ever believe. And Ethan sees that, even if you refuse to. Maybe giving him a chance is also giving yourself one."

Wiping my tears with the towel she'd given me earlier, I said, "I'm scared. Of getting hurt again. Of not being able to meet his needs. Of losing him, of losing myself . . . of all the changes."

"And that's okay," Julia reassured me, squeezing my hands. "But don't let fear dictate your future. Give him this chance. Share your fears, your hopes . . . See where it leads. Life's too short to live in doubt."

Julia's words crashed through my defenses, freeing the silent call of my own caged heart. I stood at a crossroads, one path leading back to the safety of solitude and the other into the urgency of acceptance.

Could I allow myself to be vulnerable, to truly open my heart again? It was a question only I could answer, a step only I could take. And maybe it was time to *take* that step.

"You're right," was all I could say.

Julia's expression softened. "Whatever you decide, I'm here for you. Always."

I woke up in my own bed. The emptiness had a presence of its own in the silence of my penthouse. In only my gray sweats, I wandered into the kitchen, the floor cold beneath my bare feet. Opening the fridge, I scanned it half-heartedly. Nothing looked appealing; nothing seemed worth the effort.

I approached the expansive window, remembering a time when I thought I had the best view in New York City. Now it was underwhelming. My solitary reflection stared back at me, a solemn figure set against the backdrop of a lively sprawling cityscape.

My cell vibrated. Lucas's name flashed on the screen. I stared at it for a moment, taking a deep breath before sliding my thumb to answer.

Clearing my throat, I said, "Hey."

"Hey. You good?" he asked.

"I've been better."

The line stayed quiet for a few seconds, and then Lucas said, "Let's get some food."

Getting out of this penthouse and away from my thoughts for a while sounded appealing. "Guess I should eat something."

"Be there in thirty. Be ready."

I closed my eyes for a moment. "Okay."

Hanging up, I was left in the turbulence of my own mind again. Lucas was right. I needed to get out of here, at least for a little while. Looking out at the city, I knew that no matter where I went, Mia's absence would be all-consuming.

Lucas and I slid into our usual booth at our favorite diner. The aroma of freshly brewed coffee wafted through the air, mixing with the scent of sizzling bacon from the grill. Our waitress moved around with graceful efficiency. I stirred my coffee and took a sip. But the comfort of our familiar spot did nothing to calm the despair that had been shredding the hope I was clinging to.

Lucas sat across from me, tapping his index finger on the table in a slow rhythm. "Venom is tearing it up in the studio. Their new track's gonna be a hit, man. I can feel it. And guess what? They'll be kicking off their cross-country tour with Coachella. It's gonna be fucking epic."

I forced a smile. "That's great. I wish them all the success." The words lacked the genuine enthusiasm I usually felt.

Our waitress came by and dropped off Lucas's BLT and my cheeseburger. I picked at my fries; my appetite was still nonexistent, even though I needed to eat. The ambient sounds of the diner filled the space as I took a small bite of my burger.

"So . . . you gonna pick up your stuff from Mia's today?" Lucas asked before digging into his sandwich.

I chewed and swallowed my food. "Yeah, I need to." Sitting back in my seat, I stared at my plate. Was I ready to face her after our conversation the other day?

Lucas wiped his mouth with his napkin. "Who knows. Maybe she's had enough time to think about it. Maybe she's changed her mind."

That sparked a flicker of hope, but it was quickly doused by the memory of her firm stance. "I doubt it. She seemed pretty set on her decision." Just the mere thought of going back to get my things cast more darkness on the depression that was already spiraling.

Lucas let out a long breath. "I'm sorry, man."

"It's all right," I said, my voice low. "I guess sometimes love isn't enough. Maybe our timing's off."

He tossed his napkin onto the empty plate in front of him. "Or maybe it's exactly these challenges that make the timing right. You're gonna have to prove that not being together is already more painful than your past losses."

I let his words sink in. *Already more painful than your past losses.*

"Maybe you're right." I knew that whatever the outcome, confronting Mia was the only way forward.

Lucas shrugged. "She could surprise you."

I stood in front of the living room window, my feet sinking into the plush carpet. It was midday already. I hugged myself. Despite the warmth of my apartment, an icy void had seeped into my soul. I heard the door open and close behind me, and my heart pounded in my chest.

"Hey, it shouldn't take me long to pack," Ethan said.

With a deep inhale, I found the courage to face him. His dull blue gaze locked on to mine. My eyes drifted up his body, from the wrinkled gray sweats to his stained white tee. He had dark circles around his eyes, and it looked like he hadn't shaved in days.

I opened my mouth to speak, but the words were like hard stones in my throat. I managed to force them out. "Please don't leave."

His eyebrows knitted together. The hurt in his eyes was evident, the blue color slightly clouded. "I'm just trying to give you what you want."

Each step I took toward him felt like wading through a fast-moving river. "I danced at Julia's studio today."

The corners of his mouth tugged up. "How'd it feel?"

I grinned. "Great. It made me realize how much I've missed it."

"That's great, Sweetness." He started to step back toward his unpacked bags in the corner of the living room.

I grabbed his wrist, stopping him. "I was scared when you told me how you felt. Scared of how much you mean to me, of how much I've come to rely on you. But the thing I'm most afraid of is losing the people I love most."

"I'm afraid of that exact same thing," he said.

"I understand that. That's why I kept trying to set you free from me and my baggage." Letting go of his wrist, I continued, "You know, the last time I was onstage, my mom passed. And my boyfriend at the time felt that his career was bigger than my loss, so he dumped me. Everything in me was broken. And when you showed up at that bar in Newark, you were the glue that started mending all of that brokenness. When I got sick, there was no way I could live whatever life I had left knowing that I would be leaving you with that kind of brokenness again."

His eyes searched mine as though looking for truth in my words. "Not being able to spend that life with you, no matter how short, is what is breaking me now."

"I know now that pushing you away was never the answer. I'm sorry. There's no excuse for the way I've been treating you, even with my situation." Tears began to well up in my eyes. "I need you here with me."

"How do I know you won't push me away again? We can't keep doing this."

I stepped closer. "I'm done with that—you're too big, and it's exhausting. And besides, it's not even working."

His features softened. "Are you sure about this, Sweetness?"

"Yes," I whispered, my voice steadier than I felt. "Our future is uncertain, but I know one thing for sure: I want whatever future I have left to be with you."

His palm was warm and gentle against my cheek, his fingers tangling in my hair as he leaned in closer. The proximity made my heart beat faster. His breath mingled with mine, creating a charged atmosphere. "I'll stay if that's what you really want," he said, his lips just inches from mine.

My skin tingled under his touch, sending shivers down my spine. "It is."

His lips brushed against mine, and a surge of warmth spread through me, melting the icy tendrils of doubt and fear. His kiss was a featherlight caress, tentative yet filled with an underlying passion. Our mouths moved together in a hypnotic dance. Every touch ignited a spark of longing inside me, a deep desire that threatened to consume me.

The midday sun no longer cast shadows. Instead, it bathed us in an ethereal glow. His hands slid down my sides, leaving a trail of heat in their wake. They settled on my hips, pulling me closer to him until our bodies were flush.

I moaned into his mouth as his fingers gripped me tighter. He pressed himself against me. Fuck, he was hard. In one swift movement, I had my legs wrapped around his waist. Holding me by the backs of my thighs, he carried me to the couch and laid me on the soft cushions.

Ethan caressed my neck and licked my pulse. He reached beneath my sweater and squeezed my breast. "You want me to stop?"

I didn't answer.

"If you want me to stop, I will." He ground his rigid dick against my already-pulsing pussy.

A strained noise escaped me. "No. Don't you dare fucking stop."

His shirt came off before he grabbed the band of my leggings and pulled them off, along with my thong. He slid me to the edge of the couch, sinking to his knees. "God, you're wet already."

A sharp breath escaped my lips as his tongue slipped between my folds. Every muscle in my body tensed. I exhaled a moan, clinging to the cushions, desire coursing through me. With precision, he licked his way up to my swollen clit, engulfing it with his warm, wet lips and drawing it into his mouth. His hand pressed firmly against my stomach, holding me in place. He deftly slid two fingers deep inside of me, eliciting a surge of pleasurable sensations that coursed through my entire body.

"F-fuck." I nearly choked on the word, eagerly arching toward him. The pressure was building low in my core. His movements were deliberate, each one hitting the right spot with every push and every pull. He captured my lips with his with a hungry intensity that pushed me over the edge. I cried out his name as my walls pulsated around his digits.

Ethan slipped his fingers out of me, brought them to his mouth, and licked them. "Mmm . . . so fucking good." His hands continued exploring my body, lips trailing down my neck, igniting every nerve.

He traced the shape of the small scar on my stomach. "Everything about you is perfect, Sweetness," he whispered against my skin, his voice husky.

I arched my back, pressing my chest against him as he pushed his sweatpants down to his knees. He kissed me, and I could taste the lingering bittersweetness of my own arousal.

"Tell me what you want, Mia," he murmured, dragging his lips down my jawline.

"You," I gasped, unable to form a coherent thought, pleasure coursing through me.

He chuckled softly and nipped at my earlobe. "I'm already yours." His eyes darkened as I leaned back against the couch pillows, my body aching for him. With a self-assured grin, he asked, "How do you want me?"

A corner of my mouth rose. "Don't hold back."

He cocked a brow. "Are you sure?"

I widened my legs in silent confirmation.

He aligned himself with my center. My pussy lips spread as he slid the tip into me.

He stopped. "Are you okay?"

"Keep going." I grabbed his hips and pulled him deeper, causing my own breathy moan. Our bodies fit like the missing key to my soul had been found. We moved together, our sounds of ecstasy mingling in the air.

Every thrust sent pulses of pleasure through me, building and building until I was on the edge. Ethan's tongue darted out to taste the salt on my skin as his body trembled against mine. He knew exactly what he was doing.

"Fuck, I'm gonna come," I moaned.

"Not yet," Ethan growled, his hips rocking harder. Faster.

My chest heaved as he continued, taunting me with every delicious inch of him. The tension within me grew unbearable; my body begged for release.

"Please, I need you to come with me," I said, my voice hoarse.

A grin spread across Ethan's face, and he finally surrendered to my pleas, thrusting deeply into me while his tongue danced with mine in rhythm with his hips. The intensity was so overwhelming, I could feel my release closing in on me.

The rush of pleasure surged through my body with each passing second. I screamed his name, my voice cracking, muscles contracting. His sculpted abs tensed beneath my fingertips as he let out a primal moan, releasing himself inside me. We lay there together, breathless and spent, limbs intertwined and hearts beating wildly.

"That was amazing," he said, pressing his warm lips to the curve of my neck.

Completely sated, I agreed with a mere nod. As the

daylight waned, we cleaned up and returned to bed, our bodies still trembling.

THE FOLLOWING AFTERNOON, ETHAN AND I SETTLED into the plush cushions of the living room. Despite my recent treatments, I had slept soundly last night and felt somewhat refreshed. Excitement and anxiety mixed inside me as we waited for my dad's arrival from the Philippines. The apartment was filled with the delicious aroma of homemade Filipino dishes Ethan and I had prepared earlier.

I couldn't resist standing up to peer out the window, watching the bustling street below. The distant sounds of traffic filled my ears. "He should be here any minute," I whispered, my breath quickening with each passing moment. My heart fluttered like a caged bird, pounding against my rib cage. I imagined a cab pulling up to the curb and him stepping out, his face breaking into a wide beaming smile. Every second felt like an eternity, like time itself had slowed just to prolong this moment.

A knock echoed from the door, and my heart skipped a beat. Ethan stood to answer it.

My dad smiled broadly upon seeing Ethan. "Thank you for taking good care of my girl." Dad's voice was filled with genuine gratitude.

Ethan shook his hand, a respectful gesture. "It's no

problem at all, Mr. Cruz. I'm just glad I could be here for her."

As soon as my father walked into the apartment, I stood from the couch and rushed toward him. He opened his arms wide, welcoming me into a hug that felt like home. The familiar scent of his cologne mixed with a hint of aftershave brought tears to my eyes. We held each other tightly.

"*Kumusta ang pakiramdam mo?*" Dad asked, pulling back to look at me, his eyes brimming with concern. His gaze was like a gentle touch, comforting and reassuring.

"I'm doing better, Pop. Really," I assured him, squeezing his hand. "I'm just so happy you're here." The words hung in the air, filling the room with warmth.

We sat down, and Ethan excused himself, claiming he had things to do in the kitchen. But it was just an excuse to give us privacy. Dad and I talked about everything—from my upcoming surgery to life back in the Philippines. It was a conversation filled with laughter, a few tears, and an overwhelming sense of comfort.

Ethan and I had prepared a simple yet satisfying meal of chicken adobo, the tender meat coated in a rich, savory sauce. The evening wore on, Dad and I joined Ethan in the kitchen, and the three of us shared our hearty family meal.

We sat around the dining table. Our conversation danced and swirled like the steam rising from the tasty stew. My father's deep belly laughs echoed off the walls, while Ethan's gentle smile lit up his face. In the warm, cozy kitchen, surrounded by the two most important men in my life, I was filled with a surge of hope.

Dad retired to the living room, but Ethan lingered in the kitchen with me. "If you want me to go back to my penthouse, I will."

I gave him a small smile. "No. I want you here. Unless *you've* changed your mind."

He stepped closer and wrapped his arm around my waist, pulling me to him. "Nothing's changed, Sweetness." He pressed a chaste kiss to my lips before he started clearing off the table. "Go hang out with your dad. I got the dishes."

It was the morning of my surgery, and my thoughts clashed like waves in a storm. I sat in the passenger seat of Ethan's Camaro, the cityscape blurring into muted hues. Dad and Ethan's steady presence was a small anchor but couldn't completely calm my nerves.

"Everything's gonna be okay, *anak*," Dad said from the back seat. I felt his warm hand squeeze my shoulder.

I glanced back at him and smiled. "I know, Pop."

Forty-five minutes later, we arrived at the hospital. As I walked through the automatic door, the cold sterile atmosphere hit me. Everything felt like it was closing in, the walls resonating the seriousness of what was about to happen. My heart raced as I scanned the lobby.

I spotted Lucas and Julia, their worried, caring faces offering a bit of comfort. Walking toward them was like moving through quicksand, each step heavier with the reality of my surgery. Unfortunately, the warmth of their hugs and words of affirmation couldn't cut through the fear tearing me up inside.

At the reception desk, I provided my information, each detail a small step to an irrevocable change. Obeying the nurse's orders, I sat among my loved ones and waited to be called.

Ethan's hand found mine. "You're going to be okay, Sweetness."

I desperately wanted to believe him, but the path ahead was shrouded in unknowns.

"He's right, Mia-bear," Dad added, sitting on the other side.

Julia stood a few feet from me. "This is nothing compared to some of the ballet drills we had to endure," she said.

Her comment brought a small smile to my face. Ethan's grip tightened, but his assurance felt distant against the drum of my own heartbeat. The hospital's sterile chill wrapped around me, a stark contrast to the warmth of his touch. Tremors of anxiety danced through me with every name the nurse called.

It took exactly thirty minutes for the nurse to call my name. After that, everything happened in a blur, from the presurgical assessment to the anesthesia preparation. Soon I was lying on a bed, being wheeled away toward the operating room. The surgical team stopped at the waiting room, allowing family and friends to speak to me.

Ethan's hand enveloped mine once more. "We'll see you

when you get out." He placed a gentle kiss on my forehead. "I love you."

The path ahead was filled with uncertainty, but I nodded and put on a smile. "I love you too." The words almost caught in my throat. "I'll see you all after."

Dad leaned in close, his voice filled with a tenderness that only a father could possess. "You've always been a *mandirigma*—my warrior. You *will* make it through this," he said as though it were a whispered promise.

My nurse continued rolling me toward the operating room as Julia said, "We'll be right here when you get out, M. Love you!"

The doors swung open. I was met with a symphony of sights and sounds that overwhelmed my senses. The room itself was a meticulously arranged display of gleaming stainless steel and pristine white surfaces. The overhead lights blazed like celestial bodies, casting a brilliant glow upon the stage where our fates would be decided.

The surgical team, dressed in their crisp green scrubs, moved with precision and grace. One nurse's gloved hands hovered over trays filled with an array of instruments, unpackaging them from their sterile confines. The thought of them cutting me open to remove my lady parts terrified me.

Oh god . . .

Their expertise surrounded me, each step and action deliberate, as though they were all part of a carefully choreographed routine. Every person in that room had their role to play.

The anesthesiologist approached with a gentle smile.

She explained each step of the process. She attached a syringe to my IV, and seconds later, a strange taste filled my mouth. A wave of warmth coursed through my veins, like a bittersweet lullaby. My mom's face flashed before my eyes, and I heard her voice as temporary peace tugged at me.

I'm here, my love. You're going to get through this.

I let the darkness pull me under, closing my eyes and surrendering to the void. The steady beeping of the machines faded into an eerie hum, my worries and fears slipping into the depths as I drifted far away.

"Code blue, surgery suite, room 12. Code blue, surgery suite, room 12." The intercom echoed throughout the hospital.

Is that the room she's in? I couldn't sit still in the waiting room; my nerves were raw, fraying like wires as the seconds on the clock dragged by. There were two other families sharing the space with us. Julia's knuckles were white, her fingers twisted together in a grip that mirrored her evident fear and worry. Lucas paced by the waiting room window like a caged animal, his restless steps only adding to the suffocating tension. Mr. Cruz sat with a stoic mask, his eyes darting between the surgery room doors and his watch.

It's already been two hours. Frustration bubbled up inside me, and I couldn't help muttering, "How much longer?"

"They said it could be a few hours," Mr. Cruz replied calmly.

Julia's voice wavered. "I hope everything's okay."

I couldn't think straight between my crushing worry and the hushed conversations filling the space. My eyes flicked to the doors leading to the operating rooms, desperate for any sign of progress.

Seconds later, a nurse emerged, bringing all activity in the room to a halt. My heart pounded in my chest as we waited to see which family she approached.

"The Cruz family?" she asked.

Mr. Cruz nodded and stood, concern etched on his face. "Yes, I'm her father. How is she?"

The nurse came closer and replied, "Mia's surgery has proven more complicated than expected. She's lost a significant amount of blood, but she's stabilized. We are currently administering a blood transfusion."

Fear gripped me like a vise, and my blood turned icy in my veins. I had to find my breath. "But she's going to be okay, right?"

"She's stable, but we still have to complete the surgery," she reassured us, but her words brought little comfort.

Julia's face had gone pale and expressionless, and Lucas had stopped pacing. Mr. Cruz's voice shook as he asked the question we were all thinking. "When will we be able to see her?"

"If she stays stable, it may not be too much longer," the nurse said. "We'll update you as soon as possible." When she left, the room fell into a heavy silence.

The fear inside me was growing. The nurse's words

replayed in my mind. Every tick of the clock felt like an eternity. Each second filled me with paralyzing dread.

I paced back and forth, my thoughts consumed with the possibility of losing Mia. This was supposed to help her get better, to move on from all her struggles. Lightheaded, I interlaced my fingers on the top of my head, taking deep breaths. "This isn't how it's supposed to be. She doesn't deserve this."

Julia's eyes glistened with tears as we sat in the sterile waiting room.

I clung to any shred of hope I could grasp, but it was hard when faced with the gravity of the situation.

How much more can Mia endure? How much longer can she hold on? My heart was fracturing for Mia, knowing all she'd been through and all that she still had to live for.

Another hour passed while thoughts of Mia occupied my mind—our conversations, her smile, her laughter, the perfection of the intimacies we'd shared.

I tried to stay calm. I was supposed to be the rock she always said I was. Inside, I was crumbling like a sandcastle.

Julia broke the silence. "She started dancing again."

She was finding her happiness—her passion. My throat constricted with emotion. The clock on the wall seemed to grow bigger with each passing minute, as if time itself were magnifying it. "How did she do?"

"Like she never stopped." Julia's voice faltered. "She'll dance again."

God, I hope she's right.

The same nurse emerged from the operating room once

more, her shoulders slumped, face creased with lines of worry. She pulled Mr. Cruz aside this time, and they spoke out of earshot.

My entire face froze. Blood pumped through my heart at a quickening rate.

After what felt like forever, Mr. Cruz walked over to me, Lucas, and Julia.

"There's been another complication. Mia—" His voice broke, but he continued. "She's gone into hypovolemic shock."

My chest tightened. "What is that exactly?"

Mr. Cruz settled into his chair, interlacing his fingers in front of him. He took a deep breath before speaking. "She's lost a lot of blood. The surgeon is working hard to control it. The nurse said there could be organ damage."

Julia started crying into Lucas's chest.

The thought of Mia lying there on the operating table, fighting for her life, was unbearable.

Mr. Cruz raked his hands through his dark hair. "We need to stay strong for her and trust that the medical team is doing everything they can."

I paced the waiting room, every second feeling like an eternity. I wanted to be in there with her, to hold her hand, to tell her she was going to be okay. But all I could do was wait, clinging to the hope that the woman I loved, the woman who'd somehow become my entire world, would pull through.

I sank into a stiff plastic chair that dug into my spine. The clock on the wall seemed to tick louder in my ears.

Suffocating white walls closed in around me. My hands trembled uncontrollably, and tears threatened to spill down my cheeks.

Stay strong. Hold on to hope.

Desperate for a distraction, I took long, quick strides out of the waiting room and wandered aimlessly through the empty hallways of the hospital. Each step was heavy, my mind a maelstrom of thoughts I couldn't escape.

After a fifteen-minute walk, I started toward the emergency wing. *Belle should be working.* A friend of hers recognized me and led me to the nurses' station. I spotted Belle jotting something on the tablet in her hand. She was clad in green scrubs. She didn't appear busy at the moment.

Her face lit up at the sight of me. She greeted me with a smile and a hug. Hands resting on my shoulders, she pulled away and looked into my eyes. "How's Mia?"

Tears welled as I clung to her, seeking solace in my older sister. "She's lost a lot of blood," I choked out.

Belle's arms tightened around me, her touch gentle yet reassuring. She was always so strong and capable, a doctor who had seen it all. But she was also my big sister. "I'm so sorry," she murmured.

I buried my face in her shoulder, allowing myself to release the torrent of emotions I'd been holding back. She held me tight, as if absorbing my pain. In this fragile moment, she became my pillar of strength.

My tears subsided, and Belle stepped back, her eyes filled with compassion. "Mia's strong, and from what I know, she has an incredible team. We need to hold on to hope."

Deep down, I couldn't shake the utter terror—the doubt lingering in the back of my mind. "But what if . . ." I couldn't bring myself to voice the rest of that sentence.

Belle's hands cradled my face. "Don't give in to that fear," she said firmly. "Mia needs us—she needs you—to believe in her."

My sister's words stirred something inside me, a flicker of resilience that had been overshadowed by my despair. I inhaled, slow and steady. "You're right, B."

She offered a faint smile. "I have to get back to work, but keep me updated."

I nodded, overwhelmed by her never-failing support. "Thanks, I will."

Facing the maze of hospital corridors, I lifted my chin and rolled my shoulders back with newfound hope. *I'll never stop believing in you, Mia.*

My eyelids felt heavy, like they were fighting against a sea of lethargy. Soft beeps punctuated the stillness. As the fog of anesthesia lifted, a dull ache throbbed in the pit of my stomach. My throat was dry, my breathing labored.

I squirmed against the stiff mattress, my fingers finding their way to the tender spot on my belly. The incessant beeping of the heart monitor filled the room. A crushing weight suffocated me, a burden that seemed impossible to bear. It felt as though a cruel hand had reached into my chest and crushed my heart.

The choice of being able to hold a tiny bundle in my arms had been taken away from me. I blinked back my emotions, trying to clear the haze from my vision. Nurses came in to monitor me and asked how I was feeling—the usual questions. The last thing they did was check the surgery site before leaving the room.

After thirty minutes of nurses, it was refreshing to see

my dad's face even with the worry etched into every line. He leaned close, his hand gently squeezing mine. "Mia-bear. You did great." His voice trembled with relief, and his eyes were puffy, hinting at tears he must have shed. "I'm so proud of you, *anak*." His other hand brushed a stray hair from my forehead, lingering with a tenderness that sent an ache to my heart.

I cleared my throat and asked, "What happened?"

He kissed the back of my hand. "There were complications . . . We thought we were going to lose you." He buried his face in my palm and sobbed. "I don't know what I would've done."

My cheeks were wet with my own tears as I searched for the right words to say in that moment, but all I could offer was my presence.

Dad wiped his eyes with his sleeve and sniffled. "I've been such a mess. We all tried to be strong—I tried to be strong for you."

"Thank you, Pop," I rasped. "And I'm sorry to put everyone through that."

He shook his head. "No need for apologies. I'm just so thankful you're okay now." He kissed my hand again. "I promised Ethan he could visit next, but I'll be nearby if you need me."

I nodded. "*Mahal kita.*"

"*Mahal kita din, anak.*" He kissed me on the forehead and then made his way out.

A few minutes passed, and then Ethan walked in with a guitar in hand. His blue eyes met mine with an intensity that spoke volumes. "Hey, Sweetness. How're you feeling?" He pulled up a chair and sat at my bedside, leaning the guitar against the armrest.

I wanted to speak with confidence, to say something reassuring, but words failed me. Instead, I forced my lips to curve upward, a fragile smile that cost me more than it should've. Pain rippled through my body, a sharp reminder of my reality.

Ethan's hand found mine, his touch grounding me. "Don't force it. You've been in surgery for a long time."

"My dad said they almost lost me, but he didn't say how," I managed to rasp.

Ethan inhaled, brushing his fingers through his dark hair. Before he averted his gaze, I saw his glassy blue eyes had darkened with melancholy. He blew out a breath and glanced at me once more, clearing his throat. "You lost a lot of blood—" He choked on the last word. "I'm sorry." Tears streamed down his handsome face. He grabbed my hand and kissed it.

My throat tightened. "It's okay. I'm okay."

He stared at me, a hurricane of emotions swirling in his gaze. "But I'm not. Knowing you could've left me and that I couldn't be there with you really fucked me up."

"I didn't though, Ethan." I reached out and placed his hand over my chest, right where my heart was beating steadily. "I'm still here."

Silence filled the room. His chest rose and fell. He wiped the tears from his cheeks and stood, his face hovering inches from mine. "I've never loved anyone the way I love you, Mia," he said. "That will never change."

Ethan had been by my side through everything—every emotion, every treatment, every obstacle. "I love you too," I whispered, meaning every word with every beat of my heart.

His face softened, lips curving up. "It feels like forever since you've told me that." He pressed a gentle kiss to my lips, his touch sending a wave of warmth through my weary body. I held on to his hand and couldn't help but reflect on the time we'd spent together.

He sat back down, never breaking eye contact. His eyes glistened with an unspoken promise. "I know it's been difficult for both of us."

I lifted my tired eyes, searching his face.

Ethan took a deep breath. "I wrote you a song," he confessed, a hint of nervousness lingering in his voice. "Like I said, you were in there a long time."

My heart skipped a beat. Music had always been a language that resonated deeply with us both. It was the rhythm that guided us through dark times and connected us on a level that words alone couldn't reach.

Ethan reached for the guitar leaning against the chair. He positioned himself at the edge of the seat and began to strum a gentle melody, his fingers moving effortlessly across the frets. The soft notes filled the room, weaving their way into my soul, and I closed my eyes, surrendering myself to the sweet sound that emanated from his skilled touch.

As the melody unfolded, Ethan's voice joined in—a velvety tenor that held the rawness of his love. Each word he sang carried a weight that resonated within me, as if he had poured every ounce of his love and admiration into the lyrics.

> You probably know by now, I'm sure you do, but all I know is how to run from you.
> I shouldn't be okay with not taking risks, don't want to pass you up by being selfish.
>
> I keep my distance, yes it's true. I don't let you get too close.
>
> 'Cause I'm afraid that if you really knew me, would you like all that I am?
> And when you find that I'm not perfect, will you still hold my hand?
> And I've been hurt before, so I don't love so easily, but can you love someone as broken as me?
>
> For years I'd push away anyone who cared, and fake that I'm okay when deep down I'm scared. I know that it's not right, to keep you wondering, if I will ever let you in.
>
> I keep my distance, yes it's true. I can't let you get too close.
>
> 'Cause I'm afraid that if you really knew me, would you like all that I am?
> And when you find that I'm not perfect, will you still hold my hand?
> And I've been hurt before, so I don't love so easily.

But can you love someone as broken as me?

Time stood still as the song reached its crescendo. Ethan's gaze was filled with so much vulnerability. The final chords echoed through the room, lingering for a moment before fading away into silence.

A tear escaped from the corner of my eye as I opened them. "Oh my god," I whispered through the knot in my throat. "That was beautiful. Thank you."

"You're welcome." He smiled, his eyes shining with something like happiness. "I'm glad you liked it."

I reached out, my hand trembling slightly as my fingers brushed against his cheek. "And yes, I can and will love you through your brokenness. Will you love me through mine?"

Ethan leaned into my touch, his lips grazing my palm. "You never even had to ask."

I looked into his eyes, and for the first time ever, I could see a future where our love and hope would continue to guide us through whatever challenges lay ahead.

NYC's hustle faded, replaced by the quiet of Dr. Whitaker's office. I'd started therapy a few months ago, shortly after Mia went into remission. Stepping into the space was like entering another world—one where I could let my guard down. Dr. Whitaker had been a huge help in talking me through my issues, though I'd been hesitant to share anything with her at first. Now I looked forward to these sessions.

Shifting in the cushioned lounge chair, I broke the silence. "So, where should we start today?"

Important questions hung over me today. *Can I move forward and embrace the happiness Mia has brought into my life?* This was a critical turning point, trying to find a path that honored both my past and the promise of tomorrow.

"Well," Dr. Whitaker started, leaning back in her seat. "What's been on your mind? How have you been?"

I inhaled deeply as I leaned over with my elbows on my

knees. "It's been rough. Sometimes I feel overwhelmed, but then I remember your advice—to sit with it and figure out why I feel the way I do."

"And have you figured it out?"

Gazing out the big bay window of the office at the view of New York and its skyscrapers, I said, "I was getting stuck in the past again. Losing Jacob, the fallout with Hailey."

"Do you feel like you've been projecting any of it onto your loved ones?" she asked.

My eyebrows came together. "I don't think so."

She jotted something onto her tablet. "Good." Her gaze lifted to meet mine. "And what about Mia?"

"She's been incredible. She's been my rock through my darkest moments, showing me that life can still hold beauty, even after unimaginable loss. Even after what she lost."

Dr. Whitaker nodded, tucking a strand of wavy blond hair behind her ear. "It sounds like she's been a significant source of support for you. How do you feel that's impacted your journey through the grief you've been experiencing?"

"Like she's brought color back into my gray life," I said, the metaphor falling short of fully capturing Mia's impact on me. "But there's this lingering guilt I can't seem to shake. For finding happiness again without my son . . . That Jacob couldn't be part of it."

"Mmm," Dr. Whitaker murmured, acknowledging the complexity of my feelings. "Guilt is a common companion to grief, especially when we start to feel those moments of joy again. But embracing happiness doesn't diminish the love you have for Jacob or the pain of his absence. It's a testament to your ability to carry him with you in a way that keeps him alive in your heart."

I fiddled with my thumbs, letting her words sink in. "So, moving forward with Mia doesn't mean I'm leaving Jacob behind?"

"Exactly," she affirmed gently. "Having Mia in your life isn't about replacing what you've lost. It's about knowing how to allow yourself to repair what's been broken. You've come a long way, Ethan. As life goes on, there's no perfect understanding or acceptance of your emotions, but you'll at least have the tools to guide you in being open."

With a nod, I said, "And I fully intend to use them." I looked down at my clasped hands. "There's something else I think I'm ready to do . . ."

THE CEMETERY WAS A TIMELESS LANDSCAPE, headstones bearing wilted flowers and faded photos. I tilted my head toward the sky, a canvas of soft grays and blues blending effortlessly with the full green trees whispering around us. Shadows from the branches stretched across our path as Mia and I strolled down a row of grave markers.

We approached Jacob's headstone, adorned with fresh flowers and a stone carving of a musical note perched on top. I liked to think he would've loved music as much as me.

Stepping behind Mia, I wrapped my arms around her and pulled her against me. She nuzzled into me while I pressed my lips to the curve of her neck, lingering for a few seconds. An overwhelming surge of affection spread through my heart. I couldn't believe that just a few months ago we were fighting for her life.

I released her and knelt in front of his headstone. "Mia, this is my son, Jacob."

She crouched next to me, her hand grasping mine, giving me strength to share this moment with her. "Thank you for bringing me here, Ethan."

I couldn't meet her gaze. Tears brimmed in my eyes as I inhaled, taking in the crisp spring air. "There's someone I want you to meet," I started, biting back repressed tears, imagining him right there with us—curious, bright-eyed, the way I'd always pictured he'd grow up to be. "This is Mia. She's amazing, son. She taught me how to love again."

"Hello, Jacob. Your dad has told me so much about you. I think we would've been great friends. I want you to know that as long as I have air in my lungs, I'll always be here for your daddy. I promise to give him all my love and all the support he needs." Mia's voice was filled with a sincerity that was tangible.

It was at that moment I knew Mia Cruz was going to be my forever.

Sniffling, I wiped the wetness from my cheeks, took her hand, and squeezed in a silent thank-you.

The sun dipped lower, casting a golden hue over the green landscape. As the day's warmth gave way to the cool evening, serenity filled me. The weight of earlier emotions was now but a gentle whisper.

I stood next to Mia, feeling the strength of her love and the enduring presence of Jacob's memory. "Let's go home," I said.

A quiet assurance settled over me, and I knew that whatever the future held, Mia and I would face it together. *Always*.

I HAD TURNED IN MY RESIGNATION LETTER AT LV Productions—a decision that was fully supported by my friends and boyfriend. My lips curved up at the word. Ethan was my *boyfriend* now. It had been a few months since we'd finally made it official, but a sense of surrealism still caught me every once in a while.

Returning to teach ballet was like reconnecting with an old friend, and despite all the changes life had thrown my way, dance was where I found my happiness. I stood on the dance floor of Julia's studio, knowing I'd made the best decision for myself.

The familiar scent of wood polish filled my nose. Sunlight streamed through the tall windows behind me, illuminating our students' colorful paintings adorning the wall.

"Hey, M. Can you help me pick out the music for the adult classes next week?" Julia walked up next to me, holding two iced coffees. Her straight black hair was gathered into a casual bun, revealing the elegant line of her neck. She handed me my cup of energy.

"What will you do if I say no?" I took a sip, savoring the cool vanilla goodness drifting down my throat.

Julia's eyes narrowed. "I'll stop picking up your iced coffees in the morning."

My brows knitted. I gasped, feigning disbelief. "You wouldn't."

She shrugged, placing a hand to her hip. "Say no and find out."

I rolled my eyes. "You already know it's gonna get done, Jules."

We headed toward the cozy seating area nestled in the waiting area of the studio and sank into the plush couches.

Julia studied me. Her "best friend" intuition could always read me like an open book. "What's on your mind? Are you glad to be back?"

A slew of emotions surfaced. There was so much I had to be thankful for. Ethan and I had been to hell and back these past twelve months. It was crazy how much could happen in a year. My throat tightened. "Of course. I love this job."

Her gaze softened. "What's with that look, then?"

Flashes of the past year sparked in my mind. Learning to move forward from my past had been almost more painful than the cancer treatments I'd endured. Almost. "Just thinking about everything that's happened."

She reached out and placed a hand on mine, her touch

sending waves of reassurance through me. "You're so fucking strong. I knew you'd kick that cancer's ass."

There was still a chance it could come back, but I stopped myself from pointing that out. I closed my eyes, taking a moment to collect my thoughts before I spoke. "It helps to have an amazing support system. I swear, it felt like my world was ending."

Julia squeezed my hand tighter. "You put up a hell of a fight."

I nodded, gratitude flooding me. "I had to. For me—for my mama. She wouldn't have wanted me to give up. Just like I knew she would've wanted me to dance again. It took me longer to realize that." Tears welled up in my eyes as the memories came back—the countless hours spent in hospitals and clinics, the endless needle pricks and invasive procedures. But amid it all, there were four glimmers of hope that had kept me going: Dad, Julia, Lucas, and most of all, Ethan.

"Mama Cruz would be so proud, babe," Julia said.

I inhaled a deep breath, finding solace in her words. "She would."

Julia's lips tilted up, her eyes crinkling at the corners as she leaned back into the couch cushions.

A serene silence enveloped us, punctuated only by the distant sound of classical music. The stillness allowed the moment to settle.

I took a long sip of my coffee before saying, "I used to get caught up in small stuff, like chasing success and worrying about what others think of me. But facing something as big as my own mortality? That shit changes a person."

Julia leaned forward, her eyes locked on mine. "What matters to you now?"

A smile touched my lips as I considered her question. "I've realized it's the small things—laughing with friends and family, the warmth of the sun's first light, being truly in the moment. Life's too short. One minute you're worried about breaking in pointe shoes, the next minute you're on an operating table praying for a miracle."

The bells on the front door jingled. Julia rose from the couch, curiosity lighting up her features. "I wonder who that could be," she mused. "It hasn't even been an hour since you left home."

Ethan stepped into view, and my heart fluttered. His blue eyes locked on to mine, a smile spreading across his handsome face. "Hey, Sweetness." He held up a plastic container that had my salad in it. "You left your lunch."

The gesture melted my insides into pudding. I was so incredibly lucky to have this man in my life. Since we'd moved in together permanently, Ethan having given up his penthouse for my cozy Brooklyn apartment, these little acts of love had become a regular occurrence.

"You didn't have to come all this way," I said, standing to greet him with a tender kiss on the lips.

"It's no trouble at all." He encircled me in his arms.

I glanced at Julia, who was observing our interaction with a knowing smile. She said, "Don't distract my best employee, Miller. She still needs to warm up before her first class."

He offered her a mock salute. "Yes, ma'am."

She rolled her eyes and disappeared down the hallway to her office.

I pulled away, my brow furrowing. "Aren't you late for work?"

A corner of his mouth rose. "Lucas won't mind. Besides, there's not much work to do today. You're still my date for Venom's release party tonight, right?"

I nodded. "Unless you have someone else you'd rather take."

His eyes darkened as he pressed his forehead against mine. "You're *it* for me, Mia Cruz."

Ethan's lips met mine, and the world faded away. His kiss was a promise of continued unwavering support and the shared dreams we held for our future. A spark of hope and excitement ignited inside me, illuminating the possibilities of what lay ahead for us. As the gentle sunlight filtered through the big windows of Julia's studio, I thought about how far we'd come—how Ethan and I would *always* be *it* for each other.

Ethan and I lounged in the living room of our new house, soaking up the warm afternoon sunlight streaming through the big bay window. Golden rays poured in, wrapping us in a cozy embrace. I loved how the light danced on the dark wooden floors, highlighting the rustic charm of our cottage design—the exposed beams, the soft earthy colors, and the way every nook seemed to tell a story. This was the perfect home to start our family in.

My heart raced with a mix of excitement and nerves as I stood. Pacing in front of the sofa, I glanced at our wedding photo hanging on the far wall, our beautiful moment frozen in time. In the picture, Ethan's smile was radiant and filled with affection. The sight eased me a little, reminding me of our vows and the dreams we shared.

The anticipation of what was to come mingled with the peaceful atmosphere, and I couldn't help but smile at the life we were building together. It felt like a lifetime ago that I was battling to survive while pushing Ethan away, convinced that I wasn't enough. But he'd stayed, proving time and again that our love was worth fighting for.

"You're gonna burn a hole in the rug with all that pacing, Sweetness," Ethan said from the couch, an amused look on his face.

Ethan and I had spent a few months trying to adopt an adorable baby girl from the Philippines. Each step in the process was an emotional roller coaster. I paused, willing my mind to be quiet.

"What if we're not approved?" I asked, already picturing her tiny face, with her sparkling dark eyes and sweet smile. The thought that we wouldn't be able to bring her home . . .

I need to stop thinking negatively.

Ethan stood and stepped in front of me, wrapping an arm around my waist. "Then we'll try again."

Eyes blurring, I nodded. "Okay." I shifted my gaze to the hardwood floor.

Ethan placed a finger beneath my chin, drawing my eyes back to his. "Hey, it's gonna be okay. We still have each other."

He was right. I needed to trust the universe. "I love you."

His response was to press his lips to mine, and for a moment, we became lost in each other. Our kiss was broken by Ethan's cell vibrating in his pocket. He answered it with a hopeful expression. "Hello?"

As he spoke, I watched him, nibbling on the inside of my cheek. *Is this it? The moment that will change everything?* The waiting felt like a cruel tease, each second stretching out like an eternity. I tried to read my husband's expression, searching for any hint of what was being said on the other end of the line. At the same time, I didn't want to know.

After a few more minutes, he hung up and looked at me. "We're approved!"

"Really?" My response was a mixture of disbelief and excitement.

"Yes. We need to fly out ASAP," he said, setting the cell down as I absorbed the reality of his words. He held me by my arms, and I stared into his glassy blue eyes. "We're gonna be parents, Sweetness," he all but choked out.

A slow smile formed on my lips. I squealed and jumped, wrapping my legs around his waist.

Ethan's arms tightened around me. "All our waiting and hoping . . . It's finally happening," he said, his voice muffled in my shoulder.

Our love had seen us through the darkest times, and now it would guide us into this new chapter of our lives. I pressed my lips against his once more, pouring all my love and gratitude into that single profound moment.

I'm gonna be a mom.

*If you enjoyed this book, please leave a review.
It'll help the author out more than you know!*

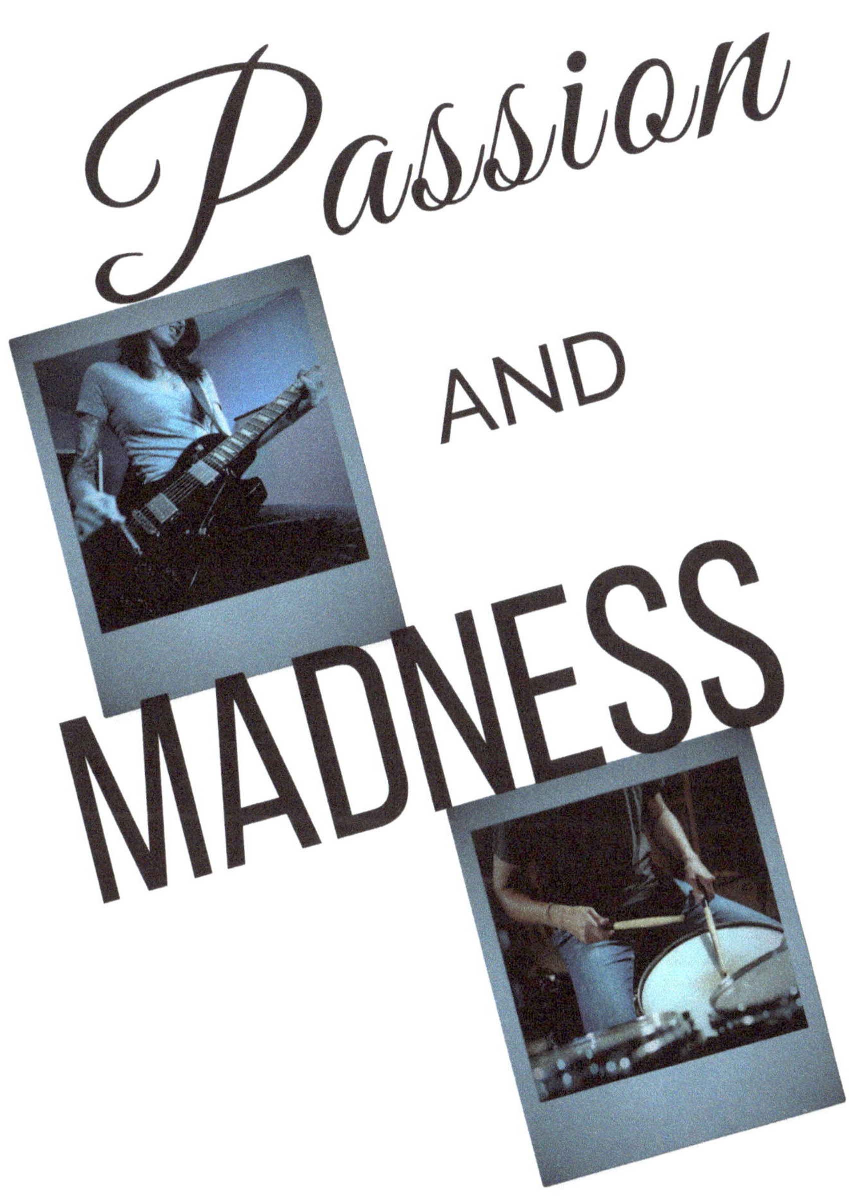

THE MAD LOVE SERIES
Passion
AND
MADNESS
ALYSSA GREEN

Chapter One

RICK

Nothing is absolute. That's one lesson life hammers into you, whether you like it or not. People drift in and out like waves at the beach. They crash into you, make a little noise, and then disappear, leaving you standing there wondering what the hell just happened. Most don't even leave a footprint behind—except for Julia, my kid.

And her.

The first time Gale Liu walked into my life, it was like someone had thrown a fucking grenade into my perfectly organized chaos. I was sitting there, half distracted, flipping through some old song sheets when the door to the garage swung open with a rusty creak. The scent of jasmine and leather hit me.

In walked this tiny woman with blond hair barely brushing her shoulders, torn jeans clinging to her legs like a second skin, and a black leather jacket at least two sizes too big. She strutted in like she owned the place, combat boots echoing on the concrete floor, not giving a damn that she was stepping into a room full of guys who thought they'd seen it all.

For a second, I wasn't sure if I was looking at a rock star or some punk kid who'd wandered in by mistake. Then she uncased her guitar and slung it over her shoulder, the strap worn and covered with band pins, and I knew—she wasn't here to fuck around.

The garage was a mess of amps and cables. Alcohol, sweat, and the lingering scent of cigarette smoke wafted through the space. Posters of classic rock bands were peeling off the walls, and empty beer bottles littered every surface.

I sat behind my drum kit, arms crossed, pretending like I wasn't fazed. But my chest tightened, and something stirred in me that I hadn't felt in years.

"I'm Gale Liu," she said, her voice rough and steady, no hesitation. "Heard you're in need of a guitarist."

I raised an eyebrow and tapped my drumstick against my thigh. "Where'd you come from?"

"Just moved here from LA. I saw your ad at my aunt's bar and, well . . . here I am." She shot me a half smirk that was infused with challenge, her brown eyes meeting mine.

Intrigue hit me, but I was determined not to show it. I scratched my stubbled chin. "Okay, let's see what you got."

She plugged in her guitar, the cord snaking across the floor. Her movements were fluid, like this wasn't just an audition but an everyday ritual.

I nodded to the guys, and we took our positions. The familiar weight of my drumsticks in my hands grounded me, but there was an electric current in the air that hadn't been there before.

The moment we started playing, it was like lightning struck. Gale's guitar wove seamlessly with Carter's bass, creating a sound that made the hair on my arms stand on end. I found myself pounding the drums harder, faster, trying to keep up with the energy pouring out of her.

Fuck, she wasn't just keeping up—she was pushing us, challenging us to go harder. Her fingers seamlessly coaxed out riffs that made my heart race. I couldn't take my eyes off her. The way she moved with the music, as though it were flowing through her veins.

Her sound hit me like a loaded dump truck, vibrating through the floor and up into my bones. Raw, gritty, alive. I felt it in my chest, my arms, my fucking teeth. My spine straightened as a shiver ran down it. I glanced over at Carter, who was struggling to keep up on his bass.

"Holy shit," Carter mouthed, his eyes wide.

Gale didn't stop. She kept playing, her fingers flying across the frets like she'd invented every note. And the way she held herself—fuck, it was like she was born with that guitar. The rest of the guys were locked in, mesmerized by the effortless power she manifested. By the time we finished, we were all drenched in sweat, breathing hard, and grinning like idiots.

Gale pushed her damp hair out of her face, her eyes bright with exhilaration. "Now that," she said, her chest heaving, "was fucking music."

I laughed, shaking my head in disbelief. "Yeah, it was."

"Well?" she asked, one eyebrow raised, a bead of sweat trickling down her temple. "Did I make the cut?"

The round leather seat groaned beneath me as I tried to keep my cool even though she had rattled me to the fucking core. "Not bad. But you're not the only guitarist in New York."

She let out a low giggle, stepping toward me, her jasmine scent filling my nose. I could make out the hint of hazel in her eyes. "You're right," she said, voice dripping with confidence. "But I'm the only one you want."

My gaze drifted to her burgundy lips. Damn, she was sexy. "Are you now?" I shot back, fighting a grin. This girl had guts—I'd give her that.

"Unless you've got someone else in mind who can actually keep up with you." She nodded toward my drums.

Carter let out a bark of laughter, the sound echoing off the garage walls. "Never gonna happen," he said, clearly enjoying the show.

I narrowed my eyes, glancing between her and Carter, but it was useless. The truth was right in front of me—all five feet, four inches of it, staring me down with her fierce gaze. She wasn't just good. *She's perfect.*

"All right, you're in," I said, trying to sound casual, like I hadn't just had my entire world tilted on its axis. "Don't make me regret it."

Gale smirked. "Trust me, you won't." She unplugged her guitar, the sudden silence almost deafening. "Same time tomorrow?" she asked, slinging her instrument over her shoulder.

"You bet your fine ass," Carter chimed in.

Gale nodded, a small smile playing on her lips. She turned to leave, her boots scuffing against the concrete, but paused at the door. "Oh, and Blackwell?"

I raised an eyebrow. "Yeah?"

"Next time, try a little harder to keep up," she said with a wink, mischief glinting in her eyes.

Before I could respond, she was gone, the door swinging shut behind her with a metallic clang. The garage felt emptier without her in it, like she'd taken some of that electricity with her.

Carter let out a low whistle, still staring at the door. "Well, that was fun," he said, grinning from ear to ear. "I think we may have found our missing link."

I grinned and shook my head, trying to process what had just happened. My heart was still racing, my palms slick with sweat. But it had nothing to do with the music and everything to do with the woman. Gale Liu wasn't just any guitarist. *She's my perfect kind of trouble.*

Sign up for my newsletter to stay informed on upcoming releases!

<u>The Akrani Gods series</u>

Book I: Of Flesh and Steel

Book II: Of Blood and Onyx

Book III: Of Wrath and Chaos (coming soon!)

<u>The Mad Love series</u>

Book I: Sunshine and Madness

Book III: Passion and Madness (coming soon!)

<u>Standalones</u>

Half Blood: The Tale of Samara

Saints and Sinners (coming soon!)

Acknowledgments

I wrote this story for my grandma Lucia, who passed away from cancer back in the early 2000s. It's crazy how long grief lasts. My only hope is that Ethan and Mia's story helps others cope as well. I know the story is far from perfect, but writing it has been so good for my mental health.

Thank you to Brittany, Lana, and Kasey for working so hard to help me develop and edit this in such a profound way. You all have contributed so much to my author career.

To my beta reader, Veronica H., my OG, thank you so much for your feedback!

As usual, I'd like to thank my husband, Bobby, for supporting me through this journey. You truly are a rock in my life.

Mom, Dad, Amber, Alex, Annamarie, Angelica, and Aliyah, you all are my heart!

Alyssa Green

Alyssa is a US Navy veteran with a degree in psychology. She's a multifaceted person who enjoys a variety of activities. When she's not writing or reading, she can be found editing for clients, traveling the United States with her husband and dog, Fiona, or hiking and exploring the outdoors. She's also a lifelong learner who has been taking classes through the Editorial Freelancers Association to improve her skills as a freelance editor.

WWW.AUTHORALYSSAGREEN.COM

facebook.com/authoralyssagreen

instagram.com/author_alyssa_green

tiktok.com/@authoralyssagreen

amazon.com/author/alyssagreen